W9-AFK-884

the power of one

Also by Bryce Courtenay

The Power of One
Tandia
April Fool's Day
A Recipe for Dreaming
The Family Frying Pan
The Night Country
Jessica
Smoky Joe's Cafe
Four Fires
Matthew Flinders' Cat

The Australian Trilogy

The Potato Factory
Tommo & Hawk
Solomon's Song
Also available in one volume, as
The Australian Trilogy

bryce courtenay

the power of one

young readers' condensed edition

DELACORTE PRESS

Published by
Delacorte Press
an imprint of
Random House Children's Books
a division of Random House, Inc.
New York

First published by William Heinemann Australia in 1989
This condensed version originally published by Penguin Books,
Australia Ltd, in 1999

Visit us on the Web! www.randomhouse.com/teens
Educators and librarians, for a variety of teaching tools, visit us at
www.randomhouse.com/teachers

Library of Congress Cataloging-in-Publication Data

Courtenay, Bryce.
The power of one / Bryce Courtenay.
p. cm.
Summary: Follows Peekay, a white British boy in South Africa during World War II, between the ages of five and eleven, as he survives an abusive boarding school and goes on to succeed in life and the boxing ring, with help from a chicken, a boxer, a pianist, black African prisoners, and many others.
ISBN 0-385-73254-6 (trade)—ISBN 0-385-90274-3 (glb)
[1. Self-confidence—Fiction. 2. Conduct of life—Fiction. 3. South Africa—History—1909–1961—Fiction. 4. Boxing—Fiction. 5. Prejudices—Fiction. 6. Apartheid—Fiction. 7. Prisons—Fiction. 8. World War, 1939–1945—South Africa—Fiction.]
I. Title.
PZ7.C83157Po 2005
[Fic]—dc22
2004058258

The text of this book is set in 11-point Goudy.

Book design by Kenny Holcomb

Printed in the United States of America

September 2005

10 9 8 7 6 5 4 3 2 1

For

Maude Jasmine Greer and Edna Murphy.

Here is the book I promised
you so long ago.

ONE
1939: Northern Transvaal, South Africa

This is what happened.

My Zulu nanny was a person made for laughter, warmth and softness and before my life started properly she would clasp me to her breasts and stroke my golden curls with a hand so large it seemed to contain my whole head. My hurts were soothed with a song about a brave young warrior hunting a lion and a women's song about doing the washing down on the rock beside the river where, at sunset, the baboons would come out of the hills to drink.

My life proper started at the age of five when my mother had her nervous breakdown. I was torn from my black nanny with her big white smile and taken from my grandfather's farm and sent to boarding school.

Then began a time of yellow wedges of pumpkin burned black and bitter at the edges; mashed potato with glassy lumps; meat aproned with gristle in gray gravy; diced carrots; warm, wet, flatulent cabbage; beds that wet themselves in the morning; and an entirely new sensation called loneliness.

I was the youngest child in the school by two years and spoke only English while the other children spoke Afrikaans, the language of the Boers, which was the name for the Dutch settlers in

South Africa. They called the English settlers Rooinecks, which means "Redneck," because in the Boer War, which had happened forty years before between the English and the Dutch settlers, the pale-skinned English troopers got very sunburned and their necks turned bright red.

The English won this war, but it was a terrible struggle and it created a hatred for them by the Boers, which was carried over into the generations that followed. So, here I was, someone who only spoke the language of the people they hated most of all in the world. I was the first Rooineck the Afrikaner kids had ever seen and, I'm telling you, I was in a lot of trouble.

On the first night of boarding school, I was taken by two eleven-year-olds to the seniors' dormitory, to stand trial. I stood there shaking like billy-o and gibbering, unable to understand the language of the twelve-year-old judge, or the reason for the hilarity when the sentence was pronounced. But I guessed the worst. I had been caught deep behind enemy lines and even a five-year-old knows this means the death sentence.

I wasn't quite sure what death was. I knew it was something that happened on the farm in the slaughterhouse to pigs and goats and an occasional heifer and I'd seen it happen often enough to chickens. The squeal from the pigs was so awful that I knew it wasn't much of an experience, even for pigs.

And I knew something else for sure; death wasn't as good as life. Now death was about to happen to me before I could really get the hang of life. Trying hard to hold back my tears, I was dragged off to the shower room. I had never been in a shower room before; it resembled the slaughterhouse on my grandfather's farm and I guessed this was where my death would take place. I was told to remove my pajamas and to kneel inside the recess facing the wall. I looked down into the hole in the floor where all the blood would drain away. I closed my eyes and said a silent, sobbing prayer. My prayer wasn't to God but to my nanny. I felt a sudden splash on my neck and then warm blood trickled over my trembling body. Funny, I didn't feel dead. But who knows what dead feels like?

When the Judge and his council of war had all pissed on me, they left. After a while it got very quiet, just a drip, drip from someplace overhead. I didn't know how to turn the shower on and so had no way of washing myself. At the farm I had always been bathed by my nanny in a tin tub in front of the kitchen stove. She'd soap me all over and Dee and Dum, the two kitchen maids who were twins, would giggle behind their hands when she soaped my little acorn. This was how I knew it was a special part of me. Just how special I was soon to find out. I tried to dry myself with my pajamas. My hands were shaking a lot. I wandered around that big dark place until I found the small kids' dormitory. There I crept under my blanket and came to the end of my first day in life.

I awoke next morning to find the other kids surrounding my bed and holding their noses. I'm telling you, I have to admit it myself, I smelt worse than a kaffir toilet, worse than the pigs at home. The kids scattered as a very large person with a smudge of dark hair above her lip entered. It was the same lady who had left me in the dormitory the night before. "Good morning, Mevrou!" they chorused in Afrikaans, each standing stiffly to attention at the foot of his bed.

The huge woman tore back my blanket and sniffed. "Why, you wet your bed, boy! Sis, man, you stink!" she bellowed. Then, without waiting for my answer, which, of course, I didn't have, she grabbed me by the ear and led me back to the place where they'd pissed on me the night before. Making me take off my pajamas, she pushed me into a recess. I thought desperately, She's even bigger than Nanny. If she pisses on me I will surely drown. There was a sudden hissing sound and needles of icy water drilled into me. I had my eyes tightly shut but the hail of water was remorseless.

If you don't know what a shower is, and have never had one before, then it's not so hard to believe that maybe this is death. A thousand sharp pricks drilled into my skin. How can so much piss possibly come out of one person, I thought. Funny, it should be warm, but this was icy cold, but then I was no expert on these things.

Then the fierce hissing and the icy deluge stopped suddenly. I opened my eyes to find no Mevrou. The Judge stood before me, his pajama sleeve rolled up, his arm wet where he'd reached to turn off the shower. Behind him stood the jury and all the small kids from my dormitory.

The jury formed a ring around me. My teeth were chattering out of control. The Judge pointed to my tiny acorn. "Why you piss your bed, Rooinek?" he asked.

"Hey, look, there is no hat on his snake!" someone yelled. They all crowded closer.

"Pisskop! Pisskop!"—in a moment all the small kids were chanting.

"You hear, you a pisshead," the Judge translated. "Who cut the hat off your snake, Pisskop?"

I looked down. All seemed perfectly normal to me. I looked up at the Judge, confused. The Judge parted his pajama fly. His large "snake" seemed to be a continuous sheath brought down to a point of ragged skin. I must say, it wasn't much of a sight.

More trouble lay ahead of me for sure. I was a Rooinek and a pisskop. I spoke the wrong language. And now I was obviously made differently. But I was still alive, and in my book, where there's life, there's hope.

⚙ ⚙ ⚙

By the end of the first term I had reduced my persecution to no more than an hour a day. I had the art of survival almost down pat. Except for one thing: I had become a bed wetter. It is impossible to become a perfect adapter if you leave a wet patch behind you every morning.

My day would begin with a bed-wetting caning from Mevrou, a routine that did serve a useful purpose. I learned that crying is a luxury good adapters have to forgo, and I soon had the school record for being thrashed. The Judge said so. I wasn't just a hated Rooinek and a pisskop, I was also a record holder.

The Judge ordered that I only be beaten up a little at a time, and if I could stop being a pisskop he'd stop even that, although he added that, for a Rooinek, this was probably impossible. I was inclined to agree. No amount of resolve on my part seemed to have the least effect.

The end of the first term finally came. I was to return home for the May holidays: home to Nanny, who would listen to my sadness and sleep on her mat at the foot of my bed so the bogeyman couldn't get me. I also intended to inquire whether my mother had stopped breaking down so I would be allowed to stay home.

I rode home joyfully in Dr. "Henny" Boshoff's shiny Chevrolet coupé. As we choofed along, I was no longer a Rooinek and a pisskop but became a great chief. Life was very good. It was Dr. Henny who had first told me about the nervous breakdown, and he now confirmed that my mother was "coming along nicely" but she wouldn't be home just yet. Sadly this put the kibosh on my chances of staying home.

When I arrived at the farm Nanny wept and held me close. It was late summer. The days were filled with song as the field women picked cotton, working their way down the long rows, singing in perfect harmony while they plucked the fluffy white fiber heads from the sun-blackened cotton bolls.

When Nanny couldn't solve a problem for me she'd say, "We must ask Inkosi-Inkosikazi, the great medicine man, he will know what to do." Now Nanny sent a message to Inkosi-Inkosikazi to the effect that we urgently needed to see him on the matter of the child's night water. The message was put on the drums and in two days we heard that Inkosi-Inkosikazi would call in a fortnight or so on his way to visit Modjadji, the great rain queen. The whites of Nanny's eyes would grow big and her cheeks puff out as she talked about the greatness of the medicine man. "He will dry your bed with one throw of the shinbones of the great white ox," she promised.

"Will he also grow skin over my acorn?" I demanded. She clutched me to her breast, her answer lost as she chortled all over me.

The problem of the night water was much discussed by the field women. "Surely a grass sleeping mat will dry in the morning sun? This is not a matter of proper concern for the greatest medicine man in Africa." It was all right for them, of course. They didn't have to go back to the Judge and Mevrou.

Almost two weeks to the day, Inkosi-Inkosikazi arrived in his big black Buick, symbol of his enormous power and wealth, even to the Boers, who despised him yet feared his magic.

All that day the field women brought gifts of food: kaffir corn, squash, native spinach, watermelons, bundles of dried tobacco leaf—and six scrawny kaffir chickens, mostly tough old roosters, their legs tied and their wings clipped.

One scrawny old cock with mottled gray feathers looked very much like my granpa, except for his eyes. Granpa's eyes were pale blue, intended for gazing over soft English landscapes; that old rooster's were sharp as beads of red light.

My granpa came down the steps and walked toward the big Buick. He stopped to kick one of the roosters, for he hated kaffir chickens. His pride and joy were his one hundred black Orpington hens and six giant roosters.

He greatly admired Inkosi-Inkosikazi, who had once cured him of his gallstones. "Never a trace of a gallstone since," he declared. "If you ask me, the old monkey is the best damned doctor in the lowveld."

The old medicine man, like Nanny, was a Zulu. It was said he was the last son of the great Dingaan, the Zulu king who fought both the Boers and the British to a standstill. Two generations after the Boers had finally defeated his *Impi* at the Battle of Blood River, they remained in awe of Dingaan.

Two years after the battle, Dingaan, reeling from the combined forces of his half brother Mpande and the Boers, had sought refuge among the Nyawo people on the summit of the great Lebombo mountains. On the night he was treacherously assassinated by Nyawo tribesmen he had been presented with a young virgin, and his seed was planted in her womb.

"Where I chose blood, this last of my sons will choose wisdom. You will call him Inkosi-Inkosikazi, he will be a man for all Africa," Dingaan had told the Nyawo maiden.

This made the small, wizened black man who was being helped from the Buick one hundred years old.

Inkosi-Inkosikazi was dressed in a mismatched suit, the jacket brown, the trousers blue pinstripe. A mangy leopard-skin cloak fell from his shoulders. In his right hand he carried a beautifully beaded fly switch, the symbol of an important chief. His hair was whiter than raw cotton, tufts of snowy beard sprang from his chin and only three yellowed teeth remained in his mouth. His eyes burned sharp and clear, like the eyes of the old rooster.

My granpa briefly welcomed Inkosi-Inkosikazi and granted him permission to stay overnight on the farm. The old man nodded, showing none of the customary obsequiousness expected from a kaffir, and my granpa shook the old man's bony claw and returned to his chair on the *stoep*.

Nanny, who had rubbed earth on her forehead like all the other women, finally spoke. "Lord, the women have brought food and we have beer freshly fermented."

Inkosi-Inkosikazi ignored her, which I thought was pretty brave of him, and ordered one of the women to untie the cockerels. With a squawking and flapping of stunted wings all but one rose and dashed helter-skelter toward open territory. The old cock who looked like Granpa rose slowly, then, calm as you like, he walked over to a heap of corn and started pecking away.

"Catch the feathered devils," Inkosi-Inkosikazi suddenly commanded.

With squeals of delight the chickens were rounded up again. The ice had been broken as five of the women, each holding a chicken upside down by the legs, waited for the old man's instructions. Inkosi-Inkosikazi squatted down and with his finger traced five circles, each about two feet in diameter, in the dust, muttering incantations. Then he signaled for one of the women to bring over a cockerel. Grabbing the old bird and using its beak as a marker, he retraced the first circle on the ground, then laid the cockerel inside the circle, where it lay unmoving. He proceeded to do the same thing to the other four chickens until each lay in its own circle. As each chicken was laid to rest there would be a gasp of amazement from the women.

Inkosi-Inkosikazi squatted cross-legged in the center of the *indaba* mats and beckoned that I should join him. Nanny pushed me gently toward him. "You must go, it is a great honor, only a chief can sit with a chief on the meeting mat."

He had the strong, sweet smell of African sweat, mixed with tobacco. After all I had been through in the smell department, it wasn't too bad and I sat cross-legged beside him.

Inkosi-Inkosikazi leaned toward me and spoke in Zulu. "Tomorrow I will show you the trick of the chickens. It's not really magic, you know."

"Thank you, sir," I said softly. I was pleased at the notion of sharing a secret. Even if it was only a trick, it was a damned clever one. My confidence in his ability to change my status as a pisskop was growing by the minute.

Inkosi-Inkosikazi indicated to Nanny that she should begin the matter of the night water. The field women settled down around the *indaba* mats, taking care not to touch even the tiniest part of the edge.

African stories are long, with every detail cherished. It was a great moment for Nanny as she stood alone in the twilight and told her story. She spoke in Shangaan so that all could share wide-eyed and groan and nod and sigh in the appropriate places.

The hugeness of Mevrou with her mustache they found amazing, the injustice of the Judge and jury they took in their stride, for they all knew how the white man passes sentences that have no relationship to what has been done. The pissing upon me by the Judge and jury had them rocking and moaning. Such an indignity was surely beyond even the white man?

In the sudden way of Africa it was dark now. A piece of green wood crackled in the fire, sending up a shower of sparks. The leaping flames lit Nanny's face; there was no doubt that they would remember this teller of a great story of misery and woe. I was hugely impressed, but when Nanny got to the part where my snake had no hat, the women cupped their hands over their mouths and started to giggle.

Nanny concluded by saying that the business of my night water was an evil spell brought upon me by the angel of death with the mustache like a man, so that she could return each morning to feed her beating *sjambok* on my frail flesh. Only a great medicine man such as Inkosi-Inkosikazi could defeat this evil spell.

Nanny finally sat down, heaving with sobs, knowing that such a tale had never been told before and that it might live forever, warped into a Shangaan legend.

I can tell you, I was mighty impressed that any person, most of all me, could go through such a harrowing experience.

Inkosi-Inkosikazi rose and yawned. With the handle of his fly switch he prodded my weeping nanny. "Get me some kaffir beer, woman," he demanded.

Dee and Dum, the twin kitchen maids, served me my dinner. They told me I was the bravest person they had ever known.

By bedtime Nanny was at my side as usual. She crushed me to her bosom and told me how I had thrust greatness upon her with the coming of the greatest medicine man in all Africa. When Nanny finally left me, she said, "Tonight Inkosi-Inkosikazi will visit in your dreams to find the way of your night water."

The morning after the night Inkosi-Inkosikazi went walkabout in my dreams, he summoned me to sit with him again on the meeting mat. From a leather bag he produced the twelve magic shinbones from the great white ox. Squatting on his haunches as he prepared to throw the bones, he commenced a deep, rumbling incantation. The yellowed dice briefly clicked together in his hands and fell onto the ground in front of him. Inkosi-Inkosikazi flicked at them with his forefinger; then with a final grunt he tossed them back into their bag.

Inkosi-Inkosikazi's eyes, sharp pins of light in his wrinkled face, seemed to look right into me. "I visited you in your dreams and we came to a place of three waterfalls and ten stones across the river. The shinbones of the great white ox say I must take you back so that you can jump the three waterfalls and cross the river, stepping from stone to stone without falling into the rushing torrent. If you can do this then the unfortunate business of the night water will be over."

I nodded, not knowing what to say.

"Now, listen to me carefully, boy. Watch and listen. Watch and listen," he repeated. "When I tell you to close your eyes you will do so."

Anxious to please him, I shut my eyes tightly. "Not now! Only when I tell you. Not tight, but as you do when your eyes are heavy from the long day and it is time to sleep."

I opened my eyes to see him crouched in front of me, his beautiful fly switch suspended slightly above my normal sightline. The fall of horsehair swayed gently before my eyes.

"Watch the tail of the horse." My eyes followed the switch as it moved to and fro. "It is time to close your eyes but not your ears. You must listen carefully, *infaan*. . . ."

A sudden roar of water filled my head and then I saw the three waterfalls. I was standing on an outcrop of rock directly above the highest one. Far below, the river rushed away, tumbling into a narrow gorge. Just before the water entered the gorge I noted the ten stepping-stones strung across it.

Inkosi-Inkosikazi spoke to me, his voice soft. "It is late; the bush doves, anticipating nightfall, are already silent. You are standing on a rock above the highest waterfall, a young warrior who has killed his first lion and is worthy now to fight in the legion of Dingaan. Worthy even to fight in the Impi of Shaka, the greatest warrior king of all.

"You are wearing the skirt of lion tail as you face into the setting sun. Now the sun has passed beyond Zululand, and now it leaves the Shangaan and the royal *kraal* of Modjadji, the rain queen, to be cooled in the great dark water beyond. You can see the moon rising over Africa and you are at peace with the night."

As I stood on the great rock waiting to jump, I could see the new moon rising above the thundering falls.

"You must take a deep breath and say the number three to yourself as you leap. Then, when you surface, you must take another breath and say the number two as you are washed across the rim of the second waterfall, then again a deep breath as you rise and are carried over the third. Now you must swim to the first stone, counting backward from ten to one, counting each stone as you leap from it to the next to cross the rushing river." The old medicine man paused. "You must jump now, little warrior of the king."

I took a deep breath and launched myself into the night. The cool air rushed past my face and then I hit the water below, sank briefly, and rose to the surface. With scarcely enough time to take a second breath I was swept over the second waterfall and then again I fell down the third to be plunged into a deep pool at its base. I swam strongly to the first of the great stones glistening in the moonlight. Jumping from stone to stone, I crossed the river, counting from ten to one, then leaping to the pebbly beach on the far side.

Inkosi-Inkosikazi's voice cut through the roar of the falls. "We have crossed the night water to the other side and it is done. You must open your eyes now, little warrior." Inkosi-Inkosikazi brought me back from the dreamtime and I looked around, a little surprised to see the familiar farmyard about me. "When you need me you may come to the night country. I will always be there in the place of the three waterfalls and the ten stones across the river." Pointing to what appeared to be an empty sack, he said: "Bring me that chicken and I will show you the trick of the chicken sleep."

I walked over to the sack. Inside, the beady red eye of the chicken that looked like Granpa blinked up at me. The old man rose and called over to me to draw a circle in the dirt. He showed me how to hold the rooster, by securing its body under your right armpit like a set of bagpipes and grabbing it high up its neck with your left hand so that its head is held between forefinger and thumb. Getting a good hold of its feet with your free hand, you dip the chicken toward the ground at an angle, with its beak not quite touching the rim of the circle. The beak is then traced around the perimeter three times and the bird laid inside the circle.

The old man made me practice it three times. The old rooster lay within the circle docile as a sow in warm mud. To bring the chicken back from wherever chickens go in such circumstances, all I needed to do was touch it and say, "Chicken sleep, chicken wake, if chicken not wake then chicken be ate!" A pretty grim warning, if you ask me.

I did not ask Inkosi-Inkosikazi how a Shangaan chicken could understand Zulu because you simply do not ask such questions of the greatest medicine man in all of Africa.

"The chicken trick is our bond. We are now brothers bound in this common knowledge and the knowledge of the place in the dreamtime."

I'm telling you, it was pretty solemn stuff. With a yell the old man called for his driver, who was asleep in the back of the Buick. Together we walked toward the big black car.

"You may keep this chicken to practice on," Inkosi-Inkosikazi said as he climbed into the backseat.

As if from nowhere, the car was surrounded by field women who loaded the boot with tributes. Nanny handed the old man a square of brightly colored cloth with several coins knotted into one corner. Inkosi-Inkosikazi declined the offer of what was, for Nanny, two months' salary.

"It is a matter between me and the boy. I am on my way to the Molototsi River, where I go to see Modjadji, the rain queen." He stuck his head out of the window and gazed into the sky. "The rains have not come to Zululand, and in this matter her magic is greater than mine."

With a roar from its mighty V8 engine, the Buick shot down the road, raising a cloud of dust behind it.

By the time the holidays were over Granpa Chook, for that was what I called my chicken, and I were practically inseparable. Calling a chicken a chook was a private joke my mother and I had shared. We had received some photos from a cousin in Australia, one of which had shown a small boy feeding the chickens. On the back was written: "Young Lennie, feeding the chooks on the farm in Wagga Wagga." We had called the two old drakes who quacked around the farmyard Wagga Wagga, and started referring to Granpa's black Orpingtons as the chooks.

Granpa Chook came running the moment I appeared at the kitchen door. There was no doubt about it, that chicken had fallen for me. I felt pretty powerfully attracted to him as well.

We practiced the chicken trick, but he got so smart that the moment I drew a circle in the dust he stepped into it and settled down politely. I think he was trying to be cooperative, but it meant that I had lost all my power. Granpa Chook was the first living creature over which I held power and now this not-so-dumb cluck had found a way of getting back on even terms.

TWO

The holidays came to an end. My bed-wetting had been cured but my apprehension at returning to boarding school remained. Nanny and I had a good weep on the last evening at home. She packed my khaki shorts and shirts, pajamas and a bright red jumper my mother had sent. We all went barefoot at school.

Next day we set out after breakfast in Granpa's old Model A Ford truck. I was in the back with Nanny, and Granpa Chook concealed in a *mealie* sack.

We stopped at the school gates and Nanny handed me the suitcase and the sack.

"What have you got in the bag, son?" Granpa asked.

Before I could reply Nanny called from the back, "It is only sweet potatoes, *baas*."

The tears were running down her cheeks and I wanted to rush back into her big safe arms. With a puff of blue exhaust smoke the truck lurched away and I was left standing at the gates. Ahead of me lay Mevrou, the Judge and jury and the beginning of the power of one, where I would learn that in each of us there is a flame that must never be allowed to go out. That as long as it burns within us, we cannot be destroyed.

I released Granpa Chook from the sack and gave him a bit of a pat on his bald head. Pisskop the Rooinek, possessor of a hatless snake, was back in town. But this time, for damn sure, he was not alone. Now that my bed-wetting days were over my camouflage was almost perfect, except for my you-know-what, which the kids could only see when we took a shower and sometimes they'd even forget to remember about it.

Skirting the edge of the playground, we made our way to the hostel that contained the small kids' dormitory. It looked out onto a run-down citrus orchard. No one ever came here. It was the ideal place for Granpa Chook to stay while I reported to Mevrou.

I set about making a small clearing among the weeds, then drew a circle on the ground, and Granpa Chook settled politely into it. It still annoyed me a bit that he refused to go through the whole magic rigmarole, but you can't go arguing with a chicken.

I found Mevrou in the washhouse folding blankets. She looked at me with distaste and pointed to a bucket beside the mangle. "Your rubber sheet is in that bucket. Take it," she said.

"I . . . I am cured, Mevrou," I stammered.

"Ha! Your *oupa*'s beatings are better than mine then, *ja*?"

"No, Mevrou, your beatings are the best . . . better than my granpa's. I just stopped doing it."

"My *sjambok* will be lonely." Mevrou called the bamboo cane she carried her *sjambok*. "You are too early. The other children will not be here till this afternoon."

I returned to Granpa Chook. Nanny had packed two large sweet potatoes in my suitcase and I planned to share one of these with Granpa Chook.

As I approached the orchard I could hear a fearful squawking. Suddenly Granpa Chook rose from above the weeds, then plunged back into the undergrowth. I stumbled toward the clearing. Granpa Chook stood inside the circle; held firmly in his beak was a three-foot grass snake. With a vigorous shake of his head and a snip of his powerful beak he removed the head from the snake and, to my astonishment, swallowed it.

The toughest damn chicken in the world tossed his head and gave me a beady wink. I could see he was pretty pleased with himself. I don't blame him. How can you go wrong with a friend like him at your side?

The afternoon gradually filled with the cacophony of returning kids. The supper bell went and I left Granpa Chook scratching happily away in his new home. I had spent the afternoon making his shelter from bits of corrugated iron I found among the weeds. I waited until the last moment before slipping into the dining hall to take my place at the table where the little kids sat.

Shortly after lights-out that night I was summoned to appear before the Judge and the jury. It was a full moon again, just like the first time. But also a moon like the one that rose above the waterfalls in the dreamtime when, as a young warrior, I had conquered my fears.

The Judge was even bigger than I remembered. He now sported a crude tattoo on his left arm. African women tattoo their faces, but I had not seen a tattoo on white skin before. Crude blue lines crossed at the center like two snakes wriggling across each other.

"You have marks like a kaffir woman on your arm," I heard myself saying.

The Judge's eyes seemed to pop out of his head. I felt an explosion in my head as I was knocked to the floor.

I got to my feet. Stars, just like in the comic books, were dancing in a red sky in front of my eyes and there was a ringing noise in my ears. But I wasn't crying. I cursed my stupidity: the holidays had blunted my sense of survival; adapt, develop a camouflage, try in every way to be an Afrikaner. A trickle of blood ran from my nose.

The Judge pulled me up to his face, lifting me so that I stood on the tips of my toes. "This is a swastika, man! It means death and destruction to all Rooineks. And you, Pisskop, are going to be the first."

"Yes, sir," I said, my voice barely audible.

"God has sent us this sign from Adolf Hitler, who will deliver the Afrikaner people from the hated English!" The Judge turned to address the jury. "We must all swear a blood oath to Adolf Hitler," he said solemnly. The jury crowded around, their eyes shining with excitement.

"I will swear too," I said hopefully. Blood was still running from my nose; some had dripped to the floor.

"Don't be stupid! Pisskop, you *are* the English." The Judge stood upright on the bed and held his arm aloft at an angle. "In the name of Adolf Hitler we will march every Rooinek bastard into the sea."

I had never been to the sea but I knew it would be a long march, all right. "The blood oath!" the jury chanted.

"Come here, Pisskop." I looked up at the Judge as he wiped his forefinger under my nose, then pushed me to the floor. He held up his finger.

"We will swear this oath with the blood of a Rooinek!" he announced. Two members of the jury lifted me to my feet while the others stuck their fingers into the blood running from my nose. One boy tweaked my nose to increase the flow and the last two members had to dab their fingers into the drops of blood on the floor.

The Judge, wiping the blood on his finger across the swastika tattoo, instructed the jury to do the same. "Death to all Englishmen in South Africa, the fatherland!" he cried.

"Death to all Englishmen in South Africa, the fatherland!" the jury chorused.

The Judge looked down at me. "We won't kill you tonight, Pisskop. But when Hitler comes your days are numbered, you hear?"

"When will that be, sir?" I asked.

"Soon!" He turned me toward the dormitory door and gave me a swift kick that sent me sprawling headlong across the polished floor. I got to my feet and ran.

Back in my own dormitory the little kids leapt out of bed, demanding to know what had happened. I sniffed out the story of the swastika and the blood oath and Hitler.

Eight-year-old Danie Coetzee shook his head.

"Pisskop, you are in deep shit."

"Who is this Adolf Hitler who is coming to get Pisskop?" a fellow we called Flap-lips de Jaager asked.

It was apparent nobody knew the answer.

I waited until everyone was asleep and then crept to the window. The full moon brought a soft sheen to the leaves of the orchard trees. "I didn't cry. They'll never make me cry again!" I said to the moon. Then I returned to my bed.

Granpa Chook's cover was blown the following morning. Before the wake-up bell went, the whole dormitory awoke to his raucous crowing. Startled out of a deep sleep, I saw him perched on the windowsill nearest my bed, his long scrawny neck stretched in a mighty rendition of cock-a-doodle-doooo! Then he cocked his head to one side and flew onto my bed-head. Stretching his long neck toward me, he gave my ear a gentle peck.

The kids surrounded me. "It's an old kaffir chicken come to visit Pisskop," Flap-lips de Jaager yelled.

Granpa Chook, imperious on the bedhead, fixed them with a beady stare. "He is my friend," I said defiantly. "He can do tricks and everything."

"No he can't! He's a dumb kaffir chicken. Wait till the Judge hears about Pisskop's new friend," Danie Coetzee said, and everyone laughed.

The wake-up bell went, which meant Mevrou would arrive in a minute, so we all scrambled back into bed to await her permission to get up. I barely had time to push Granpa Chook out of the window before her huge form loomed through the door.

Mevrou paced the length of the dormitory, her *sjambok* hanging from a loop on the leather belt of her blue uniform. She stopped as she reached my bed, whipped off the blanket and examined the dry mattress. Suddenly her eyes seemed almost to pop out of her head: "Pisskop! There is chicken shit on your pillow!"

I looked down at my pillow in horror: Granpa Chook had neatly deposited his green and white calling card.

"Explain, man!" Mevrou roared.

Shaking with terror, I told her about Granpa Chook.

Mevrou slipped the cane from her leather belt. "Pisskop, I think you are sick in the head, like your poor mother. First you come here and piss in your bed every night. Then you come back and fill it with chicken shit!" She pointed to the end of the bed. "Bend over," she commanded.

She blasted me four strokes of the *sjambok*. Biting back tears, I forced myself not to grab my bum.

"Clean up your pillow and bring this devil's chicken to the kitchen after breakfast, you hear?"

Granpa Chook and I were in a terrible jam, all right. After breakfast I slipped out to find him. He was scratching around the orchard looking for worms. I explained the latest disaster to him. So much for my resolution not to cry, I could feel the tears running down my cheeks. I picked him up and took him to a low fence that marked the hostel boundary. I looked over the fence and my heart gave a leap; in the distance I could see three kaffir huts. For sure they'd keep chickens and Granpa Chook could board with them.

I explained this new plan to Granpa Chook and pushed him over the fence. Granpa Chook, though, had other ideas. With an indignant squawk and a flap of his wings he was back on my side of the fence. It was clear that the toughest damn chicken in the whole wide world had no intention of deserting his friend, even if his own life was at stake.

We waited at the kitchen door. Mevrou appeared. "So this is the chicken that shits in your bed, Pisskop?"

"It wasn't on purpose, Mevrou. He's a very clever chicken."

"Whoever heard of a clever chicken?"

"I'll show you, Mevrou." I quickly drew a circle in the dust and Granpa Chook immediately hopped into it and settled down as though he were laying an egg, which he couldn't, of course. "He'll stay in that circle until I say to come out."

For a moment Mevrou looked impressed; then she scowled. "This is just some dumb thing kaffir chickens do that white chickens don't," she said. Just inside the kitchen stood a butcher's block with a large cleaver resting on it. "Give me that bed-shitting kaffir chicken!" she yelled, grabbing the cleaver.

Two cockroaches resting under the cleaver on the block raced up the back of Mevrou's hand. She let out an almighty scream, dropping the cleaver. One cockroach fell to the polished cement floor; the other ran up her arm and disappeared down her bodice.

With a delighted squawk, Granpa Chook came charging into the kitchen and scooped up the cockroach crossing the floor. Mevrou was waving her arms and making little gasping noises as she danced from one foot to the other. The second cockroach fell from under her skirt and Granpa Chook had it in a trice.

"It's orright, Mevrou, the other one fell out and Granpa Chook got it," I said, pointing to Granpa Chook strutting around looking very pleased with himself.

Mevrou had turned a deep crimson. I fetched a chair and she plopped down into it like an overripe watermelon. When she had recovered somewhat she pointed a trembling finger at Granpa Chook.

"You are right, Pisskop. That is a good chicken. He can stay. But he has to earn his keep."

And that's how Granpa Chook came to do kitchen duty. Every day after breakfast he checked out the kitchen for creepy-crawlies of every description. The toughest damn chicken in the world had survived, he had beaten the executioner by adapting perfectly and we were together again.

A couple of months went by. I had become a slave to the Judge. In return for being at his beck and call, I was more or less left to my own devices. The odd cuff behind the head or a push from an older kid was about all I had to endure. Things were pretty good, really. If the Judge needed me he would put two fingers to his mouth and give a piercing whistle and Granpa Chook and I would come running.

Although Granpa Chook was now under the protection of Mevrou, he still needed to be on the alert. Farm kids just can't help chucking stones at kaffir chickens. He would cluck around the playground during lessons. The moment the bell went he would come charging over to my classroom, skidding to a halt in the dust, cackling his anxiety to be with me again.

No class existed for my age and so I had been placed with the seven-year-old kids, all of whom were still learning to read. I had been reading in English for a year and the switch to reading in Afrikaans wasn't difficult. I already spoke Zulu and Shangaan and, like most small kids, found learning a new language simple enough. I was soon the best in the class. Yet I quickly realized that survival means never being best at anything, and I learned to pause and stumble over words that were perfectly clear to me. Our teacher, Miss du Plessis, wasn't anxious for a five-year-old Rooinek to shine in a class of knot-headed Boers. She put my poor results down to my inability to grasp the subtlety of the Afrikaans language as well as being the youngest in the class.

It became increasingly hard for the other kids to think of me as being different. Except, of course, for my hatless snake; but even this, like a kid with a birthmark, started to go unnoticed.

Then, on September 3, 1939, Neville Chamberlain, Prime Minister of England, declared war on Germany. We all knew by now that Adolf Hitler was the leader of the German people.

We were in the dining room when the headmaster announced the news. After the meal, when the staff had retired, the Judge jumped to his feet and stepped onto the bench at the top table. He rolled up the sleeve of his shirt so we could all see his swastika tattoo. "Adolf Hitler is the King of Germany and God has sent him to take South Africa back from the English and give it to us." He jabbed at the swastika on his arm. "This is his sign . . . the swastika will make us free again." His right hand shot up in salute. "Heil Hitler!" he cried.

We all jumped to our feet and, thrusting our arms out, yelled, "Heil Hitler!"

It was all very exciting. Then the words of the Judge on the first night at school roared back into my consciousness . . . "Don't be stupid! Pisskop, you *are* the English!"

"Some of us have sworn a blood oath to Adolf Hitler," the Judge continued, "and the time has now come to march the Rooineks into the sea. After school we will meet behind the shithouses for a council of war!"

I don't suppose any of us had much idea of where the sea was, somewhere across the Lebombo mountains and probably over the Limpopo River. A long, long way away. I could understand why the march would take some planning.

The dining room buzzed with excitement. Then the Judge pointed directly at me. "Pisskop, you are our first prisoner of war!" He raised his arm higher. "Heil Hitler!"

"Heil Hitler!" the rest of the dining hall chorused back.

It was the most exciting day in the school's history, although my own prospects looked pretty bleak. What was certain was that Granpa Chook and I needed to make some pretty urgent escape plans. I was in despair. Even if I did know how to get home, which I didn't, how far could a little kid and a chicken travel without being spotted by the enemy?

That afternoon in class Miss du Plessis rapped my knuckles sharply with her long steel-edged ruler. She grew totally exasperated when, deep into escape plans, I simply didn't hear her ask what three times four came to.

"*Domkop*! You will have to stay in after school!" The idea was impossible. Granpa Chook and I had to escape before the council of war met behind the shithouses.

"Please, miss! I'm sorry, miss." In a desperate attempt to make amends I blew my camouflage. I recited the nine times table, then the ten, eleven and twelve. I had carefully concealed my knowledge of anything beyond the four times table. The effect was profound. Miss du Plessis was consumed by anger.

"You wicked, rotten, lying, cheating child!" she screamed, raising her ruler. The blows rained down on me and with one swipe the thin metal strip in the ruler sliced into the top of my ear. The blood started to run down my arm.

The sight of blood snapped Miss du Plessis out of her frenzy. She looked down at me and brought her hand to her mouth. Then she screamed and fell to the floor.

The shock of seeing Miss du Plessis drop dead at my feet was so great that I was unable to move. The blood dripped from my ear onto her spotless white blouse until a crimson blot stained the area just above her heart.

"Cripes! You've killed her," I heard Flap-lips de Jaager say as he ran from the classroom. All the others followed, screaming as they vacated the scene of the crime.

I was unaware of anyone entering the room until a huge hand lifted me and hurled me across the classroom, where I landed against the wall. Stunned, I sat there like a discarded rag doll. Mr. Stoffel, the master who taught the Judge's class, was bending over Miss du Plessis. His eyes grew wide as he observed the blood on her blouse. "Shit, he's killed her!" I heard him say.

Just then Miss du Plessis opened her eyes and sat up. "Oh, oh, what have I done!" she sobbed.

Quite suddenly the classroom, grew very dark. I could dimly see Mr. Stoffel coming toward me, as though in slow motion. Then I must have passed out.

I awoke in my bed, to find Mevrou at my side. "Are you awake, Pisskop?" she asked, not unkindly.

"Ja, Mevrou." My head was swathed in a thick crêpe bandage and I was wearing my pajamas. My shoulder ached where I'd landed against the wall.

"Now listen to me, Pisskop. When the doctor comes you must tell him you fell out of a tree, you hear?"

"Ja, Mevrou."

"What tree did you fall out of, Pisskop?"

"It—it was the big mango tree next to the playground."

"Ja, that's good, the mango tree. Remember to tell the doctor when he comes."

To my joy Dr. Henny entered the dormitory. He unwound the bandage around my head. "What's the matter, son? You look pretty done in."

Even if Dr. Henny wasn't a Rooinek I knew he was on my side, and I longed to burst into tears and tell him all my troubles. But I had already blown my camouflage once that day with disastrous results. Choking back the tears, I told him how I had fallen from the big old mango tree.

He turned to Mevrou and in Afrikaans he said: "Hmm, except for the cut between the ear and the skull there are no contusions or abrasions. Are you quite sure this child fell from a tree?"

"The other children saw it happen, Doctor. There is no doubt." Mevrou said this with such conviction that I began to wonder myself.

"It's true, sir. I fell out of the tree and hurt my shoulder against the wall."

Dr. Henny didn't seem to notice that I'd replied in Afrikaans. "The wall?"

Fear showed for a moment in Mevrou's eyes but she quickly recovered. "The child doesn't speak Afrikaans very well, he means the ground."

"Ja, the ground," I added.

"Okay, let's look at your shoulder, then." He rotated my shoulder, then checked my heart and chest and my back with his stethoscope, which was cold against my skin. "Seems fine. We'll just put in a couple of stitches and you'll be right as rain," he said in English.

"Can I go home, please?"

"No need for that, old son." He dug into his bag and produced a yellow sucker, pineapple, my favorite after raspberry. "Here, this will make you feel better, you get stuck into that while I fix up these stitches."

A moment later he was dabbing my stitches with Mercurochrome. "I'll be back in a week to remove these." He handed me a second sucker. "That's for being extra brave."

"Thank you, sir. Doctor Henny, are you English?" I asked.

His expression changed and I could see that he was upset. "We are all South Africans, son. Don't let anyone tell you otherwise." He spoke with a quiet vehemence, then repeated: "Don't let anyone tell you anything else!"

I had certainly had better days, but a two-sucker day doesn't come along very often so it wasn't all bad.

Despite my prisoner-of-war status, the kids were pretty good for the next few days. My stitches made me a kind of hero in the small kids' dormitory, as if I'd been in the war and was wounded.

THREE

But Rooineks are not designed to be permanent heroes. The night after I had my stitches out I was summoned to appear before the Judge and jury. My temporary reprieve was over. Here I was again, being marched straight into another calamity.

"Stand to attention, prisoner Pisskop," the Judge snarled. "Tonight we must get you ready for your march into the sea." He pointed to the corridor between the beds and gave me a push. I tripped over my pajama pants and fell to the floor. One of the jury reached down and pulled the pants away from my ankles. I rose bare-arsed and looked uncertainly at the Judge. "March!" he commanded. I started to march, swinging my arms high. "*Links, regs, links, regs, halt!*" he bawled. Then again: "Left, right, left, right, halt! Which is your left foot, prisoner Pisskop?" I had no idea but pointed to a foot at random. "Domkop! Don't you even know your left from your right?"

"No, sir," I said, feeling stupid.

"Every day after school you will march around the playground for five thousand steps, you hear?" I nodded. "You will count backward from five thousand until you get to number one."

I couldn't believe my luck; no one had laid a hand on me. I retrieved my pajama pants and scurried back to my dormitory.

Being a prisoner of war and learning to march wasn't such a bad thing. But I must admit, counting backward from five thousand isn't much of a way to pass the time. It's impossible anyway, your thoughts wander and before you know it you're all jumbled up and have to start over again. Mostly I did the Judge's homework in my head. Carrying his books from school, I would memorize his arithmetic lesson and then work the equations out in my head as I marched along. If things got a bit complicated, I'd make sure nobody was looking and work out a more complex sum using a stick in the dirt. It got so I couldn't wait to see what he'd done in class each day.

The Judge was an awful *domkop*. In the mornings, carrying his books, I'd check his homework. It was always a mess and mostly all wrong. I began to despair for him and for myself as well. You see, he could only leave the school if the work he did during the year gave him a pass mark. So far, he didn't have a hope. If he failed I'd have him for another year. That is, if Hitler hadn't come by then to march me away.

Escape seemed impossible, so I'd have to think of something else. A plan began to form. It was breathtakingly simple though fraught with danger. If I blew my camouflage and helped the Judge with his homework so that he would pass, would he not be forced to spare Granpa Chook and me if Adolf Hitler arrived before the end of term?

After a long talk with Granpa Chook, we agreed it was a chance worth taking.

After breakfast the following morning, when I was folding the Judge's blanket and arranging his towel over his bed rail, I broached the subject. He was sitting on his bed, trying to do some last-minute arithmetic.

"Can I help you, sir?" My heart thumped like a donkey engine, though I was surprised how steady my voice sounded.

"Push off, Pisskop. Can't you see I'm busy, man?" The Judge was doing the fractions I'd done in my head the previous afternoon and getting them hopelessly wrong.

Gulping down my fear, I said, "What happens if you don't pass at the end of the year?" The Judge looked at me. I could see the thought wasn't new to him. He reached out and grabbed me by the shirtfront.

"If I don't pass, I'll kill you first and then I'll run away!" He went back to chewing his pencil, his brow furrowed as he squinted at the page of equations. I pointed to the one he'd just completed. "That's wrong. The answer is seven-ninths." I moved my finger quickly. "Four-fifths, six-eighths, nine-tenths, five-sevenths . . ." I paused as he looked up at me, openmouthed.

"Where did you learn to do this, man?"

I shrugged. "It's just easy for me, that's all." I hoped he couldn't sense how scared I was.

A look of cunning came into his eyes. He handed me the book and the pencil. "Just write the answers very softly and I'll copy them, you hear?"

From knowing to hide my brains for camouflage, I'd now moved up to the next stage and had learned to use them. Granpa Chook and I were one step further away from the sea.

But I knew if a domkop like the Judge went from bottom to top of his class overnight, Mr. Stoffel would soon smell a rat. Telling the Judge he was a duffer was more than my life was worth.

"We have a problem," I said.

"What problem, man? You just write in the answers very soft, that's all."

"Judge, arithmetic doesn't interest you, does it? I mean, if it did you could do it"—I snapped my fingers—"just like that!"

"Ja, if I wanted to I could. Only little kids like you are interested in all that shit!"

I grew bolder. "So you can't just get ten out of ten today when yesterday you only got two sums right. Mr. Stoffel will know there's some monkey business going on." I paused. "You will get better a little bit each week and you'll tell Mr. Stoffel that you suddenly got the hang of doing sums."

The Judge grinned slyly. "*Jy is 'n slimmertjie*, Pisskop."

The Judge had called me clever. Me! Pisskop the Rooinek! I was beside myself with pride. The thrill of the compliment almost caused me to forget my other anxiety.

"What will happen if Adolf Hitler comes before the end of term?" I asked, my heart beating overtime.

The Judge understood the reason for my question. "Okay, man, you got me there. I will say nothing until I've passed at the end of the year." He shook his head. "I'm sorry, Pisskop, after that I will have to tell him about you. You and your stupid kaffir chicken are dead meat when he comes."

I had won: my plan had worked. Granpa Chook and I were safe for the remainder of the term.

The Judge had come to the end of his copying. I had never seen him quite so happy. I saw my opportunity and, taking a sharp inward breath, said quickly, "It will be difficult to march every afternoon and still do your homework, sir."

Had I gone too far? I'd won the battle and here I was risking all on a minor skirmish.

The Judge wiped his nose on the back of his hand. "Orright, no more marching."

Victory was mine a second time.

One thing is certain in life. Just when things are going well, soon after, they are certain to go wrong.

Mrs. Gerber, another teacher, told us that day in class, there had been an outbreak of Newcastle's disease on a chicken farm near Merensky Dam. Her husband, who was a Government vet, had left to visit all the surrounding farms.

Even the youngest kids know what havoc a disease can cause with poultry or other livestock. Rinderpest and foot-and-mouth disease among the cattle were the worst, but every farm keeps at least fifty chickens for eggs, so Mrs. Gerber's news was met with consternation. My mother had once said that if my granpa lost all his black Orpingtons it would break his heart.

It was pretty depressing to think of poor old Granpa slowly dying of a broken heart. That was, if Adolf Hitler didn't arrive first. If he did, I knew Granpa wouldn't have the strength to make escape plans and then what would become of me?

Maybe I could live with Nanny in Zululand? This thought cheered me up a lot. Adolf Hitler would never look for a small English person in the middle of Zululand. Inkosi-Inkosikazi would hide me with a magic spell. As for Granpa Chook, Adolf Hitler would never be able to tell an English-speaking chicken apart from all the other kaffir chickens. I decided I would put this excellent plan to Nanny when I got back to the farm.

From what we could gather from the Judge, who was allowed to listen to the news on Mr. Stoffel's wireless, the war was going pretty badly for the English. Adolf Hitler had taken Poland, which I took to be a place somewhere in South Africa, like Zululand, but where the Po tribe lived. The Judge made it sound as though Hitler could be expected any day now in our neck of the woods.

I had no idea that South Africa was on England's side. From where I sat the English were most definitely the local enemy.

Most of my information came from the regular war councils the Judge held behind the school shithouses. All the senior hostel boys were storm troopers and Danie Coetzee, as head of the small kids' dormitory, was also allowed to attend. As the official prisoners of war, Granpa Chook and I were dragged along for the purposes of interrogation and torture.

I was blindfolded and tied to the trunk of a jacaranda tree with a rope around my chest and waist, leaving my arms and legs free. Most torture sessions began with the iron bar, which I was required to hold out in front of me while the Judge timed each session. I would have to hold the bar up longer than the previous time before dropping it.

The second main torture that required my hands to be free was "shooting practice." Every storm trooper carried a catapult as his deadly weapon. Farm kids all have catapults for shooting birds and grow very skilled at using them. All the senior boys had one stashed away and they would wear these around their necks at Nazi Party meetings.

For shooting practice I was required to stretch my arms out on either side of me with my palms open and turned upward. An empty jam tin was placed on either hand and each of the storm troopers was allowed two shots to try to knock the tins down. The six best results for the day earned the right to beat me up on the next occasion it became necessary.

I must say this for those Nazis: while they hit the tins from twenty feet often enough, only once did I collect a stone which thudded into the butt of my left hand, which I was unable to use for several days.

Granpa Chook would fly up onto a branch of the jacaranda, where he would keep a beady eye on the proceedings. He was known to the Nazi Party as Prisoner of War Kaffir Chicken Rooinek. As Mevrou's leading kitchen insect exterminator, Granpa Chook was pretty safe. Tough as the Judge was, he wasn't willing to take Mevrou on. Granpa Chook had it easy up there in the jacaranda tree, while I was the one who suffered at ground level.

The Nazi Party sessions were held twice a week. Although they would leave me trembling for hours afterward, the physical damage wasn't too bad. I only got hit if I dropped the iron bar too soon or failed to answer one of the Judge's ranting questions fast enough for his liking.

"What are you, Pisskop?"

"A piece of shit!" I would respond.

"Not shit! Dog shit!" they would all chorus back.

Halfway through an interrogation I would be blindfolded. Then, sooner or later, someone would throw a bucket of water over me. Knowing it might come but not knowing when meant that I would get an awful shock. The imagination is always the best torturer.

Or they would release half a dozen red ants down my shorts and watch me frantically trying to find them as the ants bit painfully into the soft inner parts of my legs. If I tore my blindfold away it would mean a double clout from every member of the Party. I soon learned that a red ant tends to bite only once if you leave it alone. But, let me tell you something, that one bite isn't a very nice experience.

If some new trick, like the red ants, worked, they would yell with laughter as my legs pumped up and down and my hands searched frantically to rid me of the ants.

One thing got to all of them more than anything else. They

couldn't make me cry. I suspect they even began to admire me a bit. Many of them had little brothers of my age at home and they knew how easy it is for a five-year-old to cry. In fact I had turned six but nobody had told me, so in my head I was still five.

In truth, my willpower had very little to do with my resolve never to cry. I had learned a special trick and, in the process, had somehow lost the knack of turning on the tap.

Behind the blindfold I had learned to be in two places at once. I could easily answer their stupid questions, while with another part of my mind I would visit Inkosi-Inkosikazi. Down there in the night country I was safe from the storm troopers.

As they tied the dirty piece of rag over my eyes, I would take three deep breaths. Immediately I would hear Inkosi-Inkosikazi's voice, soft as distant thunder: "You are standing on the rock above the highest waterfall, a young warrior who has killed his first lion. . . ."

I stood in the moonlight on the rock above the three waterfalls. Far below I could see the ten stones glistening and the white water as it crashed through the narrow gorge beyond. I knew then that the person on the outside was only a shell, a presence to be provoked. Inside was the real me, where my tears joined the tears of all the sad people in the whole world to form the three waterfalls in the night country.

The last term of the year had come to an end; only one more day remained, just one more interrogation, then freedom.

The Judge had pleased Mr. Stoffel with his efforts in the final term. He was top of his class by the time term ended. He showed me his report card, which said, in black and white, that he had passed.

Therefore I had no reason to expect anything but a light going-over at the last interrogation and torture session before the Judge would disappear from my life forever. After all, he owed me something.

Prisoners of War Pisskop and Kaffir Chicken Rooinek were marched off to the jacaranda tree for the last session. This time I was blindfolded immediately I was tied to the tree. I could hear Granpa Chook squawking away above me. I was about to visit the night country when the Judge's voice rang out harshly.

"This is the last time, English bastard!"

With a sudden certainty I knew today would be different. That, in his mind, the Judge owed me nothing. The bad times were back. I tried to get to the safety of the night country, but the fear rose in me and I was unable to detach myself from it.

"Today, Englishman, you eat shit." His use of the word "Englishman" rather than the familiar, almost friendly "Rooinek" added greatly to his menace.

"Hold out your hands." I held them out, palms upward. He grabbed my wrists and held them so tightly I couldn't move them. "Bring it here, Storm Trooper Van der Merwe," I heard him say.

A soft object was dropped first into one hand and then into the other. "Close your hands, bastard," the Judge commanded.

The pain in my wrists was almost unbearable. Slowly I closed my hands. "Take his blindfold off," the Judge commanded again. The rest of the Nazis had grown very quiet and one of them unknotted the blindfold. My nose as well as my eyes had been covered and a terrible smell rose up at me. My hands were sticky and I opened them to see that they contained two squashed human turds.

The Judge released my wrists. "Now, lick your fingers," he demanded. "I am going to count to three. If you haven't licked your fingers I'm going to knock your *blerrie* head off!" The Judge stood pop-eyed in front of me and I could see he was trembling.

I was too deeply shocked to react.

"*Een . . . twee . . . drie!*" he counted. I remained with my hands held out in front of me, quaking with terror. He made a gurgling sound deep in his throat; then he grabbed me by the wrists and forced my hands up to my mouth. My teeth were clamped shut in fear, and the shit was rubbed all over my face and close-cropped hair.

Then he grabbed the tree trunk about two feet above my head. First he tried to shake the tree. Then he began beating at it with his clenched fists. Suddenly he threw his head back, so that he was looking directly upward into the tree.

"Heil Hitler!" he screamed.

In the tree high above Granpa Chook dropped a perfect bomb of green and white chicken shit straight into the Judge's open mouth.

Granpa Chook had waited until the last day of term to give his opinion of the Nazi Party.

The Judge spat furiously, bent double, racing round in circles clutching his throat and stomach, and finally throwing up. He raced for the tap and filled his mouth and spat out about six times.

"Run, Granpa Chook! Run, man, run!" I screamed up into the tree. "The bastard will kill you!"

But Granpa Chook had done enough running for one old kaffir chicken. Sitting up there among the purple blossom, he sounded as though he were laughing his scraggy old head off.

Then, to my horror, he flew onto my shoulder. I grabbed him, but as I lifted him to throw him on his way, there was an explosion of feathers in my face. Granpa Chook let out a fearful squawk as he was blasted from my hands and fell to the ground. The Judge stood with his empty catapult dangling in his left hand.

Granpa Chook made several attempts to get up but the stone

from the powerful catapult had broken his ribcage. After a while he just sat there, looked up at me and said, "Squawk!"

"No *blerrie* kaffir chicken shits on me! Hang him up by the legs next to Pisskop," the Judge commanded. He was still wiping his mouth on the back of his hand. Two storm troopers slung a piece of rope over a branch and Granpa Chook soon hung upside down just beyond my reach.

"Please, sir. I will do anything! Please don't kill Granpa Chook!"

The Judge, his eyes cruel, bent down and looked into my face. "Now we'll see who'll cry," he said, grinning.

I was seized by panic. "Kill me!" I begged. "But don't kill Granpa Chook!"

"You're shit and your kaffir chicken is shit. Did you see what he did to me? Me, Jaapie Botha!"

Still dazed, I tried another desperate tack. "I'll tell Mevrou!" I shouted.

The Judge turned to the storm troopers. "Prisoner of War Kaffir Chicken Rooinek will be executed, two shots each!" He moved to take his place in the shooting line as the storm troopers loaded up their catapults.

"I'll tell Mr. Stoffel how I did your arithmetic for you!" I screamed at the Judge.

I heard the pfflifft of his catapult at the same time as I felt the stone slam into my stomach. The pain was terrible. The shock to my system was enormous; my eyes bugged out of my head and my tongue poked out in involuntary surprise, tasting the dry shit on my lips.

"Fire!" A series of dull plops tore into the fragile bones of Granpa Chook's breast. Spots of blood dropped into the dry dust and among the fallen jacaranda blossoms. Granpa Chook, the toughest damn chicken in the whole world, was dead.

The Judge untied the rope from around my waist and I dropped to my haunches at his feet. He placed his bare foot on my shoulder.

"What are you, Englishman?"

"Dog shit, sir."

"Look at me when you say it!" he barked.

Slowly I looked up at the giant. High above him I could see a milky moon hanging in the afternoon sky. We had got so close, Granpa Chook and I, to making it through to the end, just a few more hours.

I spat at him, "You're dog shit!"

He pushed violently downward with his foot, sending me sprawling. Then he let out a howl, a mixture of anger and anguish. "Why don't you cry, you bastard!" he sobbed, and started to kick blindly at me.

The storm troopers rushed to restrain him, and the Judge allowed himself to be led away. Granpa Chook and I were left alone behind the shithouses under a white moon set in a pale blue sky.

I untied his broken body and placed him on my lap. We sat there under the jacaranda tree among the fallen purple blossoms and I stroked his bloodstained feathers. No more early cock-a-doodle-doo to tell me you are there, my faithful chicken friend. Who will peck my ear? Who will be my friend? I sobbed and sobbed. The great drought was over, the inside man was out, the rains had come to Zululand.

After a long, long while, when the crying was all out of me, I carried Granpa Chook to the orchard and laid him in the place I had made for him. Then I climbed through the dormitory window to fetch my red jumper.

I gathered as many rocks as I could find and then I pulled my red jumper over Granpa Chook's body; his wings poked out of the armholes and his long neck stuck out of the head part and his feet poked out of the bottom.

He looked the best I'd ever seen him. I took the jam tin I had used for his water and collected twenty little green grasshoppers, which are the very best chicken scoff there is. I placed the tin beside his body so that he'd have a special treat on the way to heaven. Finally I covered his body with the stones.

I sat there on my haunches beside the pile of stones as the sun began to set. Now the sun was passing beyond Zululand, even past the land of the Swazi, and now it leaves the Shangaan and the royal *kraal* of Modjadji, the rain queen, to be cooled in the great, dark water beyond.

The bell for supper sounded. I moved to the tap and began to wash away the blood and shit. The last supper. Everything comes to an end. Tomorrow I would be going home for Christmas and Nanny. Wonderful, soft, warm Nanny. Only hours remained before my liberation; nothing the Judge, Mevrou and, for the moment anyway, Adolf Hitler could do would alter that.

But life doesn't work that way. I, most of all, should have known this. At supper *Boetie* Van der Merwe told me Mevrou wanted to see me in the dispensary. "If you tell about this afternoon, we'll kill you," he said through his teeth.

I didn't know then that what seemed like the end was only the beginning. All children are flotsam driven by the ebb and flow of adult lives. Unbeknown to me, the tide had turned and I was being driven out to sea.

FOUR

I waited for Mevrou outside the dispensary. "*Kom!*" she said as she brushed past me. I entered and waited with my hands behind my back, my head bowed in the customary manner.

"Why is there blood on your shirt, Pisskop?"

My shirt was stained with Granpa Chook's blood and a biggish spot where the stone had torn into me.

Mevrou sighed. "Take off your shirt."

I hurriedly removed my shirt and Mevrou made a cursory examination. "Ag, is that all?" She prodded at the wound the stone had made and I flinched.

"Please, Mevrou, I fell on a rock." Mevrou removed the cork from a bottle of iodine and upended it onto a wad of cotton wool.

"Yes, I can see that." She dabbed at my wound and the iodine stung like billy-o and I hopped up and down in dismay, wringing my hands to stop the burning pain. "You can't go getting blood poisoning on the train," she said.

"What train, Mevrou?" I asked, confused.

"Your *oupa* called on the telephone from a *dorp* in the Eastern Transvaal called Barberton. You are not going back to the farm. He says Newcastle's disease had made him kill all his chickens and he has sold the farm."

My head was swimming; my whole world was coming apart at the seams. If Granpa had sold the farm and was making telephone calls from some town in the Eastern Transvaal, where was Nanny? Without Granpa Chook and Nanny, life was not possible.

Mevrou reached into her bag and held up an envelope. "In here is the ticket. Tomorrow night you will catch the train to Barberton. Two days and two nights. I will take you to the train." She dismissed me with a wave of the envelope.

As I reached the door Mevrou called me back. "You can't take the chicken, you hear? South African Railways won't let you take a kaffir chicken, not even in the goods van. I will take the chicken, he will earn his keep."

"He is dead, Mevrou. A dog ate him today." I managed somehow to keep the tears out of my voice.

"That is a shame, he was good in the kitchen. I'm telling you, man, a kaffir chicken is no different from a kaffir. Just when you think you can trust them, they go and let you down."

I had never owned a pair of shoes. In the Northern Transvaal a farm kid only got boots if he had rich parents or if he had turned thirteen. That's when the Old Testament of the Bible says a boy becomes a man.

On the last day of term Mevrou summoned me. After lunch we would be going into town to buy a pair of *tackies* at Harry Crown's shop.

"What are *tackies,* Mevrou?"

"Domkop! *Tackies* are shoes made of canvas with rubber bottoms. Make sure you have clean feet."

From the old mango tree, I watched the kids leave. Parents arrived in beaten-up *bakkies* and mule carts. The Judge left in a mule cart. He made the black servant sit on the tailboard; then he took up the reins and the whip and set off at a furious pace. I breathed a huge sigh of relief. As my mother used to say, "Good riddance to bad rubbish."

Finally everyone had gone and I climbed down and crossed the playground. It wasn't the same without Granpa Chook. It wasn't ever going to be the same again. I saved the need to grieve for a later time. I had enough on my mind with the prospect of going to buy a pair of shoes and catching the train. I'd never owned a pair of shoes and I'd never been on a train. Two nevers in one day is enough to fill anyone's mind.

After a lunch of bread and jam with a mug of sweet tea, I hurried to meet Mevrou, stopping to give my feet a good scrub. The same shower that had been dripping that first night when I thought I was in a slaughterhouse was still sounding drip, drip, drip, like a metronome. It all seemed such a long time ago; I sure had been a baby then.

Mevrou arrived wearing a shapeless floral cotton dress and a funny black straw hat with two cherries on it. A third wire stem stuck up where a cherry had once been.

The town I knew to be about two miles from the school. Mevrou walked three paces ahead of me all the way. Her huge shape sort of rocked along; she stopped every once in a while to catch her breath. The early-afternoon sun beat down on us. "Tonight I must do this all over again for you, Pisskop," she complained, red in the face as a turkey's wattle.

Harry Crown's shop was closed. "Everyone is having their lunch, we must wait," she explained. With great effort she climbed up to the *stoep* of the shop and sat down on a bench beside the padlocked door. "Go and find a tap and wash your feet," she panted.

I crossed the street to the Atlantic Service Station, washed my feet under a tap and walked back across the road on my heels. At the far end of the verandah there was a second entrance to the shop. Above was written "Blacks only." I wondered briefly why whites were not allowed to enter.

"The Jew is late, who does he think he is?" Mevrou said impatiently.

Just then the sawmill hooter sounded. It blew at one o'clock and again at two.

Almost on the dot a big black Chevrolet drove up and parked outside the shop. It was the most beautiful car I had ever seen. Obviously being a Jew was a very profitable business. Maybe I could be one when I grew up.

Harry Crown was a fat man in his late fifties. He wore his trousers high so that his tummy and most of his chest were covered with trouser top, held up by a pair of red braces. When he smiled he showed two gold front teeth.

"A thousand apologies, Mevrou. Have you been waiting long?" he said, unlocking the doors to the shop.

"Ag, it was nothing," Mevrou said, all smiles.

In the part boarded off for white customers, two ceiling fans whirred overhead and the shop was dark and cool.

"What can I do for you, Mevrou?" Harry Crown asked; then, turning to me, he bowed slightly. "And for you, mister?" he said solemnly.

I dropped my eyes to avoid his gaze.

Observing my shyness, he produced a raspberry sucker wrapped in cellophane from a glass jar on the counter. I took the delicious prize and put it into my shirt pocket.

"Thank you, meneer," I said softly.

"Ag, eat it now, boy. When we have finished business you can have another, a green one maybe." He turned to Mevrou. "I have had this shop for thirty years and I can tell you with God's certainty that children like raspberry first and green second." He snapped his braces with his thumbs and gave a happy snort. He was wrong, of course, pineapple was second.

I felt intimidated, so I left the raspberry in my pocket.

"What is your name, boy?" Harry Crown asked.

"Pisskop, sir," I replied.

"Pisskop? This is a name for a nice boy?" he asked in alarm.

Mevrou interrupted sharply. "Never mind his name, what have you got in *tackies*? The boy must have some *tackies*. He is going on the train alone tonight to his *oupa* in Barberton."

Harry Crown gave a low whistle. "Barberton, eh? That is two days away in the train, a long journey alone for a small boy." He was looking at my feet. "We have nothing so small, Mevrou."

"Show me what you got, Mr. Crown. His *oupa* did not send enough money for boots."

Harry Crown shrugged. "It makes no difference, boots, smoots, *tackies,* smackies, I'm telling you, the boy's foot is too small."

"Let the boy try them," Mevrou insisted.

He moved behind the counter and pulled a cardboard box from the shelf. From it he withdrew a pair of dark brown canvas shoes.

"Let the boy try them," Mevrou said.

The big man sighed. "These *tackies* are four sizes too big for him already. Maybe in five or six years they will fit him like a glove. In the meantime they will fit him like the clown in a circus." He slapped his stomach. "Very amusing," he said to himself in English.

"We will try them on. With newspaper we can fix them."

"Mevrou, with the whole *Zoutpansberg Gazette* we couldn't stuff these *tackies* to fit. He has very small feet for a Boer child."

"He is a Rooinek!" Mevrou said, suddenly angry. She grabbed the *tackies* and turned to me. "Put your foot on my lap, child," she ordered.

With my heel on Mevrou's lap the first *tacky* slipped around my foot without touching the sides.

Mevrou pulled the laces tightly until the eyelets overlapped. "Now the other one," she said.

The *tackies* seemed to extend twice the distance of my feet.

"Walk, child," Mevrou commanded.

I took a step forward and managed to drag the right tackie forward by not lifting my foot.

"Bring some paper." Mevrou cunningly fashioned two little boats from newspaper. She then put the paper boats in the *tackies* and instructed me to insert my feet into them and tied the laces. This time they fitted snug as a bug in a rug. When I walked they made a phlifft-floft sound where the *tackies* bent at the end of my toes.

"We will take them," Mevrou announced triumphantly. "How much?"

Harry Crown sighed again. "Half a crown, for you only two shillings," he said, adjusting the price automatically, his heart obviously not in the sale.

I tugged at the end of the lace and to my relief the bow collapsed. I did the same for the second *tackie,* then slipped carefully out of the newspaper boats and handed the *tackies* to Harry Crown.

"You poor little bugger," he said in English. He slipped the *tackies* back into the box and when he saw Mevrou wasn't looking, quickly put two green and two red suckers in and handed it to me. "I wish you health to wear them." Speaking out of the corner of his mouth he added, "Can she understand English?"

I shook my head almost imperceptibly.

"Inside is for the journey, green and red, the best! So long, Peekay." He patted me on the shoulder and then spoke in English. "Pisskop is not a nice name for a brave person who is traveling all by himself to the lowveld to meet his granpa. Peekay, that is much better, hey?"

I nodded, not answering.

Drawing up to his full height, gold teeth flashing, he grinned. "Maybe the *tackies* don't fit, but I think your new name fits perfect!"

Mevrou threw two shillings on the counter and marched out of the shop. I followed with the precious box of loot under my arm. At the door I turned.

"Goodbye, sir!" I said in English.

Mevrou turned furiously. Grabbing me by the ear, she whispered fiercely, "Do not talk to that . . . that dirty Jew in the accursed language. You will hear from my *sjambok* when we get home!"

"Ouch! You have my sore ear, Mevrou." I knew she'd feel guilty, even though my ear was completely healed.

Mevrou let go of my ear immediately. You've got to be quick on your feet in this world if you want to survive.

Mevrou stormed ahead and I fell some five paces behind her. I hoped I'd given her enough guilt for her to withdraw the promised thrashing. I took the raspberry sucker out of my pocket. Taking off the cellophane wrapper, I licked the crimson sugar crystals that had stuck to it before throwing it away, then settled down to suck my way back to the school.

The *sjambok* was not mentioned on our return. I spent the remainder of the afternoon making a border with white pebbles around the pile of rocks on Granpa Chook's grave. I must say the toughest damn chicken in the world had a very impressive grave.

The cook boy packed me a big brown paper bag of sandwiches for the train journey. We left to catch the seven o'clock train. My suitcase, though large, contained very few things. Two shirts, two pairs of khaki shorts, my pajamas and my new *tackies* with the paper boats in them. I'd buried Granpa Chook in my mother's red jersey so he'd look pretty. The four suckers I'd hidden in a pair of shorts. There was plenty of room for the sandwiches. The suitcase wasn't really heavy and besides, with all the iron bar torture sessions, my muscles were pretty big.

The station turned out to be a raised platform upon which sat a building facing the railway line. Outside the stationmaster's office there were three truck tires painted white and in the middle of these grew dusty red cannas. Mevrou seemed to know the stationmaster. He brought her a cup of coffee in the waiting room.

"Don't worry, Hoppie Groenewald is the guard on this train, he will take good care of the boy." He turned to me. "He is champion of the railways, you know. That Hoppie, he laughs all the time, but if you get into a fight, I'm telling you, man, you better pray he's on your side!"

I wondered what a champion of the railways was. I liked the idea of having someone on my side who was good in a fight. My life seemed to be made for trouble and it would make a nice change when the next lot hit, as was bound to happen.

Sometimes the slightest things change the directions of our lives, a random moment that connects like a meteorite striking the earth. Hoppie Groenewald was to prove to be a passing mentor who would set my life on an irrevocable course. He would do so in little more than a day and a night.

Mevrou produced a ticket from an envelope and inserted a large safety pin into the hole at one end. She pinned the ticket to my shirt pocket. "Listen carefully to me now, man, this ticket will take you to Barberton but your *oupa* only sent enough money for one breakfast and one lunch and one supper on the train. Tonight you eat only one sandwich, you hear?" I nodded. "Tomorrow for breakfast another one and for lunch the last one. And also eat the meat first because the jam will keep the bread soft. Then you can eat on the train. Do you understand?"

"Ja, Mevrou."

She took out a small white hanky and placed it on her lap. In the center she placed a shilling.

"Watch carefully now, Pisskop. I am putting this shilling in here and tying it so." She brought the two opposite corners together and tied them, then did the same with the remaining two. She took a second safety pin from her handbag, then pinned the *doek* inside the pocket of my shorts.

"It is for an emergency. Only if you have to can you use some of it. But you must tie up the change like I just showed you and put it back in your pocket with the safety pin. If you don't need it you must give it to your *oupa*."

The stationmaster entered and told us we had five minutes.

"Quick, man, get your *tackies*," Mevrou said, giving me a push toward the suitcase.

I was seized by a sudden panic. What if she saw my suckers? I placed the case on the floor and opened it so the lid was between Mevrou and me, preventing her from seeing inside. Just as well, a green sucker had worked out of its hiding place and my heart went thump. Phew! I removed the *tackies* and quickly snapped the case shut. I slipped each foot into a paper boat and Mevrou tied the laces. I tried desperately to memorize how she did this.

"Please, Mevrou, will you teach me how to tie laces so I can take my *tackies* off in the train?"

Mevrou looked up, alarmed. "You must not take your *tackies* off until you get to Barberton. If you lose them your *oupa* will think I stole the money he sent. You keep them on, do you hear me now?"

The train could be heard a long way off and we left the waiting room to watch it coming in. Real walking in my *tackies* was very different from the three or four steps I had taken in Harry Crown's shop. I stumbled several times as I went phlifft-floft, phlifft-floft to the edge of the platform. Bits of newspaper crept up past my ankles and I had to press them back in.

With a deafening choof of steam, immediately followed by two short sharp hisses and a screeching sound, the huge train pulled into the station, and carriage after carriage of black people went by. They were laughing and sticking their heads out of windows and having themselves a proper good time. Finally the last two carriages and the goods van came to a halt neatly lined up with the platform. The two end carriages read South African Railways First Class and Second Class, respectively. I had seen pictures of trains, of course, and sometimes at night as I lay in the dormitory I had heard a train whistle carried in the wind, the beautiful sound of going to faraway places away from Mevrou, the Judge and his storm troopers. But I wasn't prepared for anything quite as big and black and blustering with steam, brass pipes and hissing pistons.

Africans appeared as if from nowhere. They carried bundles on their heads, which they handed up through the third-class carriage windows to the passengers inside, and then climbed aboard laughing with the excitement of it all. From inside came song and more laughter and good-natured banter. I knew at once that I would like trains.

The guard leapt down onto the platform carrying a canvas bag with Mail stamped on the outside. He handed it to the stationmaster, who gave him an identical bag in return.

The stationmaster introduced the guard. "This is Hoppie Groenewald, he is guard and conductor until you get to Gravelotte. He will look after the boy."

Hoppie Groenewald grinned down at me and tipped his navy blue guard's cap to Mevrou. "No worries, Mevrou, I will look after him until Gravelotte. Then I will hand him over to Pik Botha, who will take him through to Kaapmuiden." He opened the door of the second-class carriage and put my suitcase into the train and indicated that I should enter. The three steps up into the carriage were fairly high and as I put my weight on the bottom step the toe of the tacky buckled and I fell on my bum on the platform. Wearing shoes was a much trickier business than I had first supposed.

"Get up, man!" Mevrou said. "Even now you make trouble for me."

Bending down, Hoppie Groenewald grabbed me under the armpits and hoisted me high in the air through the door to land inside the carriage.

"No worries, little brother, I too have fallen up those *verdomde* steps many a time. I, who am a guard and soon to be a conductor, and who should know better."

Then he hopped up the steps without even looking and unhooked a neatly rolled green flag from above the door of the carriage. He unfurled the flag and pulled a large silver whistle from his waistcoat pocket.

"Watch the kaffirs get a fright," he said with a grin. He showed me how to hold on to the handrail inside the door and lean out of the carriage so I could see down the full length of the train. He then jumped back onto the platform and began to wave the flag, giving a long blast on his whistle.

You should have seen the kerfuffle. Africans who had left the train to stretch their legs scrambled frantically to get through the doors of the carriages as the train began slowly to move, laughing and yelling and climbing on top of each other. Hoppie Groenewald gave two more short blasts on his whistle and hopped aboard the train.

"Goodbye, Mevrou. Thank you," I shouted, waving at her.

"Keep your *tackies* on, you hear!" Mevrou shouted back.

It was a dry-eyed farewell on both sides. I hoped the Rooinek and Mevrou would never have to see each other again.

Hoppie Groenewald closed the carriage door as the train began to gather momentum. He refurled the flag. Then he picked up my suitcase and opened the door to the nearest compartment. The train was moving along smoothly now and I enjoyed the comforting clackity-clack, clackity-clack of the carriage wheels.

The empty compartment had two bright green leather seats facing each other, each seat big enough for three adults. A small table was positioned between the two windows. The compartment was paneled in varnished wood and above each seat was a framed photograph. It was all very posh. Hoppie Groenewald turned on the compartment lights.

"It's all yours until we get to Tzaneen. After that who knows? No worries, Hoppie will take good care of you." He looked down at my *tackies;* bits of newspaper were sticking out of the sides.

"The old cow can't get you now. Take them off," the guard said. I tugged the canvas shoes off. My feet were hot and had turned black from the newsprint rubbing off on them. It felt delicious to squiggle my toes again. Hoppie Groenewald stuck his hand out. "Shake a paw. You know my name but I haven't had the pleasure."

I'd already thought about what Harry Crown had said and had decided to take his advice and call myself Peekay. "Peekay," I said tentatively.

I suddenly felt new and clean. Nobody ever again would know that I had been called Pisskop. Granpa Chook was dead and so was Pisskop.

"All the best, Peekay. We will be pals."

"Thank you for taking care of me, Mr. Groenewald," I said politely.

He grinned. "Ag, man, just call me Hoppie."

Hoppie left to check the tickets in the African carriages but promised he would return soon.

It was almost totally dark outside, as I sat alone in a lighted room, flying through the African night, lickity-clack, lickity-clack. I had defeated the Judge and his Nazi storm troopers, survived Mevrou, and I had grown up and changed my name, lickity-clack, lickity-clack.

Opening my suitcase, I took out one of Harry Crown's green suckers. Harry Crown was right after all—the green ones were a very close second to raspberry; pineapple was definitely third. I examined the photographs above the seats, sepia-toned pictures of a flat mountain with a streak of white cloud resting just above it. The caption underneath one read "World famous Table Mountain wearing its renowned tablecloth." All there was, was a big white cloud; I couldn't see a tablecloth. Another showed a big city seen from the air with the caption "Cape Town, home of the famous

Cape Doctor." I wondered what the doctor had done to be famous and rich enough to own a big town for his home. Years later I discovered that the Cape Doctor was a wind that blew in spring to clean out the germs that had gathered during the winter. Another photograph was captioned "Truly one of the world's natural wonders."

Well, I thought, this will be a pretty good journey if we visit all those places!

Hoppie returned after what seemed ages but probably wasn't very long. On a train, with the darkness galloping past, time seemed to disappear; the lickity-clack of the wheels on the track gobbled up the minutes.

He plonked himself on the seat opposite me, then gave me a big grin and a light playful punch to the point of my chin.

"When we get to Tzaneen in an hour we'll have some dinner. We stop for forty-five minutes to take on coal and water and there's a café across the road from the station. From Tzaneen I'm only the guard and another conductor takes over. What's your favorite food, Peekay?"

"Sweet potatoes."

"How about a mixed grill? A two-bob special, heh?"

"I've only got a shilling and it's for emergencies. Is a mixed grill an emergency?" I asked.

Hoppie laughed. "For me it is. Tonight I'm paying, old mate. The mixed grills are on me."

I didn't want to ask him what a grill was so I asked him about the pictures on the wall. "When are we going to see Table-Mountain-one-of-the-natural-wonders-of-the-world?" I pointed to the picture above his head.

Hoppie turned around to look. "It's just pictures showing where

South African Railways go, but we are not going there, Peekay." He started to study all the pictures. "I almost went to Cape Town last year to fight in the finals but I was beaten in the Northern Transvaal championships. Split decision but the referee gave it to the fighter from Pretoria. I'm telling you, man, I beat the bastard fair and square. It was close, I've got to admit that, but I knew all the time I had him on points."

I listened, astonished. What on earth was he talking about?

Hoppie looked me straight in the eyes. "You're almost looking at the railways boxing champion of the Transvaal, you know." He brought his finger and thumb together in front of my face. "That close and I would of been in the National Railway Boxing Championships in Cape Town."

"What's a boxing champion?" I asked.

It was Hoppie's turn to look astonished. "What a domkop you are, Peekay. Don't you know what boxing is?"

"No, sir." I dropped my eyes, ashamed of my ignorance.

Hoppie Groenewald put his hand under my chin and lifted my head up. "It's nothing to be ashamed of. There comes a time in everything when you don't know something." He grinned. "Okay, man, settle down, make yourself at home, we're in for a long talk."

"Wait a minute, Hoppie," I said excitedly. I clicked open my suitcase. "Green or red?" I asked, taking out a sucker of each color. I had decided that I would have one sucker in the morning and one at night; that way they would last me the whole journey. But a friend like this doesn't come along every day and I hadn't heard a good story since Nanny.

"You choose first, Peekay."

"No, Hoppie. You're the one who is going to tell the story so you get first choice," I said with great generosity.

"Green," he said. He took the green sucker and I put the raspberry one back and clicked the suitcase shut.

"I've just had one," I said, grateful that I had two of the best raspberry ones left.

"We will share, then," he said. "You lick first because I'm going to be too busy doing the talking." He watched me as I unwrapped the cellophane and licked it clean. "When I was your age I used to do the same." He looked at his watch. "One hour to Tzaneen, just about time for a boxing lecture and maybe even a demonstration."

I settled back happily into the corner of the seat and proceeded to lick the sucker. One and a half suckers in less than an hour was an all-time happiness and having a real friend was another. What an adventure this was turning out to be.

"Boxing is the greatest sport in the world," Hoppie began, "even greater than rugby. The art of self-defense is the greatest art of all and boxing is the greatest art of self-defense. Take me, a natural welterweight, there isn't any man I have to be afraid of. I'm fast and I can hit hard and in a street fight a little bloke like me can take on any big gorilla." He jabbed once or twice into the air to demonstrate his lightning speed.

"How little can beat how big?" I asked, getting excited.

"Big as anything, man. If you've got the speed to move and can throw a big punch as you're moving away. Time, speed and footwork, in boxing they are everything. To be a welterweight is perfect. Not too big to be fast, not too small to pack a punch. A welterweight is the perfect fighter, I'm telling you for sure, man!" Hoppie's eyes were shining with conviction.

I stood up on the seat and lifted my hand about another eight inches above my head. Which, of course, was about the height of the Judge. "A little kid like me and a big kid, big as this?"

Hoppie paused for a moment. "With small kids it's a bit different. Small kids don't have the punch. Maybe they're fast enough to stay out of the way, but one punch from a big gorilla and it's all over, man. Kids are best to fight in their own division." He looked at me. "What big kid gave you a bad time? Just you tell me, Peekay, and he'll have to reckon with Hoppie Groenewald. I'm telling you, man, nobody hurts a friend of mine."

"Just some boys at school," I replied. I wanted to tell him about the Judge and his Nazi storm troopers, but Hoppie Groenewald didn't know I was a Rooinek and he might think differently if he found out. "It's all over now," I said, handing him the sucker.

He started to lick it absently. "Peekay, take my advice. When you get to Barberton, find someone who can teach you to box." He looked at me. "I can see you could be a good boxer; your arms are strong for a little bloke. Let me see your legs."

I stood up on the seat again. "Not bad, Peekay, nice light legs, you could have speed. With a boxer speed is everything. Hit and move, one two one, a left and a left again and a right." He was sparring in the air, throwing lightning punches at an invisible foe. It was scary and exciting at the same time.

"Wait here," he said suddenly, and left the compartment. He returned in a couple of minutes carrying a pair of funny-looking leather gloves.

"These are boxing gloves, Peekay. These are the equalizers. When you can use them well you need fear no man. In the goods van I have a speedball. Tomorrow I will show you how to use it." He slipped the huge gloves over my hands, which disappeared halfway up to my elbows. "Feels good, hey?" he said, tying the laces.

My hands in the gloves were just as lost as my feet had felt in the *tackies*. Only this was different. The gloves felt like old friends, big, yes, and very clumsy, but not strangers.

"C'mon, kid, hit me," Hoppie said, sticking out his jaw. I took a jab at him and his head moved away so my glove simply whizzed through the air. "Again, hit me again." I pulled my arm back and let go with a terrible punch that landed flush on his chin. Hoppie fell back into the seat opposite, groaning and holding his jaw. "Holy macaroni! You're a killer. A natural-born fighter." He sat up rubbing his jaw and I began to laugh. "That's the way, little *boetie*, I was beginning to wonder if you knew how to laugh," he said with a big grin.

And then I started to cry, not blubbing, just tears that wouldn't stop rolling down my cheeks. Hoppie Groenewald picked me up and put me on his lap and I put my arms with the boxing gloves around his neck and buried my head in his blue serge waistcoat.

"Sometimes it is good to cry," he said softly. "Now tell old Hoppie what's the matter."

I couldn't tell him, of course. It was a dumb thing to cry like that, but it was as far as I was prepared to go. I got off his lap. "It's nothing, honest."

Hoppie picked up the sucker and held it out to me. "You finish it. It will spoil my appetite for my mixed grill. You're still going to have a mixed grill with me, aren't you?"

I reached for the sucker but the gloves were still on my hands and we laughed together at the joke. He pulled the gloves off.

"No worries, Peekay. When you grow up you'll be the best damn welterweight in South Africa and nobody . . . and I mean no-bod-ee, will give Kid Peekay any crapola. I'm telling you, man."

When we reached Tzaneen, to my amazement Hoppie pulled down a bunk with blankets and sheets concealed in the wall above my head. From a slot behind the bunk he took out a pillow and a towel. He put my suitcase on the bed to reserve it, in case other folk came into the compartment at Tzaneen.

Opposite the station was a lighted building with a big window on which Railway Café was written. Inside were lots of little tables and chairs.

A pretty young lady behind the counter looked up as we entered and gave Hoppie a big smile. "Well, well, look who's here. If it isn't Kid Louis, champion of the railways." An older woman came up to Hoppie, wiping her hands on her apron, and he gave her a big hug.

"So when's your next fight, champ?" the young lady asked.

"Tomorrow night at the railway club in Gravelotte. It's the big time for me at last." Hoppie smiled.

The pretty young lady giggled. "Put two bob on the other bloke for me." One or two of the other customers laughed, but in a good-natured way. The older woman was clearing a table for us. Hoppie turned toward me, and held my arm aloft. "Hello, everyone. I want you to meet Kid Peekay, the next welterweight contender," he said.

I dropped my eyes, not knowing what to do.

The pretty young woman smiled at me. "How would the contender like a strawberry milk shake?" she asked.

I looked at Hoppie. "What's a milk shake, please, Hoppie?"

"A milk shake is heaven," he said. "Make that two." He turned to the older woman. "Two super-duper mixed grills, please, *ounooi.*"

Hoppie was right, a strawberry milk shake is heaven. When the mixed grill arrived I couldn't believe my eyes. Chop, steak, sausage, bacon, liver, chips, a fried egg and a tomato. What a blowout! I was quite unable to finish it, although I slurped the milk shake, in its aluminum shaker, right down to the last gurgling drop.

I had never been up as late as this before and my eyelids felt as though they were made of lead.

The next thing I remembered was Hoppie tucking me into my bunk between the clean, cool sheets and the pillow that smelt of starch. "Sleep sweet, old mate," I heard him say.

The last thing I remembered before I fell asleep again was the deep, comforting feeling of my hands in the boxing gloves. "The equalizers," Hoppie had called them. Peekay had found the equalizers.

FIVE

I woke early and lay in my bunk listening to the lickity-clack of the rails. Outside in the dawn light lay the gray savannah grasslands; an occasional baobab stood hugely sentinel against the smudged blue sky with the darker blue of the Murchison range just beginning to break out of the flat horizon. The door of the compartment slid open and Hoppie came in carrying a steaming mug of coffee.

"Did you sleep good, Peekay?" He handed me the mug.

"Ja, thanks, Hoppie. I'm sorry I couldn't stay awake."

"No worries, little *boetie,* there comes a time for all of us when you can't get up out of your corner."

I didn't understand the boxing parlance but it didn't seem to matter. To my amazement Hoppie then lifted the top of the compartment table to reveal a washbasin underneath.

"When you've had your coffee you can have a wash and then I'll take you to breakfast," he said.

"It's okay, Hoppie, I have my breakfast in my suitcase," I said hastily.

Hoppie looked at me with a grin. "Humph, this I got to see. In your suitcase you have a stove and a frying pan and butter and eggs and bacon and sausages and tomato and toast and jam and coffee?" He gave a low whistle. "That's a magic suitcase you've got there, Peekay."

"Mevrou gave me sandwiches for the first three meals because my *oupa* didn't send enough money. I should have eaten the meat one last night," I said in a hectic tumbling out of words.

Hoppie stood looking out of the carriage window; he seemed to be talking to himself. "Sandwiches, eh? I hate sandwiches. By now the bread is all turned up at the corners and the jam has come through the middle of the bread." He stooped down and clicked open my suitcase and removed the brown paper package.

"As your manager, it is my duty to inspect your breakfast. Fighters have to be very careful about the things they eat." He unwrapped the parcel. He was right, the bread had curled up at the corners. He removed the slice of bread uppermost on the first sandwich and sniffed the thin slices of meat. He dug down to the bottom two sandwiches; the jam had oozed through the bread.

He looked up at me. "I have sad news for you, Peekay. These sandwiches have died a horrible death. We must get rid of them immediately before we catch it ourselves." With that, he slid down the window of the compartment and hurled the sandwiches into the passing landscape. "First-class fighters eat first-class food. Hurry up and wash, Peekay, I'm starving and breakfast comes with the compliments of South African Railways."

I flung the blanket and sheet back and looked down at my headless snake in horror. Hoppie had removed my pants before putting me to bed. My heart pounded. Maybe it had been dark and he hadn't noticed I was a Rooinek. If he found out, everything was spoiled, just when I was having the greatest adventure of my life.

"C'mon, Peekay, we haven't got all day, you know."

"I am still full from the mixed grill last night, Hoppie. I can't eat another thing." I quickly pulled the blanket back over me.

"Who you trying to bluff?" He ripped the blanket and sheet off me in one swift movement. My hatless snake was exposed. I cupped my hands over it but it was too late, I knew that he knew.

"I'm not the next welterweight contender, Mr. Groenewald, I'm just a *verdomde* Rooinek," I said, my voice breaking as I fought to hold back my tears.

Hoppie stood in front of me, saying nothing until his silence forced me to raise my eyes and look at him. His eyes were sad; he shook his head as he spoke. "That's why you're going to be the next champ, Peekay, you've got the reason." He smiled. "I didn't tell you before, man. You know that bloke who beat me for the title in Pretoria? Well, he was English, a Rooinek like you. He had this left hook, every time it connected it was like a goods train had shunted into me." Hoppie lifted me out of the bunk and put me gently down beside the washbasin. "But I think you're going to be even better than him, little *boetie*. C'mon, wash up and let's go eat."

I can tell you things were looking up, all right. Hoppie took me through to the dining car, which had a snowy cloth on every table, silver knives and forks and starched napkins folded to look like dunces' caps. The coffee came in a silver pot. A man with a napkin draped across his arm said good morning and showed us to a table. He asked Hoppie if it was true that the light-heavy he was to fight that night had a total of twenty-seven fights with seventeen knockouts to his credit?

Hoppie said it was the first he'd heard of it. Then he shrugged his shoulders and grinned. "First he's got to catch me, man." He asked him about something called odds and the man said two to one on the big bloke. Hoppie laughed and gave the man ten bob and the man wrote something in a small book.

The man left and soon returned with toast and two plates of bacon and eggs and sausages and tomato, just the way Hoppie said it would happen. I decided that when I grew up the railways were most definitely for me.

"Are you frightened about tonight?" I asked Hoppie. Although I couldn't imagine him being frightened of anything, it was obvious the man he was going to fight was to him just as big as the Judge was to me.

Hoppie washed the sausage he was chewing down with a gulp of coffee. "It's good to be a little frightened. It's good to respect your opponent. It keeps you sharp. In the fight game, the head rules the heart. But in the end the heart is the boss," he said, tapping his heart with the handle of his fork. I noticed he held his fork in the wrong hand and he later explained: a left-handed fighter is called a southpaw. "Being a southpaw helps when you're fighting a big gorilla like the guy tonight. Everything is coming at him the wrong way round. It cuts down his reach, you can get in closer. A straight left becomes a right jab and that leaves him open for a left hook."

Hoppie might as well have been speaking Chinese, but it didn't matter: like the feel of my hands in the gloves, the language felt right. A right cross, a left hook, a jab, an uppercut, a straight left. The words and the terms had a direction, they meant business. "You work it like a piston, with me it's the right, you keep it coming all night into the face until you close his eye, then he tries to defend what he can't see and in goes the left, pow, pow, pow until the other eye starts to close. Then whammo! The left uppercut. In a southpaw that's where the knockout lives."

"Do you think I can do it, Hoppie?" I was desperate for his confidence in me.

"Piece sa cake, Peekay. I already told you. You're a natural." Hoppie's words were like seedpods with wings. They flew straight out of his mouth into my head, where they germinated in the fertile soil of my mind.

The remainder of the morning was taken up with Hoppie writing up some books in the guard's van, where he had a bunk, table and washbasin all to himself. Attached to a hook in the ceiling was a thing he called a speedball, for sharpening your punching. I was too short to reach it but Hoppie punched it so fast he made it almost disappear. I was beginning to like the whole idea of this boxing business.

Hoppie explained that at Gravelotte the train had to take on antimony from the mines. There would be a nine-hour stop before the train left for Kaapmuiden at eleven o'clock that night. "No worries, little *boetie*. You will be my guest at the fight and then I will put you back on the train."

At lunch my eyes nearly popped out of my head. We sat down at the same table as before and the man who had been at breakfast, whose name turned out to be Gert, brought Hoppie a huge steak and me a little one.

"Compliments of the cook, Hoppie. The cook's got his whole week's pay on an odds-on bet with four miners. He says it's rump steak, red in the middle to make you mean."

At lunch the dining compartment was full and everyone was talking about the fight. Gert was moving from table to table, and in between serving was taking ten-shilling and pound notes from passengers and writing it down in his book.

Hoppie looked up at me. "You a betting man, Peekay?"

I looked at him confused. "What's a betting man, Hoppie?"

Hoppie explained about betting. He signaled for Gert to come over. "What odds will you give the next welterweight contender?" he asked, pointing at me.

Gert asked me how much I had.

"One shilling," I said nervously.

"Ten to one," Gert said, "that's the best I can do."

"Is this an emergency?" I asked, fearful for Granpa's shilling.

"At ten to one? I'll say so!" Hoppie answered.

It took ages to get the safety pin inside my pocket loose and then undo the doek Granpa's shilling had been tied into. I handed Gert the shilling and he wrote something down in his little book. Hoppie saw the anxiety on my face. It wasn't really my shilling and he knew it.

"Sometimes in life doing what we shouldn't is the emergency, Peekay," he said.

We arrived at Gravelotte at two-thirty on the dot. The heat of the day was at its most intense. Hoppie said the temperature was one hundred and eight degrees and tonight would be a sweat bath. Our train was moved off the main track into a siding.

"This is where I got my shunting ticket. When the ore comes in from Murchison Consolidated and you got to put together a train in this kind of heat, I'm telling you, Peekay, you know you're alive, man," Hoppie said, pointing to a little shunting engine moving ore trucks around.

We crossed the tracks and walked through the railway workshops. The men working there talked to Hoppie and wished him luck and said they'd be there tonight, no way were they going to work overtime. Hoppie called them grease monkeys and said they were the salt of the earth.

We arrived at the railway mess where Hoppie lived. We had a shower and Hoppie opened a brown envelope that a mess servant brought to him. He read the letter inside for a long time and then, without a word, put it into the top drawer of the small table in his room.

"We are going shopping, little *boetie,* and then to the railway club to meet my seconds and have a good look over the big gorilla I'm fighting tonight. Bring your *tackies*, Peekay, I have an idea."

We set off with my *tackies* under my arm. The main street was a few hundred yards from the mess. Every time a truck passed it sent up a cloud of dust, and by the time we got to the shop Hoppie was looking for I could taste the dust in my mouth. It sure was hot.

The shop we entered had written above the door, G. Patel & Son, General Merchants. On its verandah were bags of mealie meal and red beans and bundles of pickaxes, a complete plow and four-gallon tins of paraffin. Inside, it was dark and hot.

"It smells funny in here, Hoppie."

"It's coolie stuff they burn, man, it's called incense."

A young Indian woman dressed in bright swirls of almost diaphanous cloth came out of the back. She was a mid-brown color, her straight black hair was parted in the middle and a plait hung over her shoulder almost to the waist. Her eyes were large and dark. On the center of her forehead was painted a red dot.

Hoppie nudged me. "Give me your *tackies*, Peekay," he whispered. I handed him the two brown canvas shoes, which showed no sign of wear.

"Good afternoon, meneer, I can help you, please?"

Hoppie did not return her greeting and I could tell from the way he looked at her that she was somehow not equal. I thought only kaffirs were not equal, so it came as quite a surprise that this beautiful lady was not also. "*Tackies*, you got *tackies*?" he demanded.

The lady looked at the *tackies* Hoppie was holding. "Only white and black, not brown like this."

"You got a size for the boy?" Hoppie said curtly. The lady looked at my feet and brought a whole lot of *tackies* tied together in a

Patel seemed to have become very excited and was pointing to Hoppie. "Meneer Kid Louis, I am very-very honored to meet you! All week, my golly, I am hearing about you and the fisticuffs business. My goodness gracious, now I am meeting the person myself!"

Hoppie laughed. "Bet the ninepence you rooked out of me on me, Patel."

"No, no, we are going much better. Ten pounds we are wagering on Kid Louis."

"Ten pounds! That's twice as much as I win if I win."

Patel proffered the ninepence he had been holding. "Please take it back, Meneer Kid Louis, it will bring very-very bad luck if I am keeping this money."

Hoppie shrugged and pointed to me. "Give it to the next welterweight contender."

"You are a boxer also?"

I nodded gravely; in my head it seemed almost true. Patel dug into his pocket and produced a handful of change. "Here is for you a shilling," he said.

Hoppie grinned at him. "You don't know what you just did, Patel, but it is a very good omen."

"Thank you, Mr. Patel," I said, my hand closing around the silver coin. Granpa's change was safe again and I must say it was a load off my mind.

As we left the shop Hoppie gave me a bump with his elbow. "You don't call a blerrie coolie "mister," Peekay. A coolie is not a kaffir because he is clever and he will cheat you anytime he can. But a coolie is still not a white man!"

We stopped at a café and Hoppie bought two bottles of red stuff. On the sides were the words American Cream Soda. The old lady behind the counter took them out of an icebox, opened them, popped a sort of pipe made of paper into the tops and handed them to us. I watched to see how Hoppie did it and then I did it too. It tasted wonderful.

We arrived at the railway club just before five o'clock. The temperature was still in the high nineties. The club was cool, with polished red cement floors and ceiling fans. The manager told us the boys from the mine had already arrived and the railway boys, including Hoppie's seconds, were with them in the billiard room. Hoppie took my hand and we followed the manager into the billiard room, which contained three large tables covered in green stuff on which were lots of colored balls. Men with long sticks were knocking the balls together all over the place. In the far corner some twenty men were seated at a long table on which were lots of beer bottles. They all stopped talking as we walked in. Two of them put down their glasses, rose from the table and came toward us smiling. Hoppie seemed very happy to see them. He turned to me and said: "Peekay, this is Nels and Bokkie. Nels, Bokkie, this is Peekay, the next welterweight contender." Both men grinned and said hello and I said hello back. We walked over to the group of men who had remained sitting around the table.

Bokkie put his hand on Hoppie's shoulder. He was a big man with a huge tummy and a red face with a flat nose that appeared to have been broken several times. I noticed that Hoppie was staring at a man sitting at the table with a jug of beer in front of him. The man was looking straight back at Hoppie, and their eyes were locked together for a long time. Hoppie was still holding my hand and although his grip didn't seem to increase I could feel the sudden tension. At last the man dropped his eyes and reached out for his glass.

"Gentlemen," Bokkie said, "this is Kid Louis, the next welterweight champion of the South African Railways." The men at the side of the table nearest to us cheered and whistled, and a man on the other side of the table stood up and pointed to the man Hoppie and I had been staring at.

"This is Jackhammer Smit." The miners surrounding Jackhammer whistled and cheered just as the railway men had a moment before. Jackhammer rose slowly to his feet. He was a giant of a man with his head completely shaved. Hoppie's grip tightened around my fingers momentarily and then relaxed again. "This is one big gorilla, Peekay," he said out of the corner of his mouth. Jackhammer took a couple of steps toward us. His nose was almost as flat as Bokkie's and one ear looked mashed.

Hoppie stuck his hand out but the big man didn't take it. The men all fell silent. Jackhammer Smit put his hands on his hips, and tilting his head back slightly, he looked down at Hoppie and me. Then he turned back to the miners. "Which of the two midgets do I fight?" The miners broke up and beat the surface of the table and whistled. Jackhammer Smit turned back to face us. "Kid Louis, huh? Tell me, man, what's a Boer fighter doing with a kaffir name? Kid Louis? I don't usually fight kids and I don't fight *kaffirboeties*, but tonight I'm going to make an exception." He laughed. "You the exception, railway man. Every time I hit you you're going to think a bloody train shunted into you!" The seated miners shouted and cheered again; then he walked back to his chair, where he took a deep drink from the jug of beer.

Hoppie was breathing hard beside me but quickly calmed down as the men turned to see his reaction to Jackhammer's taunts. He grinned and shrugged. "All I can say is, I'm lucky I'm not fighting your mouth, which is a super heavyweight."

Jackhammer exploded and sprayed beer all over the railway men opposite him. "Come, Peekay, let's get going," Hoppie said, moving toward the door to the cheers, whistles and claps of the railway men.

Bokkie and Nels followed quickly. Hoppie turned at the door. "Keep him sober, gentlemen, I don't want people to think I beat him 'cause he was drunk!"

Jackhammer Smit half-rose in his chair as if to come after us. "You blerrie midget, I'll kill you!" he shouted.

"You done good," Bokkie said, "it will take the bastard two rounds just to get over his anger." He told Hoppie to get some rest, that they'd pick us up at the mess at seven-fifteen to drive to the rugby field where the ring had been set up. "People are coming from all over, even as far as Hoedspruit and Tzaneen. I'm telling you, man, there's big money on this fight."

We walked the short distance to the railway mess. The sun had not yet set over the Murchison range and the day baked on, hot as ever. "If it stays hot then that changes the odds." Hoppie squinted up into a sky the color of pewter. "I think it's going to be a real Gravelotte night, Peekay, hot as hell."

When we got to the mess Hoppie told me his plan. "First we have a shower, then we lie down, but every ten minutes you bring me water, Peekay. Even if I beg you "no more," you still bring me a glass every ten minutes, you understand? And you make me drink it, okay, little *boetie*?"

"Ja, Hoppie, I understand," I replied, pleased that I was playing a part in getting him ready. Hoppie took his railway timekeeper from his blue serge waistcoat hanging up behind the door and began to undress for his shower.

The window of Hoppie's room was wide open and a ceiling fan

moved slowly above us. Hoppie lay on the bed wearing only an old pair of khaki shorts. I sat on the cool cement floor with my back against the wall, the big railway timekeeper in my hands. In almost no time Hoppie's body was wet with perspiration and after a while even the sheet was wet. Every ten minutes I brought him a mug of water. After five mugfuls Hoppie turned to me, resting on his elbow.

"It's an old trick I read about in *Ring* magazine. Joe Louis was fighting Jack Sharkey. It was hot as hell, just like tonight. Joe's manager made him drink water all afternoon just like us. To cut a long story short, by the eighth round the fight was still pretty even. Then Sharkey started to run out of steam in the tremendous heat. You see, Peekay, the fight was in the open just like tonight and these huge lights were burning down into the ring; the temperature was over one hundred degrees. In a fifteen-round fight a man can lose two pints of water just sweating and if he can't get it back, I'm telling you, he is in big trouble. I dunno just how it works but you can store water up like a camel, sort of, that's what Joe did and he's the heavyweight champion of the world."

"What did Mr. Jackhammer mean when he said you were a kaffir lover, Hoppie?"

"Ag, man, he's just trying to put me off my stride for tonight. You see, Joe Louis is a black man. Not like our kaffirs. Black, yes, but not stupid and dirty and ignorant. He is what you call a Negro. That's different, man. He's sort of a white man with a black skin. But that big gorilla is too stupid to know the difference."

It was all very complicated, beautiful ladies with skin like honey who were not as good as us and black men who were white men underneath and as good as us.

"I've got a nanny just like Joe Louis," I said to Hoppie as I rose to get his sixth mug of water.

Hoppie laughed. "In that case I'm glad I'm not fighting your nanny tonight, Peekay."

After a while Hoppie rose from the bed and went to a small dresser and returned with a mouth organ. We sat there and he played *Boeremusiek*. He was very good and the tappy country music seemed to cheer him up.

"A mouth organ is a man's best friend, Peekay. When you're sad it will make you happy. When you're happy it can make you want to dance. If you have a mouth organ in your pocket you'll never starve for company or a good meal."

Just then we heard the sound of a piece of steel being hit against another. "Time for your dinner," Hoppie said, slipping on a pair of shoes and putting on an old shirt.

Dinner at the railway mess was pretty good. I had roast beef and mashed potatoes and beans and tinned peaches and custard. Hoppie had nothing except another mug of water. Other diners crowded round our table and wished Hoppie luck. They all told him they had their money on him. They almost all said things like "Box him, Hoppie. Wear him out. They say he's carrying a lot of flab, go for the belly, man." When they left, Hoppie said they were nice blokes but if he listened to them he'd be a dead man.

"You know why he's called Jackhammer, Peekay? A jack-hammer is used in the mines to drill into rock; it weighs one hundred and thirty pounds. Two kaffirs work a jackhammer, one holds the end and the other the middle as they drill into the sides of a mine shaft. I'm telling you, it's blerrie hard work for two big kaffirs. Well, Smit is called Jackhammer because, if he wants, he can hold a jackhammer in place on his own, pushing against it with his stomach and holding it in both hands. What do you think that would do to his stomach muscles? I'm telling you, hitting that big gorilla in the solar plexus all night would be like fighting a brick wall."

"I know," I said excitedly, "you keep it coming all night into the face until you close his eye, then he tries to defend against what he can't see and in goes the left, pow, pow, pow until the other eye starts to close. Then whammo!"

Hoppie rose from the table and looked at me in surprise. "Where did you hear that?"

"You told me, Hoppie. It's right, isn't it?"

"Shhhh . . . you'll tell everyone my fight plan, Peekay! My, you're the clever one," he said as I followed him from the dining hall.

"You didn't say what happened to Jack Sharkey in the heat when Joe Louis fought him and drank all the water?"

"Oh, Joe knocked him out, I forget what round."

Bokkie and Nels picked us up in a one-ton *bakkie*. Hoppie said the truck was Bokkie's pride and joy. Nels and I sat in the back, and with me was a small suitcase Hoppie had packed with his boxing boots and red pants made of a lovely shiny material and a blue dressing gown. Hoppie was very proud of his gown. He'd held it up to show me the "Kid Louis" embroidered on the back.

"You know the young lady in the café at Tzaneen?"

"The pretty one?" I asked, knowing all along whom he meant.

"Ja, she's really pretty, isn't she? Well, she done this with her own hands."

"Is she your *nooi*? Are you going to marry her, Hoppie?"

"Ag, man, with the war and all that, who knows." He had walked over to the dressing table and taken the brown envelope from the top drawer. "These are my call-up papers. I have to go and fight in the war, Peekay. A man can't go asking someone to marry him and then go off to a war, it's not fair."

I was stunned. How could Hoppie be as nice as he was and fight for Adolf Hitler? If he had got his call-up papers that must mean that Adolf Hitler had arrived and Hoppie would join the Judge in the army that was going to march all the Rooineks, including me, into the sea.

"Has Hitler arrived already?" I asked in a fearful voice.

"No, thank God," Hoppie said absently, "we're going to have to fight the bastard before he gets here." He must have seen the distress on my face. "What's the matter, little *boetie*?"

I told Hoppie about Hitler coming and marching all the Rooineks right over the Lebombo mountains into the sea and how happy all the Afrikaners would be.

Hoppie came over and, kneeling down, he clasped me to his chest. "You poor little bastard." He held me tight and safe. Then he took me by the shoulders and held me at arm's length, looking me straight in the eyes. "I'm not going to say the English haven't got a lot to answer for, Peekay, because they have, but that's past history, man. You can't go feeding your hate on the past, it's not natural. Hitler is a bad, bad man and we've got to go and fight him so you can grow up and be welterweight champion of the world. But first we've got to fight the big gorilla. I tell you what, we'll use Jackhammer Smit as a warm-up for that bastard Hitler. Okay by you?"

We had a good laugh and he told me to hurry up and put my *tackies* on and he'd show me how to tie the laces like a fighter.

The sudden sound of a motor horn outside made Hoppie jump up. He put the dressing gown in the suitcase with his other things. "Let's go, champ, that's Bokkie and Nels."

"Wait a minute, Hoppie. I nearly forgot my suckers." I hurriedly retrieved them from my suitcase.

SIX

The rugby field was on the edge of town. We parked the *bakkie* with all the other cars and trucks under a stand of blue gums, their palomino trunks shredded with strips of gray bark. In the center of the field the men from the railway workshop had built a boxing ring that stood about four feet from the ground. The miners, who were responsible for the electrics, had rigged two huge lights on wire that stretched from four poles, each one set into the ground some ten feet from each corner of the ring.

Huge tin shades were fitted over the lights and in the dusk the light spilled down so that it was like daylight in the ring. Hundreds of moths and flying insects spun and danced about the lights. The stands, a series of tiered benches, were arranged in a large circle around the ring. It meant everyone had a ringside seat. There looked to be about two thousand men packing the stands, while underneath them, looking through the legs of the seated whites, the Africans stood or crouched, trying to get a view of the ring as best they could.

Bokkie and Nels led us to a large tent. We entered to find Jackhammer Smit, his seconds and four other men, three of them ordinary size and one not much bigger than me. Hoppie whispered that they were the judges and that "the dwarf is the referee." I was fascinated by the tiny little man with the large bald head. "Take it from me, he knows his onions," Hoppie confided.

Jackhammer Smit had already changed into black shiny boxing shorts and soft black boxing boots. In the confines of the tent, lit by two hurricane lamps, he seemed bigger than ever. As we'd entered he'd turned to talk to one of his seconds. My heart sank; Hoppie was right, I had seen his stomach muscles as he turned; they looked like plaited rope.

Hoppie clipped open his small suitcase, and taking off his shorts and shirt, he quickly slipped on a jockstrap. He looked tough, tightly put together, good knotting around the shoulders and tapered to the waist, his legs slight but strong. He slipped on his shiny red shorts and sat to put on his boxing boots.

Jackhammer Smit now stood in the opposite corner of the tent facing us, with the light behind him. He looked black and huge and he kept banging his right fist into the palm of his left hand, a solid, regular smacking sound that seemed to fill the tent.

The referee, who only came halfway up Jackhammer Smit's legs, called the two boxers together. I wondered if all dwarfs had such deep voices. He asked them if they wanted to glove up in the tent or in the ring.

"In the ring," Hoppie said quickly.

"What's wrong with right here, man?" Jackhammer shot back.

"It's all part of the show, brother," Hoppie said with a grin. "Some of the folk have come a long way."

"Ja, man, to see a short fight. Putting on the blerrie gloves is going to take longer than the action."

"Now, boys, take it easy." The referee pointed to a cardboard box. "Them's the gloves, ten-ounce Everlasts from Solly Goldman's gym in Jo'burg."

Bokkie took the two pairs of gloves out, and moving over to Smit's seconds, he offered both sets to them. They each took a pair, examined and kneaded them between their knees before making a choice. The gloves were shiny black; they caught the light from the hurricane lamps and, even empty, they looked full of action.

Bokkie held the gloves out for Hoppie to inspect. "Nice gloves, not too light," he said softly.

Hoppie put a towel around his neck and then slipped into his dressing gown. Bokkie slung the gloves around Hoppie's neck. "Let's kick the dust," Hoppie said, moving toward the open tent flap.

Suddenly Jackhammer barked, "What you say, Groenewald, okay by you, winner takes all?"

Hoppie turned slowly. "I wouldn't do that to you, Smit. What would you do for hospital expenses?" He took my hand.

"That kid of yours is gunna be a blerrie orphan by the time I'm through with you t'night," Jackhammer yelled at Hoppie's departing back.

Hoppie squeezed my hand and laughed softly. "I reckon that was worth at least another two rounds, Peekay. Never forget, sometimes, very occasionally, you do your best boxing with your mouth."

A small corridor by which the patrons and the fighters entered the brilliantly lit ring intersected the stands on either side. It at once became obvious that one semicircle contained only miners, the other railway men. I had never been at a large gathering of people before and the tension in the crowd was quite frightening. I held onto Nels' hand tightly as he took me to the top tier of a stand and handed me into the care of Big Hettie.

Big Hettie seemed to be the only lady at the fight. She was the cook at the railway mess and Hoppie had introduced us earlier at dinner. Big Hettie had given me a second helping of peaches with custard. She patted the place beside her. "Come sit here, Peekay. You and me is in this together."

Hoppie was seated on a small stool in the corner of the ring with Bokkie bandaging his hands ready for the gloves. When Jackhammer Smit entered, he didn't look up.

"Ho, ho, ho, have we got a fight on our hands!" Big Hettie said gleefully.

Now the fighters had both been gloved up, and while Hoppie remained seated, Jackhammer Smit continued to stand, looking big and hard as a mountain. While my faith was invested in Hoppie, I'd been around long enough to know the realities of big versus small. Big, it seemed to me, always finished on top and my heart was filled with fear for my newfound friend.

"Look at that sparrow fart!" Big Hettie exclaimed, pointing to the tiny referee. "How is he going to keep them men apart?"

"Hoppie says he knows his onions, Mevrou Hettie."

Jackhammer Smit began to move around the ring, snorting and snuffing and throwing imaginary punches in the air, grunting each time he threw a punch as though it had mysteriously connected to the body of an invisible opponent who was soon to become my new best friend, Hoppie. Jackhammer seemed to be increasing in size by the minute, while Hoppie, crouched on his stool, looked like a small frog. Nels was putting Vaseline over Hoppie's eyebrows while Bokkie seemed to be giving him some last-minute instructions.

The tiny referee said something and the seconds left the ring and the fighters moved to the center. The crowd grew suddenly still. Standing between the two men, the referee looked up at them and said something. They both nodded and touched gloves lightly and then turned and walked back to their corners. The crowd began to cheer like mad. The referee held his hands up, turning slowly in a circle to hush the crowd, his head just showing above the top rope of the ring. Soon a three-quarter moon, on the wane, would rise over the Murchison range, though as yet the night was black, with only a sharp square of brilliant light etching out the ring with the three men in it. It was as though the two fighters and the dwarf stood alone, watched by an audience of a million stars.

The referee addressed the stilled crowd, his surprisingly deep voice carrying easily to where we sat. "*Dames en Heere,* tonight we are witnessing the great biblical drama of David and Goliath." He paused for his words to take effect. "Will history repeat itself? Will David once again defeat Goliath?" The railwaymen went wild and the miners hissed and booed. The referee held his hands up for silence. "Or will Goliath have his revenge?" The miners cheered like mad and this time it was the railway men who booed and hissed.

"Introducing in the blue corner, weighing two hundred and five pounds and hailing from Murchison Consolidated Mines, the ex-light-heavyweight champion of the Northern Transvaal, Jackhammer Smit. Twenty-two fights, eleven knockouts, eleven losses on points, a fighter with an even stevens record in the ring. Ladies and gentlemen, put your hands together for Jackhammer Smit!" The miners cheered and whistled.

"What's eleven losses on points mean, Mevrou Hettie?" I asked urgently.

"It means he's a pug, a one-punch Johnny, a slugger. It means he's no boxer."

The referee turned to indicate Hoppie, who raised his hands to acknowledge the crowd. "In the red corner, weighing one hundred and forty-five pounds, from Gravelotte, Kid Louis of the South

African Railways, Northern Transvaal welterweight champion and the recent losing contender for the Transvaal title; fifteen fights, fourteen wins, eight knockouts, one loss." He cleared his throat before continuing, "Let me remind you that the fighter he narrowly lost to on points in Pretoria went on to win the South African title in Cape Town." He raised his voice. "Let's hear it for the one and only Kid Louis!" It was our turn to cheer until the referee orchestrated us back to silence. Hoppie had once again calmly seated himself on the stool, while Jackhammer Smit was still snorting, and throwing punches at the air in front of his body.

"This is a fifteen-round contest. May the best man win." The referee had already assumed the authority of the fight and he didn't look small anymore. He moved to the edge of the ring where the light spilled sufficiently to show three men seated at a small table. "Ready, judges?" They nodded and he turned to the two fighters. "At the sound of the bell come out fighting, gentlemen."

Out of the darkness the bell sounded for round one.

Hoppie jumped from the stool as Nels pulled it out of the ring and Jackhammer Smit stormed toward him. The big boxer's torso was already glistening with sweat. I had earlier unwrapped my first sucker, the yellow one the beautiful Indian lady with the diamond in her tooth had given me, and the wrapper tasted of pineapple.

Hoppie danced around the big man and Jackhammer Smit let go two left jabs and a right uppercut, all of which missed Hoppie by a mile. He followed with a straight left, which Hoppie caught neatly in his glove as he was going away. Hoppie feinted to the right as Jackhammer tried to catch him with two left jabs; then he stepped in under the last jab and peppered Jackhammer's face with a lightning two-handed attack. Two left, then two stabbing rights to the head. Hoppie had moved out of reach by the time Jackhammer

Smit could bring his gloves back into position in front of his face. Hoppie continued to backpedal most of the time, making Smit chase him around the ring. Occasionally he darted in with a flurry of blows to the head and then danced out of range again. Jackhammer came doggedly after him, trying to get set for a big punch, but Hoppie was content to land a quick left and a right and then move quickly out of harm's way. The first round saw him land a dozen good punches, most of them just above Jackhammer's left eye, while the big man only managed a long straight left that caught Hoppie on the shoulder.

It was clear that Jackhammer Smit was having trouble with the southpaw and was showing his frustration. The bell went for the end of the first round and the fighters returned to their corners. This time Jackhammer sat down, breathing heavily. He drank deeply, straight from a bottle of water one of his seconds held up to his mouth. The other second sponged him, dried him and smeared Vaseline above his left eye.

Hoppie looked composed, breathing lightly. He drank from a bottle with a tiny bent pipe coming out of it, rinsing his mouth and spitting the water into a bucket Bokkie held for him. Nels was massaging his shoulders and Hoppie was nodding his head at something Bokkie was saying.

"Is Hoppie winning, Mevrou Hettie?" I asked anxiously.

"It's early times yet, Peekay. In the early rounds the Kid will be too fast for the big guy, but one thing's for sure, Hoppie's punches are too short to hurt Smit."

The bell went for round two, a round much the same as round one except that Jackhammer Smit landed three punches to Hoppie's head, all glancing blows, but each time the miners went wild. After the second round a red blotch began to appear above

Jackhammer's left eye. The next three rounds saw Hoppie leading Smit all around the ring, making him throw punches that nearly always missed and then darting in with a quick flurry of blows before bounding back out of harm's way.

The bell went for the sixth round and Jackhammer shuffled to the center of the ring, his gloves rotating slowly in front of his chest. He was getting the hang of the southpaw and was going to make Hoppie take the fight to where he stood.

Jackhammer dropped his gloves, leaving his head a clear target, knowing he could take anything Hoppie dished out. Hoppie was forced to move in close enough for Smit to hit him in the gut and around the kidneys. Hoppie had to take a couple of vicious blows to the body every time he moved in to hit the spot above Jackhammer's left eye. By the end of the sixth the eye was almost closed but deep red welts showed on Hoppie's ribs where Jackhammer had caught him. Both men were breathing hard as they returned to their corners.

"It's not looking good for the Kid. The big ape has found his mark and he's going to wear him down with body punches. You could of fooled me. He got more brains than I would have given him credit for," Big Hettie said.

"Don't let him have brains, Mevrou Hettie. Brains is one thing you've got to have to win," I said in anguish. Big Hettie was fanning herself with a bright Chinese paper fan, the perspiration running down her face and neck.

"He hits awful hard, Peekay," she said.

The bell went for the seventh and Jackhammer shuffled back to the center of the ring. The heat was plainly telling on him and his gloves were held even lower than before. This left enough of his body exposed for Hoppie to hit him at long range, getting a lot more power behind his punches. The left eye was closed and Hoppie was beginning to work on the right, jabbing straight lefts right on the button every time. Near the end of the round he attempted a right cross to Jackhammer's jaw just as the big man had moved back slightly to throw a punch. Hoppie missed with the right and was thrown slightly off balance as Smit followed through with an uppercut that caught the smaller man under the heart. Hoppie's legs buckled under him as he toppled to the canvas.

"Oh, shit! One-punch Johnny has found the punch. Goliath wins in seven," Hettie said in dismay as the miners went wild. The tiny referee was standing over Hoppie and yelling at Jackhammer Smit to get into a neutral corner, but the big man just stood there, his chest heaving, waiting for Hoppie to rise so that he could finish him off. The referee wouldn't start the count and precious seconds passed as the big man stood belligerently over the fallen welterweight. Jackhammer's seconds were screaming at him to move away and when finally he did so a good thirty seconds had passed.

The referee started to put in the count. Hoppie rose onto one knee and waited until the count of eight before getting to his feet. The referee signaled for the fight to continue and Jackhammer Smit lumbered across the ring to finish Hoppie off. The almost forty-second respite had been enough to stave off disaster and Hoppie simply kept out of harm's way as Jackhammer, energy leaking out of him with every assault, kept charging like an angry bull. The bell went just as Hoppie landed a hard left uppercut to Jackhammer's eye.

"Dammit, Peekay! That was lucky. Thank the Lord Sparrow Fart knows the blerrie rules, or the Kid was out for a ten count for sure." Big Hettie removed a dishtowel that covered the basket and mopped her face and bosom. "Smit's just another stupid Boer after all. Hoppie can thank his lucky stars for that."

In all the excitement I had bitten the sucker clean off its stick and crunched it to bits, shortening its life by at least half an hour. Big Hettie took a thermos flask from the basket and, using the lid, which was shaped like a cup, poured it full of hot, sweet, milky coffee and handed it to me. Then she opened a large tin and handed me a huge slice of chocolate cake. My eyes nearly stood out on stalks. This was going to be a night to remember, all right. If Hoppie, beloved Hoppie, could just keep away from the big gorilla. The way he danced around the big man, seeming only to get out of the way of a punch at the last second, reminded me of how Granpa Chook used to dodge when stones were thrown at him. I only hoped Hoppie had the same survival instinct. For an instant I grew sad. In the end even Granpa Chook's highly developed sense of survival couldn't save him; the big gorilla finally got him.

The eighth round saw another change in the fight. Jackhammer Smit had chased Hoppie too hard and too long. The gorilla's great strength had been sapped by the heat and he was down to barely a shuffle, both eyes nearly closed. Hoppie was hitting him almost at will and Jackhammer pulled the smaller man into a clinch whenever he could, causing the referee to stand on the tips of his toes and pull at his massive arms, yelling "Break!" at the top of his voice.

The ninth and the tenth rounds were much of the same but Hoppie didn't seem to have the punch to put Jackhammer away. Early in the eleventh Smit managed to get Hoppie into yet another clinch, leaning heavily on the smaller man. As the referee moved in to break them up, Jackhammer Smit stepped backward into him, sending the ref arse over tip to the floor. Still holding Hoppie, Smit head-butted him viciously. On the railway side of the ring we saw the incident clearly, but all the miners, like the ref, saw was Hoppie's legs buckling and the welterweight crashing to the floor as Jackhammer broke out of the clinch.

This time Smit moved quickly to the neutral corner and the referee, bouncing to his feet like a rubber ball, started to count Hoppie out.

Pandemonium broke loose. The railwaymen, shouting "Foul!", began to come down from the stands shaking their fists. At the count of six the bell went for the end of the round and Bokkie and Nels rushed into the ring to help a dazed and wobbly Hoppie to his corner.

A score of railwaymen had reached the ring and were shouting abuse at Jackhammer. The miners were yelling and coming down from their stands and, I'm telling you, the whole scene was a proper kerfuffle.

Jackhammer was vomiting into a bucket and Bokkie and Nels were frantically trying to bring Hoppie round, holding a small bottle under his nose. I had begun to cry and Big Hettie drew me into her bosom while hurling abuse at Jackhammer Smit. "You dirty bastard!" she screamed. I could hear her heart going boom, boom, boom.

Several fights had started around the base of the ring and the judges' table had been overturned. The referee stood in the center of the ring, his hand raised. He didn't move and this seemed to have a calming effect on the crowd. Others rushed in to stop the ringside brawling, pulling their mates away. Not until there was complete silence did the referee indicate that both fighters should come to the center of the ring. Hoppie, meanwhile, seemed fully recovered, while Jackhammer, huge chest still heaving and both eyes puffed-up slits, looked a mess. The referee took Hoppie's arm and raised it as high as he was able. "Kid Louis on a foul in the eleventh," he shouted.

The railway men went wild with excitement, while the miners started to come down from their stands again. "Shit, it's going to be on for one and all!" Big Hettie screamed.

Hoppie jerked his arm away and started an animated argument with the referee, pointing his glove at the near-blind Jackhammer. Finally the referee held his hands up for silence. "The fight goes on!" he shouted, and both boxers moved back to their corners. The bell began to clang repeatedly and in a short while the ringside fighting stopped and the men, still shaking their fists at each other, returned to their seats.

"That Hoppie Groenewald is mad as a meat-ax," Big Hettie declared. "He had the blerrie fight won and he wants to start all over again!" She wiped away a tear with the dishcloth.

Ten minutes passed before the bell went for round twelve, by which time Hoppie was good as gold and Jackhammer's seconds, in between his bouts of vomiting, had managed to half-open his left eye. The closed lids of his right eye extended beyond his brow so that he was forced to hunt Hoppie with only half a left eye.

It was no contest. Hoppie darted in and slammed two quick left jabs straight into the left eye and closed it again. The rest of the round was a shambles, with Jackhammer simply covering his face with his gloves and Hoppie boring into his body. Jackhammer Smit simply leaned on the ropes and took everything Hoppie could throw at him. He grunted as Hoppie ripped a blow under his heart and opened his gloves in a reflex action. Hoppie saw the opening and moved in with a perfect left uppercut that landed flush on Jackhammer's jaw. The big man sank to the canvas just as the bell went for the end of the round.

Hoppie's shoulders sagged as he walked back to his corner. It was clear he was exhausted. Jackhammer's seconds helped him to his feet, leading him to his corner.

"They gotta throw in the towel!" Big Hettie said in elation. "Hoppie's got it on a TKO." My heart was pounding fiercely. It seemed certain now that small could beat big. All it took was brains and skill and heart and a perfect plan.

But we were wrong. The bell went for the thirteenth and Jackhammer Smit rose slowly to his feet, half-dragging himself into the center of the ring. Hoppie, too exhausted to gain much from the rest between rounds, was also clearly spent. He hadn't expected Jackhammer to come out for the thirteenth. It was as though each moved toward the other in a dream. Hoppie landed a straight left into Jackhammer's face, starting his nose bleeding again. He followed this with several more blows to the head but his punches lacked strength. Jackhammer, his pride keeping him on his feet, managed to get Hoppie into a clinch, in an attempt to sap what strength the smaller man had left. When the referee shouted at the two men to break, Jackhammer pushed at Hoppie and at the same time hit him with a round-arm blow to the head that carried absolutely no authority as a punch. To our consternation and the tremendous surprise of the miners, Hoppie went down. He rose instantly to one knee, his right hand on the deck to steady him. Jackhammer, sensing from the roar of the crowd that his opponent was down, dropped his gloves and moved forward. Through his bloodied fog he may not have seen the punch coming at him. The left from Hoppie came all the way from the deck with the full weight of his body to drive the blow straight to the point of Jackhammer Smit's jaw. The giant crashed unconscious to the canvas.

"Timber!" Big Hettie screamed as the crowd went berserk. I had just witnessed the final move in a perfectly wrought plan where small defeats big. First with the head and then with the heart. To the very end Hoppie had been thinking. I had learned the most important rule in winning . . . keep thinking.

For a moment Hoppie stood over the unconscious body of his opponent; then he brought his glove up in an unmistakable salute to Jackhammer Smit. He moved slowly to a neutral corner and the referee commenced to count. At the count of ten Jackhammer still hadn't moved. Hoppie moved over to his corner and then, turning to us, he held his arms up in victory.

In my excitement I was jumping up and down and yelling my head off. It was the greatest moment of my life. I had hope. I had witnessed small triumph over big. I was not powerless. Big Hettie grabbed me and held me high above her head. In the bright moonlight we must have stood out clearly. Hoppie stood up unsteadily and, grinning, he waved one glove in our direction.

Jackhammer had been helped to his feet by his seconds and was standing in the center of the ring supported by them as the referee called Hoppie over. Holding Hoppie's hand up in victory, he shouted, "The good book tells the truth, little David has done it again! The winner by a knockout in the thirteenth round, Kid Louis!" The railwaymen cheered their heads off and the miners clapped sportingly and people started to leave the stands.

As the boxers left, Gert, the waiter who took bets in the dining car on the train, entered the ring and began to settle bets. It had been a tremendous fight and even the miners seemed happy enough and would stay for the *braaivleis* and *tiekiedraai* afterward.

Big Hettie and I walked over to the ringside where the men were lining up to be paid. She moved imperiously to the head of the queue, where Gert took five one-pound notes from his satchel and handed them down to her.

"Thank you for your business, Hettie," he said politely.

Hoppie came out of the tent just as we reached it and was immediately surrounded by railwaymen. He looked perfect, except for a large piece of sticking plaster over his left eye where Jackhammer Smit had butted him. Well, not absolutely perfect: in the light you could see that his right eye was swollen and turning a deep purple.

Bokkie and Nels were with him. Neither could stop talking and throwing punches in the air and replaying the fight. More and more railwaymen crowded around Hoppie. Big Hettie lifted me into the air. "Make way for the next contender," I heard Hoppie shout. Hands grabbed hold of me and carried me over the heads of the men to where he stood.

Hoppie pulled me close to him. "We showed the big gorilla, heh, Peekay?"

"Ja, Hoppie." I was suddenly a bit tearful. "Small can beat big if you have a plan."

Hoppie laughed. "I'm telling you, man, I nearly thought the plan wasn't going to work tonight."

"I'll never forget, first with the head and then with the heart." Hoppie rubbed his hand through my hair. The last time someone had done this, it was to rub shit into my head. Now it felt warm and safe.

It was almost three hours before the train was due to leave and most of the crowd had stayed behind to meet their wives at the *tiekiedraai*. Miners and railwaymen, as well as the passengers traveling on, all mixed together, the animosity during the fight forgotten. Only the Africans went home because they wouldn't have been allowed to stay anyway.

With a slice of Big Hettie's chocolate cake already in me I could scarcely manage two sausages and a chop. I even left some meat on the chop, which I gave to a passing dog, who must have thought it was Christmas because, from then on, she stayed with me. It had been a long day and I was beginning to feel tired. I'd never been up this late when I was happy. Hoppie found me and the dog sitting against a big gum tree nodding off. Picking me up, he carried me to the *bakkie* and put me into the back of the little truck.

SEVEN

I woke at dawn to the familiar lickity-clack of the carriage wheels. From the color of the light coming through the compartment window I could see it was the time Granpa Chook would come to the dormitory and crow his silly old neck off.

The light that fled past the compartment window was still soft, with a grayish tint; soon the sun would come and polish it until it shone. Yesterday's rolling grassland was now broken by an occasional *koppie,* a rocky outcrop with clumps of dark green bush. Flat-topped fever trees were more frequent and in the far distance a sharp line of mountains brushed the horizon in a wet, watercolor purple. We were coming into the true lowveld.

I sat up and became aware of a note pinned to the front of my shirt. I undid the safety pin to find a piece of paper with a ten-shilling note attached to it. I was a bit stunned. I'd never handled a banknote and it was difficult to imagine it belonged to me. If one sucker cost a penny, I could buy one hundred and twenty suckers with this ten shillings. On the paper was a carefully printed note from Hoppie.

❂ ❂ ❂

Dear Peekay,

Here is the money you won. We sure showed that big gorilla who was the boss. Small can beat big. But remember, you have to have a plan—like when I hit Jackhammer Smit the knockout punch when he thought I was down for the count. Ha, ha. Remember always, first with the head and then with the heart. Without both, I'm telling you, plans are useless!

Remember, you are the next contender. Good luck, little boetie.

Your friend in boxing and always,
Hoppie Groenewald

PS Say always to yourself, First with the head and then with the heart, that's how a man stays ahead from the start. H.G.

I was distressed at having left the best friend after Granpa Chook and Nanny that I had ever had, without so much as a goodbye. Hoppie had passed briefly through my life, I had known him a little over twenty-four hours, yet he had managed to change my life. He had given me the power of one, one idea, one heart, one mind, one plan, one determination. Hoppie had sensed my need to grow, my need to be assured that the world around me had not been specially arranged to bring about my undoing. He gave me a defense system and with it he gave me hope.

In the early morning the lickity-clack of the carriage wheels sounded sharper and louder as though racing toward the light. I swung down from my bunk and stood at the window watching the early morning folding back. I became aware that the lickity-clack of the carriage wheels was talking to me: *Mix-the-head with-the-heart you're-ahead from-the-start. Mix-the-head with-the-heart you're-ahead from-the-start,* the wheels chanted until my head began to pound with the rhythm. It was becoming the plan I would follow for the remainder of my life; it was to become the secret ingredient in the power of one.

Now the sun was coming up over the distant Lebombo mountains and the African veld sparkled as though it were contained in a crystal goblet.

There was a sudden rattle at the door and a single sharp word, "Conductor!" Whereupon the door slid open to reveal a slight man in a navy serge uniform just like Hoppie's. Only this man looked very neat and his boots shone like a mirror. Around the edge of the blue and white enamel badge on his cap it read South African Railways—*Suid Afrikaanse Spoorweë,* but unlike Hoppie's, which had the word Guard across the center, this badge read Conductor.

The man wore a thin black mustache that looked as though it had been drawn on with a crayon. His bleak expression suggested someone already soured by the burdens of life.

"Where's your ticket? Give it here, boy," he said.

"I have it here, meneer." I hurriedly fumbled with the safety pin where Hoppie had pinned my ticket to the clean shirt I had changed into for the fight.

"This ticket is not clipped," he said accusingly. "You got on this train who knows where? I'm not a mind reader, man."

"I didn't know I had to give it to be clipped, meneer," I said, suddenly fearful.

"It's that *verdomde* Hoppie Groenewald! He did this on purpose to make work for me. Not clipping tickets is an offense. Just because he is going into the army he thinks he can go around not clipping tickets. Who does he think he is, man? What do you think would happen if we all went around not clipping tickets?"

"Please, meneer, Hoppie clipped everybody's ticket. He only forgot mine, that's the honest truth!" I pleaded, frantic that Hoppie would get into trouble on my behalf.

"Humph! First I lose one pound ten shilling betting on that big ape from the mines and now that one who calls himself after a nigger boxer goes around not clipping people's tickets." He paused. "I'm afraid it is my duty to report this," he said, his lips drawn thinly so that his crayon mustache stretched in a dead straight line across his upper lip.

"Please, meneer, he hates kaffirs just like you do. Please don't report him."

"It's all right for you. You're his friend, you'll say anything." He paused as though thinking. "Orright, I'm a fair man, you can ask anybody about that. But mark my word. Next time that Hoppie Groenewald is going to be in a lot of trouble or my name is not Pik Botha." He withdrew a pair of clippers from his waistcoat pocket and clipped my ticket.

"Thank you, Meneer Botha, you are a very kind man."

"Too kind for my own good! But I am a born-again Christian, a member of the Apostolic Faith Mission, and not a vengeful type. Come, boy, I will take you to breakfast, your ticket says you get breakfast."

Breakfast was another feast of bacon and eggs with toast, jam and coffee. It was too early for the other passengers, and a waiter called Hennie Venter served us. He was pleased as punch because he had won five pounds on the fight. Forgetting what he had said to me about losing one pound ten, Pik Botha proceeded to give him a long lecture on the sin of fighting and the even greater evil of gambling. He ended by asking Hennie if he was ashamed and ready to repent.

Hennie put down a plate of toast covered with a napkin to keep it warm. "No, Meneer Botha, gambling is only a sin if you lose because you didn't back your own kind, but bet on the other side." He lifted the silver coffeepot and commenced to fill the conductor's cup.

"Humph! He's only a grade two railwayman and look how cheeky he is already. Young people don't know their place anymore," Pik Botha grumbled.

Outside the compartment window the bushveld baked in the hot sun. The sunlight flattened the country in the foreground and smudged the horizon in a haze of heat. Noon is a time when the cicadas fill the flat, hot space with a sound so constant it sings like silence in the brain. While I couldn't hear them for the lickity-clack of the carriage wheels, I knew they were out there, brushing the heat into their green membraned wings, energizing after the long sleep when their pupae lay buried in the dark earth, sometimes for years, until a conjunction of the moon and the right soil temperature creates the moment to emerge and once again fill the noon space.

In the heat the compartment seemed to float, lifting off the silver rails and moving through time and space.

Hoppie had explained to me that from Kaapmuiden I would have to take the branch line to Barberton, a further three hours' journey "in a real little coffeepot," he had said. He had told me the story of a washerwoman with a huge pile of freshly ironed washing on her head who was walking along the railway line when the Barberton train drew up beside her. The driver had leaned out of the train and invited her to jump aboard into the kaffir carriage. "No thank you, *baas*," she had replied, "today I am in a terrible big hurry." It was a funny story when Hoppie told it, but I knew it wasn't true because no white train driver would ever think to offer a kaffir woman a ride in his train.

It was nearly four o'clock when we arrived in Kaapmuiden. The train to Barberton left at six o'clock. The train pulled into the busy junction. Kaapmuiden served as the rail link between the Northern and Southern Transvaal and the Mozambique seaport of Lourenço Marques.

The station was all huff and puff, busier even than Gravelotte, with engines shunting, trucks banging, clanging and coupling on lines crisscrossing everywhere like neatly arranged spaghetti. Our train drew slowly into the main platform and, with a final screech of metal on metal, came to a standstill.

I had put on my *tackies,* even though I wouldn't arrive in Barberton until well into the evening. At the beginning of my journey the original oversized *tackies* had been a banal signal of the end of the Judge, his storm troopers, the school and Mevrou. Equally this second pair, fitted to my feet so perfectly by the beautiful Indian lady, with a diamond in her tooth, seemed to symbolize the unknown. The two days between the first *tackies* and the snugly fitting ones I now wore were the beginning of the end of my small childhood, a bridge of time that would shape my life to come.

It was just after ten in the evening when the train puffed into Barberton station. My head was dizzy with sleep and mussed up with the events of the day.

I climbed down the steps of the carriage onto the gravel platform with my suitcase. The platform was crowded with people hurrying up and down, heads jerking this way and that, greeting each other and generally carrying on the way people do when a train arrives.

My granpa didn't seem to be among them. I decided to sit on my suitcase and wait, too tired to think of anything else I might do. I expected any moment that I would hear my nanny's big laugh followed by a series of tut-tuts as she swept me into her apron. That was when everything would be all right again.

A lady was approaching. She bent down beside me and crushed me to her bony bosom. "My darling, my poor darling," she wept, "everything will be the same again, I promise."

My mother was here! Yet I think we both knew, everything would never be the same again.

"Where is my nanny?" I asked.

"Come, darling, Pastor Mulvery is waiting in his car to take us home to your granpa. What a big boy you are now that you are six, much too big for a nanny!" Reaching for my suitcase, my mother straightened up. "Come, darling."

Her remark about my not needing a nanny now that I was six struck me so forcibly that it felt like one of the Judge's clouts across the mouth. My nanny, my darling beloved nanny was gone and I was six. The two pieces of information tumbled around in my head like two dogs tearing at each other as they fought, rolling over in the dust.

My mother had taken my hand and was leading me to a big gray Plymouth parked under a streetlamp beside a peppercorn tree. A fat, balding man stepped out of the car as we approached. His top teeth jutted out at an angle, and peeped out from under his lip as though looking to see if the coast was clear so that they might escape. Pastor Mulvery seemed aware of this and he smiled in a quick flash so as not to allow his teeth to make a dash for it. He reached for my suitcase, taking it from my mother. "Praise the Lord, sister, He has delivered the boy safely to His loved ones." His voice was soft and high-pitched.

"Praise His precious name," my mother replied. I had never heard her talk like this before.

Pastor Mulvery stuck his hand out. "Welcome, son. The Lord has answered our prayers and brought you home safely." I took his hand, which was warm and slightly damp.

"Thank you, sir," I said, my voice hardly above a whisper. It felt strange to be speaking in English. I climbed into the backseat of the car next to my mother.

Granpa Chook was dead, Hoppie had to go and fight Adolf Hitler and maybe he would never come back again, and now my beloved nanny was gone. Like Pik Botha, my mother seemed to have entered into a relationship with the Lord that was bound to create problems. My life was a mess.

We drove through the town, which had streetlights and tarred roads. Only a few cars buzzed down the wide main street. We passed a square filled with big old trees. The street was lined with shops one after the other—McClymonts, Gentleman's Outfitters; J. W. Winter, Chemist; the Savoy Café; Barberton Hardware Company. We turned up one street and passed a grand building called the Impala Hotel that had big wide steps and seemed to have lots of people in it. The sound of a concertina could be heard as Pastor Mulvery slowed the Plymouth down to a crawl.

"The devil is busy tonight, sister. We must pray for their souls, pray that they may see the glory that is Him and be granted everlasting life," he said.

My mother sighed. "There is so much to be done before He comes again and takes us to His glory." She turned to me. "We have a lovely Sunday school at the Apostolic Faith Mission, you are not too young to meet the Lord, to be born again, my boy."

"Can we meet Him tomorrow, please? I am too tired tonight," I said.

They both laughed and I felt better. The laugh that rang from my mother was the old familiar one. "We're going straight home, darling, you must be completely exhausted," she said gently.

I had almost dropped my camouflage, but now it was back again. Pik Botha had said he was a born-again Christian and also that he belonged to the Apostolic Faith Mission. How had my mother come to this? Who was this strange man with escaping teeth? What was this new language and who exactly was the Lord?

I had seen my return to Granpa and to Nanny first as a means of escape from Adolf Hitler and then, when Hoppie had calmed my fear of his imminent arrival, the continuation of my earlier life on the farm. Living in a small town hadn't meant anything to me. Living with Granpa and beautiful Nanny had meant everything. My mother had been a nice part of a previous existence, though not an essential one; she was a frail and nervous woman and Nanny had taken up the caring, laughing, scolding and soothing role mothers play. My mother suffered a lot from headaches. In the morning when I was required to do a reading lesson and had come to sit on the verandah next to her favorite bentwood rocking chair eager to show her my progress, she would often say: "Not today, darling, I have a splitting headache."

I would find Nanny and I would read my book to her and then she would bring a copy of *Outspan* magazine and point to pictures that showed women doing things like making cakes or sewing dresses, or going to posh places. I would read what it said about the pictures and translate them into Zulu. Her mouth would fall open in amazement at the goings-on. "Oh, oh, oh, I think it is very hard to be a white woman," she would sigh, clapping her hands.

I guessed that was why my mother was always getting headaches, because it was a very hard thing to be a white woman.

We drew up beside a house that sat no more than twenty feet from the road. A low stone wall marked the front garden, and steps led up to the *stoep*, which ran the full width of the house. The place was only dimly lit by a distant streetlamp so that further details were impossible to make out. Two squares of filtered orange light, each from a window in a separate part of the house, glowed through drawn curtains, giving the house two eyes. The front door made a nose and the steps to it a mouth. Even in the dark it didn't seem to be an unfriendly sort of place. Behind the funny face would be my scraggy old granpa and he would tell me about Nanny.

Pastor Mulvery said he wouldn't come in and he praised the Lord again for my delivery into the bosom of my loved ones and said that I would be a fine addition to the Lord's little congregation at the Apostolic Faith Mission Sunday school. It was becoming very apparent to me that the Lord was a pretty important person around these parts.

We watched the red brake lights of the big Plymouth disappear down a dip in the road, for we seemed to be on the top of a rise.

Lugging my case in front of me with both hands, I followed my mother up the dark steps. Her shoes made a hollow sound on the wooden verandah and the screen door squeaked loudly on its hinges. She propped it open with her toe and pushed the front door. Sharp light spilled over us and down the front steps, grateful to escape the restrictions of the small square room.

This room, at least, was not much altered from the dark little parlor on the farm. The same overstuffed lounge and three high-backed armchairs in faded brocade with polished arms, the backs of the lounge and chairs scalloped by antimacassars, took up most of the room. The old grandfather clock stood in a new position beside a door leading into another part of the house, and it was nice to see the steady old brass pendulum swinging away quietly. On one wall was my granpa's stuffed kudu head, the horns of the giant antelope brushing the ceiling. On either side of the bookcase hung two narrow oil paintings, one showing a scarlet and the other a yellow long-stemmed rose. Both pictures were the work of my grandmother, who had died giving birth to my mother. On one wall was a colored steel engraving in a walnut frame showing hundreds of Zulu dead and a handful of Welsh soldiers standing over them with bayonets fixed. They stood looking toward heaven, each with a boot and putteed leg resting on the body of a near-naked savage. I had always thought how clean and smart they looked after having fought the Zulu hordes all night, each soldier seemingly responsible, if you counted the bodies and the soldiers in the picture, for the deaths of fifty-two Zulus. The caption under the painting read: The morning after the massacre. British honor is restored at Rorke's Drift, January, 1879. Brave men all.

The tired old zebra skin, which, along with everything else, I had known all my life, covered the floor. The only change in the room, for even the worn red velvet curtains had come along, was a small wireless in brown Bakelite on top of the bookcase.

Perhaps only the outside of things had changed and the inside, like this room, largely remained the same. For a moment my spirits lifted. Just then my granpa walked into the room, tall and straight as a blue gum pole. His pipe was hooked over his bottom lip and he stood framed by the doorway, his baggy khaki pants tied up as ever with a piece of rope, his shirtsleeves rolled up on his collarless shirt. He looked unchanged. He took two puffs from his pipe so that the smoke whirled around his untidy mop of white hair and curled past his long nose. "There's a good lad," he said. His pale blue eyes shone wet, and he blinked quickly as he looked down at me. He raised his arms slightly and spread his hands palms upward as though to indicate the room and the house in one sad gesture of apology.

"Newcastle's disease, they had to kill all the Orpingtons," he said.

"They killed Granpa Chook," I said softly.

My mother put her hand on my shoulder and moved me past my granpa. "That's right, darling, they killed all Granpa's chooks. Come along now, it's way past your bedtime."

I hadn't meant to say anything about Granpa Chook. My granpa, after all, had never known him. It just came out. One chicken thing on top of another. He had been enormously fond of those black Orpingtons. Even Nanny had said they must be Zulu birds because they stood so black and strong and the roosters were like elegantly feathered Zulu generals.

Nanny. Where was she now? Was she dead? Tomorrow I must speak urgently to my granpa. My granpa would tell me for sure. I would ask him when I returned his shilling to him in the morning.

I awakened early as always, and padded softly through the sleeping house to find the kitchen. The black cast-iron stove was smaller than the one on the farm and, to my surprise, when I spit-licked my finger before dabbing it on one of the hot plates, it was cold. On the farm it had never been allowed to go out. The two little orphan kitchen maids, Dee and Dum, had slept on mats in the kitchen and it had been their job to stoke the embers back to life. This kitchen smelt of carbolic soap and disinfectant and I missed the warm smell of humans, coffee beans and the aroma of the huge old cast-iron soup pot that plopped and steamed on the back of the stove in a never-ending cycle of new soup bones added and old ones taken out. This stove was bare but for a blue and white speckled enamel kettle.

The doorway from the kitchen led out onto a wide back *stoep*, which, unlike the front of the house, was level with the ground and looked out into a very large and well-tended garden. The fragrance of hundreds of roses filled the crisp dawn air and I observed that stone terraces, planted with rosebushes, stretched up and away from me. Each terrace ended in a series of steps and at the top of each set of steps an arbor of climbing roses bent over the pathway. Blossoms of white, pink, yellow and orange, each arbor a different color, cascaded to the ground. The path running up the center of the garden looked like the sort of tunnel Alice might well have found in Wonderland. Six huge old trees, of kinds I had not seen before, were planted one to each terrace. It was a well-settled garden and I wondered how it came to be Granpa's.

I now saw that our house was situated a little way up a large hill. Beyond a line of mulberry trees at the far end of the garden the hill of virgin rock and bush rose up steeply, its slopes dotted with aloe, each tall, shaggy plant carrying a candelabra of fiery blossoms. A crown of rounded boulders clustered at its very top.

As I walked up the path, I saw that each terrace carried beds of roses set into neatly trimmed lawns, though the last terrace was different. On one side it contained a stone wall enclosure too tall for me to see over; on the other it was planted with hundreds of freshly grafted rose stock, behind which stood the line of mulberry trees.

In this very tidy garden only the fences on either side testified to the subtropical climate. Quince and guava, lemon, orange, avocado, pawpaw, mango and pomegranate mixed with Pride of India, poinsettia, hibiscus and, covering a large dead tree, a brilliant shower of bougainvillea. At the base of the trees grew hydrangea, agapanthus and red and pink canna. It was as though the local trees and plants had come to gawk at the elegant rose garden. They stood on the edges like colorful country hicks, too polite to intrude any further.

I ducked under the canopy of dark mulberry leaves. As I walked fallen berries squashed underfoot, staining the skin between my toes a deep purple. I hadn't eaten since the previous day, and I began to feast hungrily on the luscious berries. The plumpest, purplest of them broke away from their stalks at the slightest touch. Soon my hands were stained purple from cramming the delicious berries into my mouth.

Emerging from the line of mulberry trees clear of the garden, the first of the aloe plants stood almost at my feet, its spikes of orange blossom tinged with yellow. In front of me, the African hillside rose unchanged, while behind me, embroidered on its lap, gaudy as a painting on a chocolate box, lay the rose garden.

Without thinking I had started to climb, skirting the rocks and the dark patches of scrub and thornbush. In half an hour I had reached the summit and, scrambling to the top of a huge boulder, I looked about. Behind me the hills tumbled on, accumulating height until, in the far distance, they became proper mountains. Below me, cradled in the foothills, lay the small town. It looked out across a beautiful valley that stretched thirty miles over the lowveld to an escarpment that rose two thousand feet to the grasslands of the high-veld.

It was the most beautiful place I had ever seen. The sun had just risen and was not yet warm enough to lap the dew from the grass. I could see the world below me but the world below could not see me. I had found my private place; how much better, it seemed to me, than the old mango tree beside the school playground. Above me, flying no higher than a small boy's kite, a sparrowhawk circled, searching the backyards below for a mother hen careless enough to let one of her chicks stray beyond hasty recovery to the safety of her broody undercarriage. Death, in a vortex of feathered air, was about to strike out of a sharp blue sky.

Chimneys were beginning to smoke as domestic servants arrived from the black shantytown hidden behind one of the foothills to make the white man's breakfast. The sound of roosters, spasmodic when I had started my climb, became more strident as they sensed the town start to wake. Part of the town was still in the shadow cast by the hills, but I could see it was crisscrossed with jacaranda-lined streets. My eyes followed a long line of purple that led beyond the houses clustered on the edge of the town to a square of dark buildings surrounded by a high wall perhaps a mile into the valley. The walls facing me stood some three stories high and were studded with tiny dark windows. The buildings were in a square around a center quadrangle of hard, brown earth. On each corner of the outside wall was a neat little tower capped with a pyramid of corrugated iron that glinted in the early-morning sun. I had never seen a prison, but the architecture of misery has an unmistakable look and feel about it.

My grandpa, an early riser, would be out and about soon and it took no more than twenty minutes to clamber down the hill, back into the rose garden. He was cutting away at the arbor on the third terrace, snipping and then pulling a long strand of roses from the overhang and dropping it on a heap on the pathway. He looked up as I approached.

"Morning, lad. Been exploring, have you?" He snipped at another string of roses and pulled it away from the trellis. "Mrs. Butt is an untidy old lady. If you don't trim her pretty locks, she's apt to get out of control," he announced cheerfully. I said nothing. Much of what my granpa said was to himself. I was soon to learn the names of every rose in the garden and Mrs. Butt, it turned out, was the name of this particular cascade of tiny pink roses.

I pulled the lining of my shorts pocket inside out and unclipped the large safety pin that held Mevrou's *doek*. Crouching on the ground, I unknotted the cloth to reveal Granpa's shilling and my folded ten-shilling note. I removed Granpa's shilling and once again knotted the cloth and pinned it back into the pocket. "This is your change from the *tackies*, Granpa," I said, rising and holding the shilling out to him. He paused, holding the secateurs above his head, then reached down for the coin and dropped it into the pocket of his khaki trousers. "There's a good lad, that will buy me tobacco for a week." I thought he sounded pleased so I took a deep breath and came out with it.

"Granpa, where's Nanny?" He had moved back to the roses and now he turned slowly and looked down at me. Then he walked the few paces to the steps leading up to the terrace and slowly sat down.

"Sit down, lad." He patted the space beside him. I sat down. He removed his pipe from his pocket, tapped it gently on the step below and blew through the pipe twice before taking his tobacco pouch from his pocket and refilling it. My granpa was not one for hurrying things so I waited with my hands cupped under my chin. Lighting a wax match on his thigh, he started at last to stoke up, puffing away until the blue tobacco smoke swirled about his head. For a long time we sat there, my granpa looking out at nothing, his pipe making a gurgly noise when he drew on it, and me looking at the roof of the house, which had patches of faded red paint clinging to the rusted corrugated iron.

"Life is all beginnings and ends. Nothing stays the same, lad," my granpa said at last. "Parting, losing the things we love the most, that's the whole business of life, that's what it's mostly about."

My heart sank. Was he trying to tell me Nanny was dead?

He was doing his looking-into-nothing trick again and his pipe had gone out. "She was a soft and gentle woman. Africa was too harsh a place for such a little sparrow." With this he struck another match and touched it to his pipe. Puff, puff, swirl, swirl, puff, puff, gurgle, but he did not continue. While it didn't sound a bit like big, fat Nanny, my granpa was always a bit vague about people. I waited patiently for him to continue. Taking his pipe from his mouth, he used it to indicate the rose garden around us. "I planned it for her; the roses were the ones which grew in her father's vicarage in Yorkshire, the trees too, elm and oak, spruce and walnut." He replaced the pipe in his mouth, but it had gone out again and he had to light it a third time. I had already observed that my granpa could waste a great deal of time with his pipe when he didn't want to give an answer or needed time to think. So I waited and thought it best to say nothing, though none of it made sense. Nanny, who discussed everything with me, had never once talked about roses, and I knew for a fact that she came from a village in Zululand near the Tugela River. While she had often talked about the crops and the song of the wind in the green corn, of pumpkins ripening in the sun and of the sweet *tsamma* melons that grew wild near the river, she had never mentioned anything about roses.

After another long while of looking into nothing my granpa continued. "When she died giving birth to your mother, I couldn't stay here in her rose garden." He looked down at me. "Sometimes it's best just to walk away from your memories."

I was beginning to realize that Nanny had nothing to do with my granpa's conversation.

"Her brother had come out from England and decided to stay on. A good rose man, Richard. In thirty years he hasn't changed a thing. When the roses grew old he replaced them with their own kind." He pointed to two perfect long-stemmed blossoms, the edges of their delicate orange petals tipped with red, on the terrace below. "I'll vouch that is the only Imperial Sunset standard rose left in Africa," he said with deep satisfaction. Then, picking up the secateurs, he stood and turned to look about him. "Now Dick's dead I've come home to her rose garden."

They were the most words I could recall having come from my granpa in one sitting. While he hadn't answered my urgent questions about Nanny, I could see that he had said something out loud that must have been bouncing around in his head for a long time.

"There's a good lad, off you go now." He moved over to resume the tidying up of old Mrs. Butt. I rose from the steps and started to walk toward the house. Smoke was coming from the chimney and breakfast couldn't be too far away. The clicking of the secateurs suddenly ceased. "Lad!" he called after me. I turned to look at him. "You must ask your mother about your nanny. It's got something to do with that damn fool religion she's caught up in."

Imagine my delight when I walked into the kitchen to find our two little kitchen maids, Dee and Dum. With a squeal of pleasure they rushed over to embrace me, each of them holding a hand and dancing me around the kitchen. "You have grown. Your hair is still shaved. We must wash your clothes. Your mouth is stained from the fruit. You must eat. We will look after you now that Nanny has gone. Yes, yes, we will be your nanny, we have learned all the songs." The two little girls were beside themselves with joy. It felt so very good to have them with me. While they had only been on the periphery of my life with Nanny, who had scolded them constantly but loved them anyway, I now realized how important they were to my past. They were continuity in a world that had been shattered and changed and was still changing.

"Me, Dum," one of them said in English, tapping her chest with one hand while covering her mouth with the other to hide her giggle.

"Me, Dee," the second one echoed, the whites of her eyes showing her delight as they lit up her small black face. They were identical twins and were reminding me of the names I had given them when I was much smaller. It had started as Tweedle Dum and Tweedle Dee and had become simply Dum and Dee. I laughed as they showed off their English.

The room smelt of fresh coffee and Dee moved over to a tall enamel coffeepot on the back of the stove and Dum brought a mug and placed it on the table together with a hard rusk and then walked over to a coolbox on the *stoep* for a jug of milk. She returned with the milk and Dee poured the coffee into the cup, both of them concentrating on their tasks, silent for the time being. Dee ladled two carefully measured spoons of sugar into the mug of steaming coffee. It was a labor of love, an expression of their devotion. Dum brought me a *riempie* stool and I sat down and Dee placed the mug on the floor between my legs so that I could sit on the little rawhide chair and dunk the rusk into it just the way I had always done on the farm. The two girls then sat on the polished cement floor in front of me, their legs tucked away under their skirts.

On the farm they had simply worn a single length of thin cotton wrapped around their bodies and tied over one shoulder. Their wrists and ankles had been banded in bangles of copper and brass wire that jingled as they walked. Now these rings were gone and over their slim, twelve-year-old bodies they wore sleeveless shifts of striped cotton that reached almost to their ankles.

We chatted away in Shangaan. They asked me about the night water and I told them that Inkosi-Inkosikazi's magic had worked and the problem was solved. We talked about the men who came in a big truck and lit a huge bonfire and killed and burned all the black chickens. The smell of burning feathers and roasted chickens had lingered for three days. Such a waste had never been seen before. My granpa had sat on the *stoep* at the farm for a day and a night, watching the fire die down to nothing, silently puffing at his pipe.

At last we reached silence, for the subject of Nanny had been standing on the edge of the conversation waiting to be introduced all along and they knew it could no longer be delayed.

"Where is she who is Nanny?" I asked at last, putting it in the formal manner so they could not avoid the question. Both girls lowered their heads and brought their hands up to cover their mouths.

"Ah, ah, ah!" They shook their heads slowly.

"Who forbids the answering?"

"We may not say," Dee volunteered, and they both let out a miserable sigh.

"Is it the mistress?" I asked, already knowing the answer. Both looked up at me pleadingly, tears in their eyes.

"She is much changed since she has returned," Dum said.

"She has made us take off our bangles of womanhood and these dresses make our bodies very hot," Dee added with a sad little sniff. Both rose from the floor and stood with their backs to me, sobbing.

"At least tell me, is she who is Nanny alive?" They both turned to face me, relieved that there was something they could say without betraying my mother's instructions.

"She is alive!" they exclaimed together, their eyes wide. Using their knuckles to smudge away their tears, they smiled at me.

"We will make hot water and wash you." Dum reached down beside the stove for an empty four-gallon paraffin tin from which the top had been cut; the edges had been hammered flat and a wire handle added, to turn it into a container for hot water.

"See, the water comes to us along an iron snake which comes into the house," Dee said, moving over to the sink and turning on the tap.

"I am too old to be washed by silly girls," I said indignantly. "Put on the water and I will bath myself." Apart from wiping my face and hands with a damp flannel, I hadn't really washed since the shower with Hoppie at Gravelotte.

The girls showed me a small room off the back *stoep* in which stood an old tin bath. Carrying the paraffin tin between them, they poured the scalding water into the bath. Then they fought over who should turn on the cold tap over the tub. Dum won and Dee, pretending to sulk, left the bathroom. She returned shortly with a clean shirt and pair of khaki shorts. I ordered them both to leave the room. Giggling their heads off, they jostled each other out.

That was a bath and a half, I can tell you. It soaked a lot of misery away. The thought that Nanny was still alive cheered me considerably and made the task of asking my mother about her a lot easier.

After breakfast my mother retired to her sewing room and several women turned up to see her. I could hear her talking to them about clothes. When I questioned the maids about this, they said, "The missus has become a maker of garments for other missus who come all the time to be fitted." On the farm my mother had often been busy making things on her Singer machine, and had always made my granpa's and my clothes. Now she seemed to be doing it for other people as well.

Apart from a garden boy who came in to help my granpa, Dum and Dee were our only servants. They cleaned, scrubbed, polished, did the washing and prepared most of the food, though my mother did the cooking and the general bossing around like always. The maids slept in a small room built onto the garden shed.

Later I was to realize that making enough to get by was a pretty precarious business in the little household. My granpa sold young rose trees and my mother worked all day and sometimes long into the night as a dressmaker. Between making dresses and serving the Lord she didn't have much time for anything else.

After lunch I gathered up enough courage to venture into my mother's sewing room. Dee had given me a cup of tea to take in.

My mother looked up and smiled as I entered. "I was just thinking to myself, I would die for a cup of tea, and here you are," she said. She poured the spilt tea in the saucer back into the cup and then took a sip, closing her eyes. "Heaven, it's pure heaven. There's nothing like a good cup of tea." She sounded just like she used to before she went away. For a moment I thought all the carry-on with Pastor Mulvery was exaggerated in my mind because I knew I had been very tired. "Come in for a bit of a chat, have you? You must have so much to tell me about your school and the nice little friends you made." She leaned over and kissed me on the top of the head. "I tell you what. Tonight, after supper, when your grandfather listens to the wireless, we'll sit in the kitchen and have a good old chin-wag. You can tell me all about it. I'm dying to hear, really. Dr. Henny wrote to say you'd got into some sort of scrape with your ear. Is that all right now?" I nodded and she continued, "I'm better now, quite better. The Lord reached down and touched me and I was healed." She took a sip from her cup.

"Mother, where is Nanny?" I asked, unable to contain myself any longer. There was a long pause and my mother took another sip and looked down into her lap.

Finally she looked up at me and said sweetly, "Why, darling, your nanny has gone back to Zululand."

"Did you send her there, Mother?" My voice was on the edge of tears.

"I prayed and the Lord guided me in my decision." She put down her cup and fed a piece of material under the needle, brought the tension foot down and, feeding the cloth skillfully through her fingers, zizzed away with the electric motor. Lifting the tension foot, she snipped the thread and looked down at me. "I tried to bring her to the Lord but she hardened her heart against Him." She looked up at the ceiling as though asking for confirmation. "I can't tell you the nights I spent on my knees asking for guidance." She looked down at me again. "Your nanny would not remove her heathen charms and amulets and she insisted on wearing her bangles and ankle rings. I prayed and prayed and then the Lord sent me a sign I was looking for. Your grandfather told me about the visit of that awful old witch doctor and that it had been at your nanny's instigation." Her face grew angry. "That disgusting, evil old man was tampering with the mind of my five-year-old son! How could I let a black heathen woman riddled with superstition bring up my only son?" She picked up her cup and took a polite sip. "Your nanny was possessed by the devil," she said finally.

I stood looking directly at my mother. "The Lord is a shithead!" I shouted, and rushed from the room.

I ran through the Alice in Wonderland tunnels and under the mulberry trees to the freedom of the hill, my sobs making it difficult to climb. At last I reached the safety of the large boulder and allowed myself a good bawl.

The fierce afternoon sun beat down, and below me the town baked in the heat. When was it all going to stop? Was life about losing the things we love the most, as my granpa had said? Couldn't things just stay the same for a little while until I grew up and understood the way they worked? Why did you have to wear camouflage all the time? The only person I had ever known who didn't need any camouflage was Nanny. She laughed and cried and wondered and loved and never told a thing the way it wasn't. I would write her a letter and send her my ten-shilling note; then she would know I loved her. Granpa would know how to do that.

I sat on the big rock on my hill until the sun began to set over the bushveld. I will have to become a new sort of person, I thought to myself; the old one wasn't managing life very well. But I couldn't think what sort of a person I'd have to become so that I would understand the things happening around me. It seemed to me that just as you got the hang of things in life they changed, each time for the worse, and you were left just feeling alone and not knowing what to do about anything.

EIGHT

"It is a fine sunset, ja? Always here is the best place." I looked behind me, and there was a thin, tall man, much taller than my granpa. He wore a battered old bush hat and his snowy hair hung down to the top of his shoulders. His face was clean-shaven, wrinkled and deeply tanned, while his eyes were an intense blue and seemed too young for his face. He wore khaki overalls without a shirt and his arms and chest were also tanned. The legs of his overalls, beginning just below the knees, were swirled in puttees that wound down into socks rolled over the tops of a pair of hiking boots. Strapped to his back was a large canvas bag from which, rising three feet into the air directly behind his head, was a cactus, spines of long, dangerous thorns protruding from its dark green skin. Cupped in his left hand he held a camera.

"You must excuse me, please, I have taken your picture. At other times I would not do such a thing. It is not polite. It was your expression. Ja, it is always the expression that is important. You have some problems I think, ja?"

At the sound of his voice I had stood up hastily, looking down at him from the rock, a good six feet higher than where he stood. He made a gesture at me and the rock and the sky beyond.

"I shall call it Boy on a Rock. I think this is a good name. I have your permission, yes?" I nodded and he seemed pleased. Dropping the camera so that it hung around his neck by its leather strap, he extended his right hand up toward me. He was much too far away for our hands to meet but I stuck mine out too and we both shook the air in front of us. This seemed a perfectly satisfactory introduction. "Von Vollensteen, Professor Von Vollensteen." He gave me a stiff little bow from the waist.

"Peekay," I said.

"Peekay? P-e-e-k-a-y, I like this name, it has a proper sound. I think a name like this would be good for a musician." He squinted up at me, then took a sharp intake of breath as though he had reached an important decision. "I think we can be friends, Peekay."

"Why aren't the thorns from that cactus sticking into your back?" The canvas bag was too lightly constructed to protect him.

"Ha! This is a goot question, Peekay. I will give you one chance to think of the answer; then you must pay a forfeit."

"You first took off all the thorns on the part that's in the bag."

"Ja, this is possible, also a very goot answer"— he shook his head slowly—"but not true. Peekay, I am sorry to say you owe me a forfeit and then you must try again for the answer. Now let me see . . . Ja! I know what we shall do. You must put your hands like so"—he placed his hands on his hips—"at once we will stand on one leg and say, 'No matter what has happened bad, today I'm finished from being sad. Absoloodle!' "

I stood on the rock, balanced on one leg with my hands on my hips, but each time I tried to say the words the laughter would bubble from me and I'd lose my balance. Soon we were both laughing fit to burst. Me on the rock and Professor Von Vollensteen dancing below me on the ground, the cactus clinging like a green papoose to his back. I could get the first part all right, but the "Absoloodle!" at the end proved too much and I would topple, overcome by mirth.

Spent with laughter, Professor Von Vollensteen finally sat down, and taking a red bandanna from the pocket of his overalls, wiped his eyes. "My English is not so goot, ja?" He beckoned me to come down and sit beside him. "Come, no more forfeiting, too dangerous, perhaps I die laughing next time. I will show you the secret. But first you must introduce yourself to my prickly green friend who has a free ride on my back."

I scrambled down and came to stand beside him. "Peekay, this is *Euphorbia grandicornis*. He is a very shy cactus and very hard to find in these parts."

"Hello," I said to the cactus, not knowing what else to say.

"Goot, now you can see why Mr. *Euphorbia grandicornis* does not scratch my back." I walked behind him. The part of the bag resting on Professor Von Vollensteen's back was made of leather too thick for the long thorns to penetrate. "Not so stupid, ha?" he said with a grin.

"Aaw! If you'd given me another chance I would've got it," I said.

"Ja, for sure! It is always easy to be a schmarty pantz when you know already the trick."

"Honest, Mr. Professor Von Vollensteen, I think I could've known the answer," I said, convincing myself.

"Okay, Peekay, then I give you one chance more. A professor is not a mister but a mister can be a professor. Answer me that, mister Schmarty Pantz?"

I lay down on a small rock trying to work this out. My heart sank, for I knew immediately that he had the better of me. "I give up, sir," I said, feeling foolish. "What is a professor?"

Suddenly he removed the canvas bag from his back and once again held the camera cupped in his hands. "Peekay, you are a genius, my friend! Look what we find under this rock where you are sitting. This is *Aloe microsfigma!*" I rose from the rock and joined him on his knees looking underneath it. A cluster of tiny spotted aloes grew in the grass at the base of the rock. The old man brushed the grass out of the way and, lying flat on his tummy, he focused the camera on the tiny succulents. Behind him the sunset bathed the plants in a red glow. "The light is perfect but I must work quick." His hands, fumbling with the camera, were shaking with excitement. Finally he clicked the shot and got slowly back to his knees. He used a small knife to separate four of the aloes, leaving twice as many behind. He held the tiny plants in his hand for me to see. "*Wunderbar,* Peekay, small but so perfect, a good omen for our friendship."

I must say I was not too impressed but I was glad that he was happy. "You haven't said what a professor is."

He wrapped the tiny aloes in his bandanna and placed them carefully into his canvas bag. "Ja, I like that. You have good concentration, Peekay. What is a professor?" He stood looking at the dying sun. "A professor is a person who drinks too much whisky and once plays goot Beethoven and Brahms and Mozart and even sometimes when it was not serious, Chopin. Such a person who could command respect in Vienna, Leipzig, Warsaw and Budapest and also, ja, once in London." His shoulders sagged visibly. "A professor is also some person who cannot any more command respect from little girls who play not even 'Schopstics' goot."

I could see that his previous mood of elation had changed and there was a strange conversation going on in his head. But then, just as suddenly, his eyes regained their sparkle. "A professor is a teacher, Peekay. I have the honor to be a teacher of music. You can call me Doc. You see I am also Doctor of Music, it is all the same thing. I am too old and you are too young for Mister this or Professor that. Just Peekay and Doc. I think this is a goot plan?"

I nodded, though I was too shy to say the word out loud. He seemed to sense my reluctance. "What is my name, Peekay?" he asked casually.

"Doc," I replied shyly. Hoppie was the only other adult with whom I had been on such familiar terms.

"One hundred percent! For this I give you eleven out of ten. Absoloodle!" he said, and we both started to laugh.

The sun sets quickly in the bushveld and we hurried down the hill, racing to beat the dark. Below us the first lights were coming on.

"So it is you who live now in the English rose garden," Doc said when we reached the line of mulberry trees. "Soon I will show you my cactus garden. We will meet again, Peekay." I watched his tall, shambling figure with the *Euphorbia grandicornis* sticking up beyond his head moving into the gathering darkness.

"Goodnight, Doc," I said, and then on a whim shouted, "*Euphorbia grandicornis* and *Aloe microsfigma*!"

The old man turned in the dark. "Magnificent, Peekay. Absoloodle!"

Euphorbia grandicornis, such a posh name for a silly old cactus. I wondered briefly how it might sound as a name for a fighter, but almost immediately rejected it. *Euphorbia grandicornis* was no name for the next welterweight champion of the world.

When I entered the kitchen, Dum and Dee averted their eyes and Dee said, "The missus wants to see you, *Inkosikaan*." She looked at me distressed. Dum reached out and touched me.

"We have put some food under your bed in the pot for night water," she whispered.

I knocked on the door of my mother's sewing room. "Come in," she said, and looked up as I entered. Then she bent over her sewing machine and put her foot down on the motor and sewed away for quite a while. If her saying nothing and carrying on with her machine was meant to unsettle me she had no hope. After Mevrou and the Judge, she wasn't to know she was dealing with a veteran of interrogation and punishment. I could outwait her any time of the day.

After a while she stopped and, taking off her glasses, she gave a deep sigh. "You have hurt me and you have hurt the Lord very deeply," she said at last. "Don't you know the Lord loves you?" She didn't wait for my answer. "When I had my quiet time with the Lord this afternoon," my mother continued, "He spoke to me. You will not get a beating, but you will go to your room at once without your supper."

"Yes, Mother," I said, and turned to go.

"Just a moment! You have not apologized to me for your behavior."

I hung my head just like I used to do with Mevrou. "I'm sorry, Mother."

"Not sorry enough, if you ask me. Do you think it's easy for me trying to make ends meet? I'm not supposed to get tired. I'm only your mother, the dog'sbody about the place. All you care about is that black woman, that stinking black Zulu woman!" She suddenly lost her anger and her eyes filled with tears. Grabbing the dress she had been sewing, she held it up to her eyes, her thin shoulders shaking, and began to sob.

I felt enormously relieved. This was much more like my old

mother. She was having one of her turns, and I knew exactly what to do. "I'll make you a nice cup of tea and an Aspro and then you must have a good lie-down," I said, and left the room.

Dum and Dee were delighted that I hadn't received a beating and hurriedly made a pot of tea. Dee handed me two Aspro, from a big bottle kept in a cupboard above the sink and I put them in my pocket, for I was afraid that if I put them on the saucer I'd slop tea over them.

My mother was sitting at the machine unpicking stitches as I entered the sewing room. Her eyes were red from crying but otherwise she seemed quite composed. I put the cup of tea down carefully on the table next to the machine and fished in my pocket for the Aspro, which I placed next to the cup. "Thank you," she said in a tight voice, not looking up at me. "Now go straight to your room. You may not come out until morning."

It was light punishment. I had expected far worse. In the chamberpot Dum and Dee had left three cold sausages, two big roast potatoes and a couple of mandarins, a proper feast. There wasn't much else to do but go to sleep after that. It had been a long day and a very good one. I had made a new friend called Doc and had learned several new things. *Euphorbia grandicornis* was an ugly green cactus with long, dangerous-looking thorns, *Aloe microsfigma* was a tiny, spotted aloe that liked to hide under rocks, and a professor was a teacher of music. Also, there was a rose called Mrs. Butt and another called Imperial Sunset.

I fell asleep thinking about Hoppie fighting Adolf Hitler, which would probably be an easier fight than the one against Jackhammer Smit, and how I was going to become welterweight champion of the world.

Two days later I was sitting on the front *stoep* watching army trucks passing the front door. An army camp was being set up in the valley about three miles out of town. The big khaki Bedford, Chevrolet and Ford trucks, their backs covered with canvas tarpaulin canopies, had been passing for two days. Some contained soldiers who sat in the back carrying .303 rifles. But mostly they carried tents and timber and other things needed for building an army camp.

My granpa said it was typical of the army bigwigs, putting a military camp at the end of a branch line, which couldn't move troops out fast enough to anywhere, least of all to Lourenço Marques, where the Portuguese couldn't be relied on to maintain their neutrality for a moment. I had learned that Portugal was one of a handful of European countries that had remained neutral in the war, and its neutrality extended to its possessions in Africa.

My Adolf Hitler fears returned immediately. Lourenço Marques, I discovered, was no more than eighty miles away if he came through Swaziland. I was glad that my granpa had Nanny's address in Zululand and that I had sent her a postal order for my ten shillings, my love in a letter and a photograph taken much earlier showing her holding me. If she couldn't get somebody to read the letter, she'd know it was from me and my original escape plan would still be intact.

I was also glad the army was so close at hand. Lourenço Marques, the nearest seaport, was obviously where Adolf Hitler planned to march all the Rooineks from these parts into the sea. Even an army at the end of a branch line was better than no army at all.

My mother added that Lourenço Marques was probably seething with German spies at this very moment, and they were probably using code words on Radio Lourenço Marques to relay messages to the Boer Nazis who were plotting to tear down the country from within.

I thought about the Judge and Mr. Stoffel and how they always listened to the wireless. When my granpa said that was a lot of poppycock, I was not so sure.

I thought about these things as I watched a convoy of one hundred and five army trucks go by, the biggest yet by far, so I didn't notice Doc coming up the hill until he almost reached the gate.

"Goot morning, Peekay." He was dressed in a white linen suit and wore a panama hat, so that I hardly recognized him. He carried a string bag and a fancy walking stick and under one arm was a large manila envelope.

"Good morning, Doc," I said, jumping to my feet.

"I can come in, ja?" I hurried down the steps to open the gate. "This is an official visit, Peekay. I have come to see your mother."

I felt stupidly disappointed. I hadn't known he knew my mother. I followed him up the steps. "You will introduce us, please," he said as we reached the verandah.

Unreasonably pleased that I was his first friend, I led him into the parlor. Visitors to the farm had been infrequent but the routine was unerring. First you sat people down and then you gave them coffee and cake. I asked Doc to sit down and he did so, but not before he had stood in the center of the zebra skin and slowly turned around, taking the room in. When he reached the grandfather clock he paused and said, "English, London, about 1680, a very good piece." He took a gold Hunter from his fob pocket, and snapping it open, examined it briefly. "Four minutes a month," he said. I was amazed he should know how much our grandfather clock lost, for he was right. I thought perhaps my granpa had told him.

"Do you know my granpa?" I asked.

"I have not yet had this pleasure but it will be okay. We are both men of thorns, with me the cactus, with him the rose. The English and the Germans are not so far apart. It will be all right, you will see." He said this just as I was about to leave the room to get Dum and Dee to bring coffee and cake.

I was dumbfounded. Professor Von Vollensteen was a German! What should I do? My grandfather had gone to the library in town, that was one good thing anyway. You never knew what he might do coming face to face with a German. I decided to say nothing to my mother. She might have a conniption on the spot.

Dum and Dee had somehow known we had a guest and were putting out the tea things and half a canary cake on a plate. I could hear the sewing machine zizzing away as I went to tell my mother she had a guest.

"There is someone to see you, Mother," I shouted over the sound of the whirring machine.

"Tell her to come in, darling, it must be Mrs. Cameron about her skirt."

"It is Professor Von Vollensteen. He wants to see you."

"Professor who?" she asked, removing her glasses.

"He is a teacher of music," I said urgently in an attempt to hide my confusion. She rose to her feet and patted her hair.

"Well, he can't teach music here. We haven't got that sort of money," she said. I followed behind her, not at all sure of the reception Doc would get.

But my mother was countrybred and all visitors were treated courteously. Doc rose from the lounge as she entered. "Madame," he said, bowing slightly, "Professor Karl Von Vollensteen."

My mother extended her hand and Doc took it lightly and

bowed over it, bringing his heels together. "Please sit down, professor. Will you take coffee with us?"

Dum and Dee entered, Dee carrying a tray with cups and cake and Dum carrying the china coffeepot we used for visitors. Dee set the tray on the traymobile and carefully wheeled it over to my mother, who sent her back to fetch a knife for the cake. Dum too was sent back to the kitchen, for the coffee strainer.

"You can tell them a hundred times over, it's useless. I don't know what goes on inside their heads," my mother sighed. I had been standing beside her chair and now she turned to me. "Run along now."

Doc looked up. "With your permission, madame, I would like for Peekay to stay, please?"

"Who?" my mother said.

"Your son, madame, I would much like him to stay."

My mother turned to me. "What on earth have you been telling the professor?"

"It's my new name. I, I haven't told you about it yet," I said, flustered. My mother laughed, but I knew she was annoyed.

"Why, you have a perfectly good name, my dear." She turned to Doc. "Of course he may stay, but I'm afraid our family never had much of an ear for music and lessons would be too expensive."

Without looking at Dee and Dum, who had reentered the room, she held her hand out for the knife and strainer and dismissed them with an impatient flick of her head. She lifted the coffeepot.

"Black only, no sugar," Doc said, leaning forward.

My mother poured his coffee. "A nice piece of cake, professor?"

Doc put the coffee and cake on the zebra hide between his legs and picked up the manila envelope. His eyes sparkled as he handed the envelope to my mother.

"Goodness, what can it be?" she said. She withdrew the largest photograph I had ever seen, which, to my amazement, turned out to be me sitting on the rock on top of the hill. "Goodness gracious!" My mother stared at it, momentarily lost for words. The photograph showed every detail, even the lichen on the rock. Shafts of sunlight seemed to be directed straight at the rock on which I sat. My body, half in shadow, appeared to be as one with the rock. I didn't know it at the time, but it was an extraordinary picture. At last my mother spoke. "Wherever did you take this? Why did you take a picture of him when he was looking so sad?"

Doc rubbed his chin. It was plainly not the comment he expected. Ignoring the first question, he leaned forward as he answered the second. "Ja, this is so. The smile, madame, is used by humans to hide the truth; the artist is only interested to reveal the truth." He leaned back, clearly satisfied with his reply.

"Goodness, professor, all that is much too deep for simple country people like us. He's only a very little boy, you know. I prefer him to smile."

"Of course! But sadness, like understanding, comes early in life for some. It is part of intelligence."

My mother's back stiffened. "You seem to know a lot about my son, professor. I can't imagine how. He has only been home from boarding school for three days."

Doc clapped his hands gleefully. "Boarding school! Ha, that explains I think everything. For a boy like this, boarding school is a prison, ja?"

My mother was beginning to show her impatience. Her fingers tapped steadily on the arms of the chair, a sure sign that things were not going well. "We had no choice in the matter, professor. I was ill. One does the best one can under the circumstances."

Doc suddenly seemed to realize that he had gone too far. "Forgive me, madame. It is not said to make you angry. Your son is a gifted child. I don't know how. I only pray it is music. Today I have come to ask you, please let me teach him?" He had spoken to my mother softly and with great charm and I could feel her relax.

"Humpf! I can't see how he is any different to any other child of his age," she said, though I could tell that she was secretly pleased by the compliment. My mother was a proud woman and didn't expect charity from anyone. "It is out of the question. Piano lessons don't grow on trees, professor."

"Ja, that is true. But, I think, maybe on cactus plants." Doc's blue eyes showed his amusement. "For two years I have searched everywhere for the *Aloe microsfigma.* Then, poof! Just by sitting on a rock, *Aloe microsfigma* comes. The boy is a genius. Absoloodle!"

"Whatever can you be talking about, professor? What have you two been up to?" Whereas before she had been angry, now she was plainly charmed by him.

"Madame, we met on the mountaintop. The picture will capture the moment forever. It was destiny: the new cactus man has come." He paused. "My eyes are not so goot. If the boy will come with me to collect cactus specimens, I will teach him music. It is a fine plan, ja? Cactus for Mozart!"

My mother looked pleased. "His grandmother was an artist. But I don't know if there were any musicians in the family."

The idea of a musician in the family was clearly to my mother's liking. The idea of a son who played the piano, let alone classical music, was a social triumph of the sort she had never expected to come her way. In this largely English-speaking town, a classical piano player was a social equalizer almost as good as money.

I was to learn that the Apostolic Faith Mission was deemed pretty low on the social scale in Barberton. My mother was constantly fighting the need to remain loyal to the Lord and his congregation while at the same time aspiring to the ranks of "nice people."

Old Pisskop at the piano promised to be the major instrument in balancing the family social scales. The bargain was struck just as Mrs. Cameron arrived for her fitting. In return for trekking around the hills as Doc's companion, I would receive free piano lessons. While I had no concept of what it meant to be musical, from the very beginning pitch and harmony had been a part of my life with Nanny.

The long summer months were spent mostly with Doc, climbing the hills around Barberton. Often we would venture into the dark *kloofs* where the hills formed the deep creases at the start of the true mountains. These green, moist gullies of treefern and tall old yellowwood trees, the branches draped with lichen and the vines of wild grape, made a cool, dark contrast to the barren, sun-baked hills of aloe, thorn scrub, rock and coarse grass.

Occasionally, we saw a lone ironwood tree rising magnificently above the canopy. These relics had escaped the axes of the miners who had roamed these hills fifty years before in search of gold. The mountains were dotted with shafts sunk into the hills, supported by timber.

Doc taught me the names of plants. The sugarbush with its splashy white blossoms. A patch of brilliant orange-red in the distance usually meant wild pomegranate. I learned to differentiate between species of tree fuchsia, to stop and crush the leaves of the camphor bush and breathe its aromatic smell. I recognized the pale yellow blossoms of wild gardenia. Nothing escaped Doc's curiosity and he taught me the priceless lesson of identification. Soon trees and leaves, bush, vine and lichen began to assemble in my mind in a schematic order as he explained the ecosystems of bush and kloof and high mountain.

"Everything fits, Peekay. Nothing is unexplained. Nature is a chain reaction. Everything is dependent on something else. The smallest is as important as the largest. See," he would say, pointing to a tiny vine curled around a sapling, "that is a stinkwood sapling, which can grow thirty meters, but the vine will win and the tree will be choked to death long before it will ever see the sky."

He would often use an analogy from nature. "Ja, Peekay, always in life an idea starts small, it is only a sapling idea, but the vines will come and they will try to choke your idea so it cannot grow and it will die and you will never know you had an idea so big it could have grown thirty meters through the canopy of leaves and touched the face of the sky." He looked at me and continued, "The vines are people who are afraid of originality, of new thinking; most people you encounter will be vines. When you are a young plant they are very dangerous." His piercing blue eyes looked into mine. "Always listen to yourself, Peekay. It is better to be wrong than simply to follow convention. If you are wrong, no matter, you have learned something and you will grow stronger. If you are right you have taken another step toward a fulfilling life."

Doc would show me how a small lick of water trickling from a rock face would, drop by drop, gather round its wet apron fern and then scrub and later trees and vines until the kloof became an interdependent network of plant, insect, bird and animal life. "Always you should go to the source, to the face of the rock, to the beginning. The more you know, the more you can control your destiny. Man is the only animal who can store knowledge outside his body. This has made him greater than the creatures around him. Your brain, Peekay, has two functions; it is a place for original thought, but also it is a reference library. Use it to tell you where to look and then you will have for yourself all the brains that have ever been."

Doc never talked down. Much of what he said would take me years to understand, but I soaked it up nevertheless. He taught me to read for meaning and information, to make margin notes and to follow these up with trips to the Barberton library, where Mrs. Boxall, the librarian, would give a great sigh when the two of us walked in. "Here come the messpots!" She claimed she had to spend hours erasing the penciled margin notes in the books we borrowed.

But I don't think Mrs. Boxall really minded. The books on birds and insects and plants were seldom borrowed by anyone else and besides, as most of the books in the natural history section had once belonged to him, Doc adopted a proprietorial attitude toward the library. Over the years his tiny cottage had become too small to contain them, so they had been bequeathed to the library.

We climbed the high *kranses* and the crags in search of cactus and succulents. Toward the end of summer, on the side of a mountain scarred by loose gray shale and tufts of coarse brown grass, I stumbled on *Aloe breviflora,* a tiny thorny aloe.

Doc was overjoyed. "Gold! Absolute gold!" The triumph of the rare find showed in his excited eyes: "*Brevifolia* in these parts, so high, impossible! You are a genius, Peekay. Absoloodle!"

It was the find of the summer and, to Doc, worth all the weary hours spent on the hills and in the mountains. We recorded the find with the camera and removed six of the tiny plants.

Like me, Doc was an early riser, so just after dawn all that summer he gave me piano lessons. "In one year we will tell, but it is not so important. To love music is everything. First I will teach you to love music, after this slowly we shall learn to play."

I was anxious to please Doc and worked hard, but I suspect he knew almost from the outset that I wouldn't prove an especially gifted musician. My progress, while superior to that of the small girls he was obliged to teach for a living, indicated a very modest talent. In the years that followed, it was enough to fool my mother and all the big-bosomed matriarchs who ruled the town's important families. At concerts they would applaud me loudly.

These occasions, which occurred in the spring and autumn, made my mother very proud, though they also represented a compromise with the Lord. Concerts were just the sort of thing that, like moneylending, the Lord condemned. She justified my participation and her attendance by pointing out that many of the great classical musicians wrote music for the church.

The Lord's will was equally explicit on drinking and smoking and dancing, except ballet. Ballet was another of the items cherished by the lavender-scented ladies from the town's upper-echelon families, and my piano recital—Chopin—was usually followed by Tchaikovsky's "Dance of the Swans" by gramophone record, danced to by six-year-olds in white tutus and duckbilled headdresses made of papier-mâché.

We were the cultural meat in a popular sandwich otherwise filled with amateur vaudeville acts, solo songs of an Irish nature, and piano accordion and guitar renditions of well-known Afrikaans folk songs usually performed by the Afrikaner warders from the prison.

The concert would always end with the All Saints Anglican church choir singing the patriotic wartime song "White Cliffs of Dover" with the audience joining in. To show the Rooinek majority where their unspoken loyalty lay, the warders and their families would leave the town hall prior to the mass rendition of "White Cliffs." This would be accompanied by booing and catcalls from less well-bred members of the remaining audience.

Germany had covertly helped the Boers during the Boer War. To the Boers, Germany was an old and trusted friend in a country where a contract was a handshake and declared friendship a bond that continued beyond the grave. The concept of the superiority of some races over others was never for one moment in doubt. In this context, to many Boers Adolf Hitler was only doing his job and, to some minds, doing it well.

After the warders and other Nazi sympathizers had walked out the remainder of the audience would stand up, lock arms and sing "White Cliffs of Dover" at least twice to confirm their love for a Britain facing her darkest hour. To bring the concert to a close the concert party, with warders and other Afrikaners missing, would gather on the stage, each of us holding a long-stemmed rose delivered earlier by me. We stood to rigid attention while a scratchy 78 rpm rendered "God Save the King." Whereupon the cast hurled the roses into the audience.

My granpa, my mother and I then walked home, having politely refused the mayor's invitation to the traditional postconcert party for the cast at the Phoenix Hotel. Worldly parties were pretty high up on the Lord's banned list.

The next issue of the *Goldfields News* would report the concert with the warder walkout splashed across the front page. Tongues wagged for days. Important people suggested the military be brought in to wipe out this nest of Nazi vipers or that the prison be moved to Nelspruit, an Afrikaans town forty miles away, where most of the prisoners probably came from in the first place.

My granpa, with his experience in fighting the Boers, had once been canvassed for his opinion by Mr. Hankin, the editor of the *Goldfields News*. But they didn't print what he said. What he said was: "I spent most of the Boer War shitting my breeches as a stretcher bearer. The only thing those buggers do better than music is shoot. Without them the concert wouldn't be worth a cardboard boot."

Mrs. Boxall, who was the newspaper's correspondent on matters cultural, could always be relied on to devote most of her column, "Clippings from a Cultured Garden by Fiona Boxall," to my performance. For days after it appeared my mother was in a state of dazed euphoria.

In the process of keeping faith with my mother, Doc instilled in me an abiding love for music. What my clumsy hands could never play I could hear quite clearly in my head. A love of music was, among his many gifts to me, perhaps the most important of them all, and he continued to teach me even after his calm and gentle life was thrown into turmoil, and the joy of being alone with him on the *kranses* was stolen from my childhood.

NINE

I had been enrolled at the local school when the new term began at the end of January. Six was the starting age for Grade One, but after a few days it was clear that my year spent in a mixed-age class at boarding school had put me well ahead of the rest of the kids. I was pushed up to Grade Three, where I easily held my own against kids two years older than me.

A comprehensive understanding of Afrikaans in a classroom of English-speaking kids coming to the language for the first time, and Doc's demand that I write up my field notes, gave me a hugely unfair advantage. I quickly earned a reputation, rather unjustly, for being clever. Doc persuaded me to drop my camouflage and not to play dumb. "To be smart is not a sin. But to be smart and not use it, that, Peekay, is a sin. Absoloodle!" I had needed little encouragement. Under his direction my mind was constantly hungry, and I soon found the schoolwork tedious and simplistic. Doc became my real teacher.

His cactus garden was a never-ending source of delight. It was half an acre on the flat top of a small hill that overlooked the town and valley. A ten-minute climb up a dirt road that led nowhere else. His may well have been the best private collection of cacti and succulents in the world. I, who grew up to be an expert on cacti, have never seen a better one.

Doc's cottage had three rooms and a lean-to kitchen. The three rooms were called the music room, the book room and the whisky room. Each had its specified purpose—music, study and drinking himself to sleep.

In the first year we spent together I never once witnessed him drunk, though when I arrived just after dawn for my music lesson I often had to wake him. He would come to sit beside the Steinway, his blue eyes red-rimmed and dulled from the previous night's whisky, his long fingers wrapped around the enamel mug of bitter black coffee. All he would sometimes say as I set my music out on the big Steinway was "Pianissimo, Peekay, the wolves were howling in my head last night." I would look through my music for something soft and easy on the nerves.

It was the cactus garden that testified to "his problem with Doctor Bottle," as my mother would say about any person who ever held strong drink to their lips. Bordering both sides of the path were embedded Johnnie Walker bottles, their square bases shining in the sun like parallel silver snakes winding around the cactus and aloe and blazing orange and pink portulaca. Doc made no apology for his drinking. It was always blamed quietly and politely on the wolves, which I imagined slavering away, great red tongues lolling.

It was at sunset on a Saturday afternoon late in January 1941, a little more than a year after Doc and I had first met on the hill behind the rose garden. We'd spent the day in the hills and had almost arrived back at Doc's cottage. We'd found a patch of *Senecio serpens* high up in a dry kloof, growing over the tailings of an old digging. It was a nice find, although blue chalksticks, as they are commonly called, are not too rare unless they flower in an unusual color. We had decided to plant them in the cactus garden and wait until they flowered again. That was the magic of the cactus garden: some succulents can play dumb; a common blue chalkstick can turn from a Cinderella into a princess in front of your very eyes. I was the first to notice the army van with the white-stenciled Military Police on its hood. The van was parked directly in front of the whisky bottle path that led to the cottage. Two men leaned against the front mudguard smoking, their red-banded khaki caps resting on the hood of the van.

The two men saw us approach and, dropping their cigarettes, ground them underfoot. They reached for their caps and carefully placed them back on their heads the way men do when they are about to undertake an unpleasant duty. Both wore khaki bush shirts, shorts, brown boots, puttees and khaki stockings, though one of them wore the polished Sam Browne belt of an officer while the other, a sergeant, wore a white webbing one. The officer stepped right in front of Doc, who stopped in surprise. Doc was taller than the officer, so the military man was obliged to look up at him. He had a thin black pencil mustache just like Pik Botha. From the top pocket of his tunic he removed a piece of paper, which he held up.

"Good afternoon, sir. You are Karl Von Vollensteen, Professor Karl Von Vollensteen?"

"Ja, this is me," Doc said.

The officer cleared his throat and proceeded to read from the paper he held in front of him. "Under the Aliens Act of 1939 and by the authority vested in me by the Provost Marshal of the South African Armed Forces, I arrest you. You are charged with conspiracy to undermine the security of a nation at war." He handed the paper to Doc. "You will have to come with me, sir. The civilian police, under the direction of military security, will search your premises and you will be detained at Barberton prison until your case can be heard."

To my surprise Doc made no protest. His face was sad as he looked down at the officer and handed him back the piece of paper without even glancing at it. He raised his head, his gaze following the line of the cactus garden. He turned slowly, his eyes filled with pain, taking in the hills, the marvelous aloe-dotted hills, his garden of Eden for twenty years in the Africa he so savagely loved.

"The stupidity. Already the stupidity begins again," he said softly; then he patted my shoulder. "You must plant the *Senecio serpens* to get the morning sun, they like that." He removed his bush hat and got his red bandanna from his overalls and slowly wiped his face. Then he put his bush hat on my head. I looked up at him in surprise. Doc didn't play that sort of childish game. But his eyes were sad and his voice soft, barely above a whisper. "So, now you are the boss of the cactus garden, Peekay."

Turning to the officer, Doc said, "You will please allow me first to shave and change my clothes."

The officer rolled his eyes heavenward. From the number of cigarette butts on the ground they had been waiting for some time. "Orright, professor, but make it snappy." Turning to the sergeant in an official manner, he rapped, "Sergeant! Escort the prisoner to his house for kit change and ablutions."

We walked slowly down the whisky bottle path and Doc dropped his canvas bag on the verandah. I followed him into the dark little cottage to the lean-to kitchen, where he placed an enamel basin on the hard earth floor and poured water into it from a jug. He washed himself from head to toe, then wiped himself briskly with an almost threadbare towel. He was brown all over and his thin body was hard and sinewy.

The sergeant had grown impatient and had wandered into the music room, where he was playing "Chopsticks" on the Steinway. Doc seemed not to hear as he shaved carefully, stropping his cutthroat razor until it was perfect. Then he dressed in his white linen suit and black boots. Finally he placed a spare shirt and his shaving things in a sugar bag and, walking through to the book room, he selected a large book from the top shelf of one of the bookcases. "Put it also in the bag, Peekay." I took the large leather-bound volume from him. Its binding was scuffed and mottled. The title on the spine was hard to read: *Cactaceae. Afrika und Amerika. K. J. Von Vollensteen.* I opened the heavy book to find that it was written in German. I wiped the dust from the cover and put it in the bag. On the packing case dresser next to the bed was half a bottle of Johnnie Walker and this too I put in the bag. Then, heaving it over my shoulder, I joined Doc at the front door. He removed his panama hat from a hook on the wall and picked up his silver-handled walking stick. "We are ready, sir," he said, turning slowly to the sergeant.

The sergeant rose from the piano stool. "That's a blerrie good peeano you got there, professor. Once I saw this fillim star dance on the top of a peeano just like this one, only it was all white. Okay, man, let's go." He took the sugar bag from my shoulder, and looked into it. "Hey, what's this? You can't take whisky where you going." He grinned. "If you like we can have a quick spot now, *oubas*?" he said to Doc. He gave him a conspiratorial wink and uncapped the bottle. Raising it to his lips, he took a long drag of whisky, and wiped his mouth with the back of his hand and the top of the bottle with his palm. "*Lekker*, man, that's blerrie good whisky!" He handed the bottle to Doc, who raised his hand in refusal. The sergeant shrugged. "Suit yourself, man, all the more for me." He took another long swig and walked over to the piano. "In this fillim this man was playing the peeano like at a funeral; then a drunk tipped some whisky on it and suddenly it was playing like mad." He tipped the remaining whisky over the keys of the Steinway. Doc, who had been standing passively waiting, seemed to come alive. He raised his stick and rushed at the sergeant.

"*Schweinehund!* Do not defile the instrument of Beethoven, Brahms, Bach and Liszt!" He brought his cane down hard onto the sergeant's wrist and the bottle fell from his hand to smash on the cement floor. Gripping his wrist, the sergeant danced in agony among the broken glass. Doc, using the sleeve of his linen jacket, ran his arms across the keys in an attempt to wipe them and sent the piano into a glissando. Then he turned and walked toward the front door.

"You Nazi bastard!" the sergeant yelled. I hurried after Doc and he caught up with us on the path outside the cottage. "I'll show you!" He was trying to remove a pair of handcuffs from his belt as he ran. "Stop! You're under military arrest!" But Doc, his head held high, simply continued toward the van. The sergeant grabbed Doc's arm and clicked a handcuff around his wrist. Doc just kept walking, obliging the sergeant to hang on to the other handcuff as though he were being dragged along like a prisoner. He took a swinging kick at Doc, knocking his legs from under him and bringing the old man to his knees on the path. In his fury he aimed a second kick just as, screaming, I flung myself at his legs. The army boot intended for Doc's ribs caught me under the chin, knocking me unconscious.

I awoke in Barberton Hospital with a man in a white coat shining a torch into my eyes. My head was ringing as though voices came from the other end of a long tunnel. "Well, thank God for that, he's regained consciousness," I heard him say.

"Thank you, Jesus," I heard my mother say in a weepy voice. I looked around to see her seated at the side of the bed. She looked pale and worried. My granpa was also there, sitting at the opposite side of the bed. I tried to talk but found it impossible and my jaw hurt like billy-o. My mouth tasted of blood and, running my swollen tongue around my palate, I realized that several teeth were missing.

The doctor spoke to me. "Now, son, I want you to tell me how many fingers I'm holding up in front of you." He held up two and I held up two fingers. "Again." He held up four fingers and I too held up four. He repeated this with several combinations before he finally said, "Well, he doesn't appear to have concussion. We'll have to X-ray the jaw, I think it's probably broken." He turned to my mother and granpa. "We'll be taking him into theater almost immediately, we may need to wire his jaw. He'll be sedated when he comes out so there isn't any point in your staying."

They both rose and my mother leaned over and kissed me on the forehead. "We'll see you tomorrow morning, darling. You be a brave boy, now!" My granpa touched me lightly on the shoulder. "There's a good lad," he said.

I watched them leave the emergency ward, where I appeared to be the only emergency; the other three beds were unoccupied. My jaw ached a great deal and while I think I may have been crying, I only recall being terribly concerned for Doc.

It turned out my jaw had been broken. They wired the top jaw to the bottom one in the closed mouth position, so I was unable to talk. I couldn't inquire about him. Adults decide what they want kids to know and all my mother would say when she came to visit was "You've had a terrible shock, darling, you mustn't think about what happened."

In fact, that was all I could think about. I managed to communicate to a junior nurse called Marie, who had taken to calling me her little *skattebol,* that I wanted paper and a pencil. She brought a pad and a pencil and I wrote, "What's happened to Professor Von Vollensteen?" She read the note and her eyes grew large.

"Ag no, man! Sister says we can't tell you nothing." She held out her hand for the pad and pencil but I quickly tucked it under the quilt. I felt less vulnerable with the pad and pencil beside me. I tore a single sheet from the small pad and, placing it on the cabinet beside my bed, I leaned over and wrote, "My name is not *skattebol,* it is PEEKAY." I didn't much like the endearment as I didn't see myself as a fluffy ball, which is a name you give to really small kids. I handed it to her. She read it slowly, then walked to the end of the bed.

"That's not what it says here," Marie said, looking down at the chart that hung from the foot of the bed. "Don't you know your proper name then?" she teased. "Sis, man! I never heard of a name like Peekay. Where'd you get a silly name like that?" She took a sharp breath. "Anyway, it's a rotten name for a hero who tackled a German spy when he was trying to escape." She moved her spotty face close to mine. "It says in the paper you even maybe going to get a medal!" She drew back suddenly, alarmed that she'd told me too much. "Don't you tell Sister I told you, you hear." She brought a finger up to her lips. "I promise I'll call you Peekay if you promise to stay *stom.*" I nodded my head, though I wondered how she thought I could tell anyone. The tears began to roll down my cheeks. They came because of the news about Doc. I could hear his voice when the officer had handed him the piece of paper. "The stupidity. Already the stupidity begins again."

"Don't cry, Peekay," Marie said, distressed. "I don't really think Peekay is a silly name," she said gently. "Who showed you how to write so good? I went to school up to fourteen and even I can't write so good as you."

After three days alone in the ward I was moved onto the verandah, where there were eight beds all occupied. Except for the fact that I still couldn't talk, I was much better. I had walked into the ward with the sister and with the exception of two old men who were asleep, all the others had applauded and said things like "Well done, son!" One man said that I was a proper patriot. As soon as Sister left the ward I wrote on a piece of paper, "What happened to Professor Von Vollensteen?" I jumped out of bed and took it over to the bed nearest me and gave it to the man in it. He read it and handed it back to me.

"You mean the German spy? Sorry, son, we're not supposed to tell you"—he winked at the others—"we got strict orders."

My mother came to the hospital in the mornings when Pastor Mulvery was able to bring her. She sat with me while he went around the hospital to witness for the Lord. But first he came in to see me, and he'd flash his lightning smile that prevented his two front teeth from escaping and hold my hand in his damp, warm grasp. In his soft voice he said, "We're all praying that this terrible ordeal will make you accept Jesus into your heart." Then he knelt beside the bed and my mother also knelt on the other side and Pastor Mulvery would pray aloud.

"Lord, we are gathered here in Your precious name to pray for this poor child. In his terrible affliction, show him the path to salvation."

"Hallelujah, praise the Lord," my mother would answer. And so it would go every morning.

Not long after I first met Doc, we were sitting on our rock on the hill behind the rose garden and I asked him why I was a sinner and condemned to eternal hellfire unless I was born again.

He sat for a long time looking over the valley and then he said, "Peekay, God is too busy making the sun come up and go down and watching so the moon floats just right in the sky to be concerned with such rubbish. Only man wants always God should be there to condemn this one and save that one. Always it is man who wants to make heaven and hell. God is too busy training the bees to make honey and every morning opening up all the new flowers for business." He paused and smiled. "In Mexico there is a cactus that even sometimes you would think God forgets. But this is not so. On a full moon in the desert every one hundred years He remembers and He opens up a single flower to bloom. And if you should be there and you see this beautiful cactus blossom painted silver by the moon, this, Peekay, is heaven." He looked at me, his deep blue eyes sharp and penetrating. "This is the faith in God the cactus has." We had sat for a while before he spoke again. "It is better just to get on with the business of living and maybe, if God likes the way you do things, He may let you flower for a day or a night. But don't go pestering and begging and telling Him all your stupid little sins; that way you will spoil His day. Absoloodle."

I still sometimes got a bit scared about going to hell and I used to think quite a lot about being born again. But my heart didn't want to open up and receive the Lord. All the people I knew who had opened up their hearts struck me as a pretty pathetic lot, not bad, not good, just nothing. I couldn't afford to be just nothing when I was aiming to be the welterweight champion of the world. I decided I liked Doc's God a lot more than my mother's and Pastor Mulvery's and Pik Botha's.

Pastor Mulvery got up from beside the hospital bed and gave me a flash smile and said that Jesus loved me anyway. Then he trotted off with the Bible under one arm and a handful of tracts to visit all the other patients and my mother stayed with me.

After I got the pad I wrote her a long note asking her about Doc. She took it and without reading it, asked, "Is this about the professor?" Her lips were drawn tight as I nodded. Then she scrunched the note in her hand. "I don't want you ever to mention his name again, do you hear? He is an evil man who used you to cover up the terrible things he was doing and then he nearly killed you." There were sudden tears in her eyes. "The doctor says, if he had caught you on the other side of the head he would have killed you! You've been through a terrible experience and I've prayed and prayed the Lord will make you forget it so you are not scarred for life."

"No! No!" I forced myself to say. What came out was two squeaks from the back of my throat that forced their way past my clamped mouth. They were blaming Doc for what had happened to me and I was the only one who knew the truth and I couldn't help him. It was my fault anyway. If I hadn't put the bottle of Johnnie Walker in his sugar bag this never would have happened.

"You poor little mite," my mother said, "you've been through a terrible time. We'll never talk about it again. Mrs. Boxall from the library has asked to come and see you but the doctor and I have agreed that you're not well enough to have visitors." She opened her bag and withdrew a green school report card. "Now I have some good news for you. You came first in your class. Your granpa and I are very proud of you. They've put you up another two classes. You're going to be in with the ten-year-olds. Fancy that, seven and in with the ten-year-olds!" She handed the report card to me and I took it and tore it into four pieces. For a long time my mother said nothing, looking down at the pieces of green cardboard. Finally she gave a deep sigh. I hated her sighs because they made me feel terribly guilty. "The Lord has blessed you with a good brain. I pray every day that you will take Him into your heart and use your fine mind to glorify His precious name." She gathered the pieces up and dropped them into her handbag, giving me a sort of squiffy smile. "I'm sure it can be mended. You are just not your old cheerful self at present, are you?" But her eyes weren't smiling as she spoke.

That afternoon I wrote a note to Mrs. Boxall. All it said was, "Please come! In the afternoon," and I signed it. I also wrote a note for Marie asking her if she would take the note to Mrs. Boxall at the Barberton public library. Marie had switched to night duty and came on at six p.m. with our dinner. I handed her the note. She read it and quickly hid it in the pocket of her white starched junior nurse's uniform.

"I'll only do it if it's got nothing to do with that spy," she whispered as she put my tray down in front of me. I handed her the second note. She gave me a suspicious look. "I got to read it first before I say I'll do it." She read the note and seemed assured by its contents. "I've got my day off tomorrow, I'll do it then." She seated herself on the side of the bed and, taking up a teaspoon, she filled it with pumpkin and put it through the hole in the corner of my mouth. I had lost four top and bottom teeth on the same side where the sergeant's boot had landed, and Marie called it my feeding hole.

I spent the rest of the evening writing for Mrs. Boxall a long, detailed description of what had happened. Doc, when I presented him with my botanical notes, would always stress that a botanist is concerned with detail. "Observation is what makes a scientist," he said. And so I wrote it all down just the way it happened, even the swearwords, and then I hid the three sheets of paper in my pillowslip. Mrs. Boxall came the very next afternoon. In her bag she carried a new *William* book by Richmal Crompton, a book called *Flowers from the Banks of the Zambesi* and three copies of *National Geographic*. "You are such a precocious child, Peekay, I hope they suit your catholic taste." Like Doc, Mrs. Boxall never talked down to me. With the result that I didn't always understand her and wondered what the Catholics might have to do with my taste.

I withdrew my notes from inside the pillow and handed them to Mrs. Boxall. "Well now, what have we here?" she said, taking the three pages and reaching into her bag for her glasses. She read for a long time before looking up at me. "Remarkable! You are a remarkable child. This comes just in time. A military court is being convened next week and things are looking pretty grim for our professor. The whole jolly town is up in arms about him. People are seeing Jerries in their chamberpots." She chuckled at her own joke. The Germans were nicknamed Jerries, which was also slang for chamberpots. "I tried to see him in prison but those dreadful Boers said only authorized people could see him. I've started a petition in the library but so far I only have twelve signatures and three of them are Boers and we all know where their sympathies lie. That dreadful little man, Georgie Hankin, has threatened to say some perfectly ghastly things about me in the *Goldfields News*." She paused, dug once more into her string bag and withdrew a copy of the *Goldfields News*. Taking up almost half the front page was Doc's picture of me sitting on the rock. Above the picture in huge black letters it said, THE BOY HE TRIED TO KILL! Just above the headline and below the masthead was written Special Spy Edition. Under the picture the caption read "Like Abraham's biblical sacrifice of Isaac, the innocent boy waits on the rock." No doubt the editor, Georgie Hankin, saw this as his finest professional hour.

The reason Mrs. Boxall hadn't been able to visit me was because Dr. Simpson, in resisting Georgie and his photographer's attempts to see me, had banned all visitors. She was surprised that I hadn't seen the earlier paper and promised to bring it the following afternoon.

The essence of the story reported in the *News* was that the provost officer and his sergeant had waited most of the afternoon for Doc to arrive. When he appeared with a small boy in tow, he was in a disheveled state and it was obvious to the two military policemen that he had been drinking. The sergeant, on the orders of the officer, escorted him back to his cottage to allow him to clean up. Whereupon, when his back was turned, Doc attacked the sergeant with a heavy metal-topped walking stick and attempted to run for the hills. It was pointed out that Doc knew the hills well and would be able to conceal himself indefinitely in one of the hundreds of disused mine shafts. He would then make his way across the mountains to Lourenço Marques, the nearest neutral territory.

The story had gone on to say that the sergeant was stunned from the blows he had received and Doc would have made good his escape had it not been for me, who had bravely tackled him. Hearing my scream, the officer had rushed down the path just in time to see Doc take a vicious kick at my head. The officer arrested the suspected spy at the point of his pistol.

The editorial went on to point out that Doc was a noted photographer, and that under the guise of photographing cactus he had undoubtedly taken pictures of likely enemy landing places and established landmarks, as well as mine shafts for storing food and weapons for enemy spies infiltrating South Africa from Portuguese territory. Fortuitously, inside the expensive German Leica camera the spy had used that very afternoon was exposed film of a hole in the mountainside, with the ore tailings dug from the mine heaped directly outside the shaft, making it an ideal defensive position. In Doc's notepad had been found a compass bearing and exact location of the disused mine. There had also been several pictures of a succulent, which proved how cunning and careful to cover up Doc had been.

The picture was, of course, the site where we had found *Senecio serpens,* the blue chalksticks. Doc, as he had taught me to do, always established the location of a find, the direction of the prevailing winds, by studying the bush and plants in the immediate area, the soil conditions and the surrounding rock types.

To the rumor-happy folk of Barberton it was all very feasible and few of them paused long enough to examine the evidence. Mrs. Boxall said people were going around saying, "Once a Jerry, always a Jerry!" "Goodness, Peekay, I'd suspect my dear old father before I'd suspect the professor. He doesn't have a patriotic bone in his body unless it's for Africa and has something to do with cactus." She folded my notes carefully and placed them in her handbag. "Chin up, old chap, we've got all the evidence we need to get our mutual friend out of trouble. I'll get back tomorrow with the news." She was gone, her sensible shoes clattering on the polished cement floor, her back straight as a ramrod and her bobbed head held high.

For the first time in a week I felt happy. Mrs. Boxall was not the sort to be trifled with and I had confidence that she'd sort things out. She was Doc's friend and mine as well and as Doc had so often said, "This woman, she is not a fool, Peekay."

But I didn't see Mrs. Boxall the next day. Somehow my mother had heard of her visit and had seen Dr. Simpson, who brought down a ban on visitors again. I had begun to make semi-intelligent sounds through my wired jaw and Marie, after a few trial sessions, had little trouble understanding me. She said she had a little brother who was a bit wonky in the head and I sounded a lot like him. It was nice to talk to someone again and it was Marie who told me about my mother's visit to Dr. Simpson. I was once again cut off without any news. Marie also told me that I would be going home on Tuesday and she was quite sad about it. She was fifteen and came from a farm in the valley. She lived in the nurses' home and only got one weekend a month off to go home. She wasn't very pretty or very clever and she had pimples, which she called her terrible spots, so she didn't have any friends. I told her I was her friend.

On the Monday evening she came into the ward and put a large brown paper bag on the bed. She brought a finger to her lips, signaling for me to say nothing. "Mrs. Boxall brought it to the nurses' home. She says it's the latest on you know what," she whispered, thrilled to be a part of the conspiracy but also frightened.

I looked into the paper bag, which, at first glance, seemed to contain nothing but bananas, but under the bananas was a tightly folded newspaper and a letter. After lights-out I stuffed both into my pajama jacket and walked down the corridor to the lavatories. The letter was written in Mrs. Boxall's neat librarian's hand.

Dear Peekay,

Much news from the war zone. I have been to see Mr. Andrews. He is the lawyer who comes into the library and only takes out books on birds. He read your notes and he said, "By Jove! This places a different complexion on everything." He seemed very hopeful he could get to the military judge when he arrives from Pretoria next Wednesday. He agrees with me your notes are excellent.

"Too good," he said. "Who will believe a seven-year-old can express himself in such detail?"

That's the problem he thinks we may have. He knows about your inability to speak. But he's hit on a clever plan. He wants you to take an intelligence test, a written test in front of the judge so the judge can make up his own mind. Mr. Andrews has been to see your mother but she won't hear of your having anything to do with the case. But she did say she'd pray about it so all is not lost. It's a bit of a problem really, but we're not beaten yet. I'm sure British justice will come through in the end, even if we have to write personally to Mr. Winston Churchill.

Can you come and see me when you get out of hospital? Keep your chin up!

Yours sincerely,
Fiona Boxall
Librarian

I wondered what sort of test the judge would give me. What if I failed and let Doc down? What if the Lord didn't give my mother permission for me to see the judge?

But the Lord, with a little help from Mr. Andrews, who came from one of the most important families in town, came out in favor of my being a witness at the hearing. The lawyer had pointed out that it was very much in my mother's interests to clear our family name as the prattle tongues in town might well accuse her of neglect for having allowed me to roam the hills with a German spy.

I was released from hospital on Tuesday and the following morning Mrs. Boxall called round in Charlie, her little Austin Seven, to take me down to the magistrates' court, where the military tribunal was to be held. Mr. Andrews was waiting for us and so, to my surprise, was Marie.

"She seems to be the only one who can understand you, Peekay, so we've brought her along as interpreter. It was my idea," Mrs. Boxall declared. Marie looked even more scared than I felt.

Mr. Andrews said the judge would see us privately in the magistrates' chambers and, depending on how things went, I wouldn't be required as a witness.

We had to walk down a long corridor of cork lino that smelt of floor wax. I looked into every open door in the hope that I might see Doc. We finally reached a door with Magistrate in gold lettering on it. Mr. Andrews knocked on the door and a voice said, "Come!" and we followed him in. Sitting behind a desk was a man wearing a proper uniform with a polished leather Sam Browne belt. He stood up when we entered and I could see he wore a revolver at his side. Mr. Andrews introduced him to us as Colonel de Villiers. There were four chairs arranged in front of the desk and we all sat down. My notes were on the desk on top of a file tied with purple tape. Colonel de Villiers put on a pair of spectacles that slid down his nose so he looked over the top of them as he spoke.

"Well now, young man, Mr. Andrews here tells me that you are bright enough to have written these notes." He tapped my notes with his forefinger. "How old are you?"

"Seven, sir," I rasped at the back of my throat. The colonel, Mr. Andrews and Mrs. Boxall turned to look at Marie. Her mouth opened but nothing came out. Her whole face appeared to be frozen in terror. I held up seven fingers to the colonel, who looked stern and cleared his throat.

"I see, seven. Well, you write very well for a seven-year-old. I think someone must have helped you." I shook my head. "Umph!" the colonel grunted, and looked at Mr. Andrews. "These alleged swearwords the sergeant is claimed to have said, they would seem an unlikely part of the vocabulary of a seven-year-old child who, you tell me, has a religious background. I am also a little surprised at his knowledge of Latin. *Senecio serpens* and *Glottiphyllum uncatum* seem a little esoteric for a small boy who, I imagine, like all small boys, is more interested in getting his mouth around a sucker than a Latin noun."

Mrs. Boxall said, "The professor is an amateur botanist and the child has been trained by him to take punctilious notes. Besides, he has almost perfect recall."

"Hmm . . . a bit too perfect if you ask me, madam," the colonel said.

"He did it all himself, I seen him do it in the hospital," Marie said suddenly, her voice quaking with terror.

"Well, that's one good thing. Little Miss Florence Nightingale has found her voice," the colonel said. He turned to me. "Son, I want you to tell me the whole story again, just as it happened." I repeated the story. Marie had no chance of pronouncing the Latin names of the two succulents, which I then referred to as "blue chalksticks and another succulent genus, which I can write for you, if you want?" The colonel pushed a piece of paper across the desk and I wrote the Latin names on it. "Extraordinary. It seems I owe you an apology, madam," he said, dipping his head at Mrs. Boxall. When we got to the swearwords Marie refused to say them. "Please, sir, I can't say them words, I've never said words like that in my whole life," she said fearfully but with absolute resolve.

The colonel would cut in every once in a while and ask me questions such as "What was the color of the sergeant's cap and belt?" They all involved some minor piece of detailing, but I had no trouble answering them.

When I was finished, he told Marie that she had done an excellent job and she blushed crimson and the pimples stood out on her face. Then he turned to Mr. Andrews.

"The child's statement coincides almost precisely with that of the prisoner. We have already determined that neither has been in a position to compare notes nor to have a third party coordinate a defense. Mrs. Boxall did try to see him but was not allowed to do so. The prisoner has been visited and interviewed only by military personnel and I am satisfied that the incident took place as the boy has alleged. I am quite sure the court will find for the defendant in all matters except one. I will ask that the charges of assault to a minor and attempted escape be withdrawn. Quite obviously the striking of the provost sergeant was under severe emotional provocation and the court is likely to look upon it as such. Both the army and the prison reports state that the prisoner smelt heavily of whisky but we can easily ascertain whether his coat sleeve is stained."

He pulled at the purple tape on the file and opened it up. Inside were two folded copies of the *Goldfields News*. The colonel held up one of the newspapers. "Really, this kind of hysterical nonsense makes it very difficult for us. The trial of aliens is distressing enough without having the general population turning the butcher, the baker and the music maker into enemies of the state. The only charge Professor Von Vollensteen faces is a technical one, that of not having registered as an alien." He rose from his chair and smiled briefly at me. "I only wish I could be here to have a chat with you when your jaw is better, young man. I am also beginning to form a healthy respect for the teachings of your professor."

When we got back to the waiting room Mrs. Boxall started to laugh. "We won, Peekay, we won!" she said triumphantly.

But we hadn't won. While Doc was acquitted of all the charges just as the colonel said he would be, he was charged with being an unregistered alien and the court ordered him to be detained in a concentration camp for the duration of the war. The *Goldfields News* headline read NO SPY BUT STILL A GERMAN!

TEN

Doc was to be kept in custody at the Barberton prison until arrangements could be made to send him to a concentration camp in the highveld. Two days after Doc had been sentenced I went to the library to take a bunch of roses from my mother to Mrs. Boxall. Mr. Andrews had explained to my mother how my evidence had saved Doc from a severe sentence, one that might well have killed a man of his age. My mother decided that the Lord had guided her in the matter and that His will had been clearly wrought through me.

Mrs. Boxall seemed excited when she saw me come through the door. "I'm so glad you came, Peekay, I have a letter for you." She placed the roses on a table and withdrew into her office to return with a small sealed envelope. I opened it carefully. "Do hurry, Peekay, I can't bear the suspense," Mrs. Boxall said. I withdrew a single sheet of cheap exercise paper. Doc's neat hand covered the page. "Oh dear, I'm such an awful nosy parker! May I read it with you?" Besides Hoppie's note, it was the only letter I had ever received. I would have preferred to read it alone but of course I couldn't possibly say so and I nodded my agreement.

❂ ❂ ❂

Dear Peekay,

What a mess we are in. Me in this place where they tear down a man's dignity and you with a broken jaw. But things could be worse. I could be a black man and that would be trouble and a half. I have been placed under open arrest. It means I can go anywhere in the prison grounds and my cell is not locked. Best of all, it means I can have visitors. Will you come and see me?

I do not think of myself as a German. To say a man is a German, what is that? Does it tell you if he is a good man? Or a bad man? No, my friend, it tells you nothing. Also, because I am German, I am well treated by the warders. This also is stupid. Have you planted the Senecio serpens? *Perhaps Mrs. Boxall will take the books in the cottage and put them in the library? In the meantime I am treated well and whisky is getting easier not to have. Please come soon.*

Your friend, Doc

"We will call the prison at once," Mrs. Boxall said.

The superintendent of Barberton prison, Kommandant Jaapie Van Zyl, told Mrs. Boxall that Colonel de Villiers had said Professor Von Vollensteen should be allowed access to the boy within the normal rules of the prison. He added that he had heard of my bravery and wanted to meet me himself. That if Mrs. Boxall cared to have me bring Doc library books this would be permitted. The professor was a musician and a scholar and Barberton prison was honored to have him.

Mrs. Boxall selected three botanical books and I set out with a note from her to visit Doc.

I arrived at the gates of the prison, which were locked with a huge chain and padlock. It was the biggest lock I had ever seen.

I decided that escape from inside the wall would be impossible. Set high up to the side of the gate was a church bell and hanging from it a rope. A sign fixed onto the wall said "Ring for attention." My heart beat wildly as I tugged on the rope and the noise from the bell cracked the silence. Almost immediately, a warder carrying a rifle slung over his shoulder came out of a guardhouse some twenty feet from the gate and walked toward me. His highly polished black boots made a scrunching sound on the white gravel driveway. I handed my note to him through the bars of the gate and he opened it suspiciously. He looked at the note for a bit, then looked at me.

"*Praat jy* Afrikaans?" he asked.

I nodded my head. While my voice sounded a bit gravelly I could talk quite clearly through my wired-up mouth. The young guard started to talk in Afrikaans. He asked me to read the note as he didn't have much English. "It says that I am here to visit Professor Von Vollensteen and have permission from Kommandant Van Zyl," I told him.

"I will get on the telephone and ask. Wait here." He walked over to the guardhouse and I could see him talking on the phone. Finally he stuck his head out of the door. "Kom!" he beckoned to me. But the gate was locked and he shook his head and disappeared to return with a very large key. The gates opened smoothly and closed with a clang as he locked them behind me.

The young warder told me to report to the office in the administration block and pointed it out to me. "*Totsiens* and thanks for reading the note. You are a good *kêrel*," he said.

The area between the gate and the administration block was a parade ground of sun-hardened red clay. The strip of green lawn on either side of the pathway was a brilliant contrast to the baked earth and the blue-gray walls of the buildings. I could see a warder's head in the window of a little tower jutting out from the wall. There was a walkway on either side of the tower. Two guards with rifles slung over their shoulders paced up and down it. I seemed to be the only person on the ground below them and I wondered how, on my way out, they'd know I wasn't a prisoner trying to escape. Maybe they'd give me a white flag to carry.

I could sense the oppression of the place, the terrible silence. Without trees, no cicadas hummed the air to life. No birds punctuated the stillness. My bare feet on the gravel made an exaggerated sound. There were tiny dark windows arranged three stories high. Each was divided by two vertical steel bars. I imagined hundreds of eyes hungrily devouring my freedom as they watched from the prison darkness.

The door of the administration block was open. Inside was a small hallway with three benches. A window with bars was set into the wall. Through the bars I could see an office. I sat on a bench and waited.

A door opened and a big man followed by another younger man came out. They led me into the office and after taking my name, address and age the older man made a phone call and asked to speak to the Kommandant. "The Kommandant wants to see you but he's doing an inspection now, we have to wait twenty minutes." He turned to the younger warder. "Klipkop, get Peekay here a cup of tea and a biscuit." I wondered how someone could be called Klipkop. In Afrikaans it means "stone head." But then I suppose *I* had been called Pisskop and that was far worse. Come to think of it, when I glanced at the tall, blond man, his rawboned features looked as though they could well have been carved out of stone.

Klipkop rose and held out his hand. "We might as well introduce ourselves. Oudendaal, Johannes Oudendaal," he said formally in the

Afrikaans manner. "This is Lieutenant Smit." He indicated the older warder. I wondered whether Lieutenant Smit was related to Jackhammer Smit, but I didn't have the courage to ask. After all, Smit is a pretty common Afrikaans name. "Come, I'll show you where we make tea," Klipkop said. "There's a kaffir who makes it but if we want a cup in between we make it ourselves. You got to watch the kaffir, or the black bastard pinches everything. I'm telling you, man, this place is full of thieves."

I followed him into a small kitchen behind the office and he put water into an electric jug and plugged it in. "Peekay, that's a name I haven't heard before."

"It's just a name I gave myself. Now it's my real name," I said.

"Ja, I know, man, it's the same with me. They call me Klipkop because I box and can take any amount of head punches. Now I sometimes find it hard to remember my born name."

For a moment I was stunned. "You box?" I asked.

"Ag ja, man. In this place if you want to get on you have to box, but I like it anyway. On the weekend we travel all over the place to fight." He took three mugs from a cupboard. "Lieutenant Smit is the boxing coach. He used to be a heavyweight." He spooned tea into the pot. "Next month I have my first professional fight." He poured the water from the electric jug into the teapot. "Do you box, Peekay?"

My heart was pounding as I spoke. "No, but can you teach me, please, Meneer Oudendaal?"

He looked at me in surprise and must have seen the pleading in my eyes. "First your jaw has to get better, but I think you're a bit young anyway. Lieutenant Smit teaches also the warders' kids but I think the youngest in the junior squad is already ten years."

"I'm ten in class already. I could be ten in boxing easily and my jaw will be better soon," I begged.

"Hey, whoa! Not so fast! Ten is ten. On the form we wrote you were seven years old."

"If you fight first with the head and then with the heart, you can be ten years old," I said.

"*Magtig,* you're a hard one to understand, Peekay. You'll have to ask Lieutenant Smit. He's the boss."

"Will you ask him for me?" I rasped. The excitement made me overproject so that my throat was strained.

"I'll ask him, man, but I already told you what he'll say." He poured tea into the three enamel mugs, then went to the cupboard, took out a tin and prized it open. "That blerrie kaffir! We had a packet of Marie biscuits in here, now they all gone. It's time that black bastard went back into a work gang."

"Please, Meneer Oudendaal, you won't forget to ask the lieutenant? You see, I've got to start boxing because I have to become the welterweight champion of the world."

I said it without thinking. Klipkop whistled. "Well, you're right, man. With an ambition like that you've got to get started early. Me, I'll be happy if I can beat the lieutenant's brother in Nelspruit next month." He turned and looked over his shoulder at me. "You can call me Klipkop if you like. I won't mind, man."

I followed him back into the office where Lieutenant Smit was working on some papers. Klipkop put a mug of tea down in front of him. "Peekay wants to ask you something, lieutenant," he said, and turned to me.

Lieutenant Smit gave a short grunt. "Please, sir, will you teach me how to box?" I asked, my voice down to a tiny squeak.

He didn't look at me but instead lifted the tea to his lips, and took a sip. "You are too young, Peekay. In three years come back; then we will see." He looked at me. "We read about you in the paper. You have lots of guts. That's a good start but you are not even big for seven like a Boer kid." He ruffled my hair. "Soon you will be ten, just you watch."

At that moment an African came into the room. He was quite old and very thin, wearing the coarse knee-length gray canvas pants and shirt, of a prisoner. "I have come to make tea, *baas,* but the pot she is not here," he said slowly in Afrikaans. He stood with his head bowed. In two bounds Klipkop had reached him and, grabbing him by the front of his shirt, he lifted the African off his feet and gave him a tremendous swipe across the face. The man fell at his feet, whimpering.

"You black bastard! You stole the Marie biscuits. You piece of dog shit, you stole them all!" He gave him a kick in the rump.

"No, *baas*! Please, *baas*! I not stole biscuit. I good boy, *baas*," the old man pleaded.

The warder turned to Lieutenant Smit. "Please, lieutenant, can't we transfer this black bastard to the stone quarry? First he steals sugar, now the biscuits." He looked down at the whimpering African.

Lieutenant Smit hadn't even looked up. The African scrambled to his feet and Klipkop gave him a flying kick that sent him sprawling again. Crawling on all fours, the black prisoner fled from the room.

Klipkop examined his hand. "They got heads made of blerrie cannonballs." He turned to me. "Always remember, when you hit a kaffir, stay away from his head. You can break your fist on their heads, just like that. Hit him in the face, that's orright, but never on the head, man. I got a big fight coming up, I can't afford a broken fist from a stinking kaffir's head."

Lieutenant Smit took another sip from his tea. "We can't send him to the quarry, man. He's had rheumatic fever; he'd die in a week. Besides, he is the first kaffir we've had who can make proper coffee and tea." He turned to look at Klipkop, with just the hint of a smile on his face. "Next time, man, ask before you hit. I ate the blerrie Marie biscuits."

Klipkop's mouth fell open and then he grinned. "Okay, so I hit him because he steals the sugar. So what's the difference?"

The phone rang and Lieutenant Smit picked it up and listened for a moment. "Right," he said into the receiver and replaced it. He turned to me. "The Kommandant is back. Come on, son."

Grabbing Mrs. Boxall's books, I followed the lieutenant up a set of stairs to the second floor. We entered a small outer office where a lady sat behind a desk typing on a big black machine that said Remington Corona in gold letters on its back. "Go right in, Lieutenant Smit, the Kommandant is waiting for you," she said, smiling at me.

We entered a large office, dark brown and filled with dead animals. A kudu head was mounted behind the Kommandant's desk with a sable antelope head beside it. There were gemsbok and eland heads to complete the display of larger antelope and next to them, in a cluster of five heads, were the smaller variety of buck: gray duiker, klipspringer, steenbok, reebok and springbok. I turned to face the wall behind me. A large black-maned lion looked down at me, mouth in the full roar position. Next to it were a leopard and a cheetah. All the carnivores were on one side of the door, while on the other were their most common prey, a zebra and a black wildebeest. Below these, fixed to brackets on the wall, were two Boer War rifles and a long-shafted Zulu *assegai*.

On the polished floorboards were a zebra and a lion skin. Directly behind the Kommandant's head hung two portraits. One was of King George VI and the other of Paul Kruger, the last president of the defeated Boer Republic.

Kommandant Van Zyl rose from his desk. "Good morning, Smit. So this is the boy, eh?" He walked out from behind his desk and stuck out a huge hand. "Good morning, Peekay." He was even bigger than Lieutenant Smit. Like the lieutenant and Klipkop, he wore the gray military-style uniform of a prison warder. The only differences were four stars and a crown on his shoulder tabs and a small tab of blue velvet inserted into the top of his lapels. I shook his hand shyly.

"So, you want to see our professor?"

I nodded my head. "Yes, please, sir."

"The law says he must be detained and I must follow the law, but inside this place, *I* am the law," the Kommandant told me. "In here he can come and go as he pleases provided he stays within the gates. Also he can have visitors in official visiting hours." He looked at me and smiled. "I have decided to make an exception in your case. You can come anytime you want, only not Sundays." He paused and looked at me again. "How do you like that, hey?"

"Thank you, Meneer Van Zyl," I said.

He looked at Lieutenant Smit as though he felt the need to explain his decision. "A friendship between a man and a boy is not a thing to be broken. This boy has no father. I know what that is like, man. My father died when I was the same age. Make out a permanent pass for the boy so he can come anytime except Sunday, you hear?"

"Ja, Kommandant." Smit looked at the larger man. "What about the professor's peeano?"

Kommandant Van Zyl slapped his hand on his thigh. "I clean forgot. Thank you, Smit." He turned to me. "We are going to let the professor have his peeano here; there are already many musicians among us. Everybody thinks Boers are not cultured, but I'm telling you, man, when it comes to music we leave everyone for dead. For us it is an honor to have a man such as him in our prison community. *Magtig!* A real professor of music, here, in Barberton prison. *Wonderlik!*"

"Thank you for letting me come to see him, meneer."

"The boy has nice manners. I like that," he said to Lieutenant Smit. He hesitated for a moment. "Peekay, we need just a small favor. On Monday, about one o'clock, we will be having a nice little surprise for the townsfolk in the market square. I already telephoned the mayor but I can't trust him to tell people. Will you inform Mrs. Boxall, who telephoned about you, and who, I understand, is also a friend of the professor? Ask her to tell everyone, you hear." I nodded and he seemed pleased. "*Dankie,* Peekay. Now Lieutenant Smit is going to take you to see the professor. I see you have some books for him." He stretched his hand out. "Show me." I handed the books to him. He opened the top one and leafed through it for a few moments. "Plants, I don't know much about plants. Animals, that's my specialty." He brought his hands up as though he were squinting down the barrel of a rifle, pulled an imaginary trigger and made a small explosive sound. "I've shot it." He grinned at me. He had two gold teeth. "I love wild animals," he said.

Lieutenant Smit cleared his throat loudly and the Kommandant turned back to us. "Well, it's been nice to meet you, Peekay." He patted me briefly on the shoulder. "If you want anything you just come and see me, you hear?"

It was like the time I had to decide whether to offer to do the Judge's arithmetic. Like then, I was doing pretty well. Why risk it? If I got on the wrong side of the lieutenant, I stood to lose everything, even the chance of becoming a boxer once I turned ten.

"Please, Meneer Van Zyl. Could I learn to box here?"

"You want to box?" The Kommandant looked at me. "That's the lieutenant's department."

"I already told the boy he must wait until he is ten, then maybe," Smit said, trying not to sound terse.

"When you're seven it's a long time to wait till you're ten," the Kommandant said.

"We train at five-thirty in the morning. How could he get here?"

"I will get here, I promise. I will never miss, not even once. Please, Meneer Smit?"

Lieutenant Smit looked down at his boots for a long time. "We can try when your jaw is fixed. But I must have a note from your mother to say it's okay to teach you." He looked up, appealing directly to the Kommandant. "He is too small, Kommandant."

"He will grow, Smit. As I recall you and your younger brother started very young. Is he still fighting?"

"Yes, sir, his next fight is against Oudendaal."

"That's right, the lowveld heavyweight title next Saturday." Kommandant Van Zyl ushered us to the door. "All the best, Peekay."

When we reached the bottom of the stairs Smit stopped, and getting down on his haunches, he grabbed me by the front of the shirt. He had said nothing when we left the Kommandant's office, but I was too good at listening to silence not to know I was in real trouble. I closed my eyes, waiting for the clout across the head that must inevitably come. I hadn't been hit for a year except for a few hidings from my mother that you couldn't really call hidings after what I'd been through. To my surprise the blow didn't come and I opened my eyes again to look straight into Lieutenant Smit's angry face. "I'm telling you flat, don't do that to me again, you hear? When I tell you something I mean it, man!" He shook me hard, expecting me to cry; instead I held his gaze. "You trying to be cheeky?" he asked.

"Please, meneer, I saw your brother fight in Gravelotte last year. That's when I decided."

A look of amazement crossed Smit's face. "You were there? *Wragdig?* You saw that fight?"

I nodded. "He fought Hoppie Groenewald . . . Kid Louis," I corrected. Lieutenant Smit released his grip on the front of my shirt.

"I was there also. *Magtig!* That was a fight and a half." He rose from his haunches and suddenly his eyes grew wide. "The kid with Hoppie Groenewald! I remember now. We thought you was his kid."

We had reached the office again. Klipkop was on the floor doing push-ups and stood up rather foolishly as we entered. "You know the fight in Gravelotte my brother had against Groenewald the welterweight last year?" Klipkop nodded. "Peekay saw that fight; he is a personal friend of Groenewald."

The warder laughed. "I lost a fiver on that fight."

"You mark my words, if Groenewald comes out of this war he's going to be South African champ," Smit said.

Klipkop grinned. "I'm going to do the same to your brother on Saturday as he did."

"Don't be so blerrie sure of yourself, Oudendaal. Jackhammer Smit is no pushover. This time he'll be fit."

Smit turned to me suddenly. "Okay, I changed my mind, you on the squad. But no fighting for two years, you hear? Just training and learning your punches and technique, you understand me?"

I nodded, overjoyed. My eyes brimmed with tears. I had taken the first step to becoming the welterweight champion of the world.

"Klipkop, take Peekay to see the professor. I'll make a phone call and you can meet him in the warders' mess."

We left the administration block and passed through another building. "This is the gymnasium for the prison officers," Klipkop said. We walked over to the punching bag and the boxing ring set up at one end of the room. Large leather balls lay on the floor and Klipkop bent down and scooped one up. "Here, Peekay, hold on to this." I put both my hands out and he flipped the ball lightly into them and suddenly I was sitting on the floor with Klipkop laughing over me. "It's a medicine ball and it weighs fifteen pounds. When you can throw one of these over my head you'll be strong enough to box." I got up, feeling very foolish; then I bent down and tried to pick the brown leather ball up. Using all my strength, I managed to lift it but was happy to let it drop again. "Not bad, Peekay," Klipkop said with a grin. We were standing next to the ring and I liked the smell of the canvas and the sweat. I wondered how I could possibly wait two years before I climbed into the ring to face a real opponent.

We left the gymnasium and crossed the huge indoor courtyard, an area half the size of a football field. The prison blocks rose up on every side of the square where two old lags were raking its gravel surface so all the tiny rake lines ran diagonally across the quad. "It's Friday, diagonal lines. I like Monday best, when they make a big star in the middle," Klipkop said. I was soon to learn that each day had a different pattern. It was how the prisoners knew what day of the week it was.

"Where are all the prisoners, Klipkop?" I asked. The two old lags doing the raking were the only humans I had seen since leaving the administration building.

"They're all out in work gangs. Most work on farms, some at the quarries and some at the sawmills. The people who hire them call for their gangs at four in the morning and they got to be back here by six at night. What you see around here in the daytime is just old lags, too old to work hard, like that black bastard who makes our tea."

"What about the white prisoners. Do they also work in the gangs?"

Klipkop looked surprised. "No blerrie fear! Gangs is not a white man's work. Mostly white men are only here in transit to Pretoria."

We had crossed the gravel quad and passed through an archway that led to the back of the prison. A corrugated-iron shed stretched from the main building and smoke rose from three chimneys along its length. "Kitchens. The warders' mess is on the other side," Klipkop said.

Doc was overjoyed to see me. He hugged me and his sharp blue eyes went watery. "Let me see your jaw? Tut tut tut. I wish only I could have taken the kick; then you would be okay. Can you talk?"

"My jaw is not so bad. They are going to take the wire out in six weeks, but I have learned to talk with my mouth shut."

Doc laughed. "You and I, Peekay, even when they cement our mouths, we find a way to talk."

I handed him the books from Mrs. Boxall and he held them briefly before putting them on the table beside him. "She is a goot woman. You and she, Peekay, eleven out of ten for brains. Absoloodle. Also Mr. Andrews. I do not think they would listen to a poor old German professor of music on his own. German measles was in the air and only you and Mrs. Boxall don't catch a big dose, ja?" He chuckled at his sad little joke.

"I can come and visit you as much as I like," I said happily.

Doc looked bemused. "Without the hills it will not be the same. What can I teach you here?"

"Lots of things. I could go into the mountains and find things and bring them here and then we could talk about them."

Doc gave me one of his proper grins. "You are right, Peekay. A man is only free when he is free in his heart. We will be friends like always. Absoloodle. But also one more thing: they are going to let me have the Steinway here. You can continue your lessons. You must tell your mother this. I think she will be happy. On Monday they are letting me come with them to get it. I will see my cactus garden one last time. Maybe you can be there, Peekay?"

Dr. Simpson had said that another week's recuperation was in order.

"I'll be waiting for you. I've already planted the *Senecio serpens*, just like you said, facing east."

Doc looked pleased, but then a worried expression crossed his face. "Peekay, on Monday is happening a stupid thing. It is not my decision, but please you must trust me. That is why I want you to be there. I think Kommandant Van Zyl wants to be a schmarty pantz with some people in this town. I am too old for such silly games. You will help me, please?"

"Kommandant Van Zyl said I was to tell Mrs. Boxall everyone has to be in the market square at one o'clock, but he didn't say what it was all about."

Just then Klipkop emerged from the door leading to the kitchen.

Doc went on talking. "Monday, Peekay. Be so kind as to be at the cactus garden at twelve o'clock; then I will explain. Also, tomorrow maybe find for me Beethoven Symphony Number Five, you will see on the cover is printed my name and Berlin 1925. That is the one I want." I knew where to look, for the music Doc played only to himself was kept under the seat of his piano stool. I found it strange that he would ask me to find it. After all, he knew perfectly well where it was. "Peekay, put what's above the score in my water flask, the key for the piano stool lid you will find under the pot on the *stoep* where grows the

Aloe saponara." He said all this in a perfectly straight voice in English. Klipkop appeared to be uninterested. I looked quizzically at Doc but he put his forefinger to his lips and indicated the warder with his eyes.

A hooter sounded somewhere in the prison. "Twelve o'clock, lunchtime, Peekay. We must get back to the lieutenant and the professor must go to lunch," Klipkop said.

I would have to run all the way home as my mother would expect me back from the library by now. I wasn't at all sure how she would take the news of my potential comings and goings to the Barberton prison.

After Sunday school the next day I went to the cactus garden. Dum and Dee had the afternoon off on Sundays and had excitedly agreed to come with me to clean things up a bit. They took brooms and feather dusters and other cleaning things in two buckets, which they carried on their heads, chatting away happily. There wasn't much they could do on their half-day off as they hadn't yet learned to speak Swazi. They must have felt isolated from their own kind. On the farm they had been at the center of things. Here they were two lonely girls who, outside our home, could make no contact and knew no people other than our family.

When we arrived at the cactus garden they set to, delighted to be without supervision from anyone. I went straight to the terracotta pot on the *stoep* where *Aloe saponara* was growing. With some difficulty I pushed the large pot aside to reveal the key to Doc's own piano stool.

I always used to sit at the piano on a second stool. I hurried to the stool and opened it. The recess was packed with sheets of music and handwritten music manuscripts. I dug down quite deeply into the manuscripts and sheet music without finding Beethoven's Fifth Symphony. Then, lifting another batch of paper, I revealed a bottle of Johnnie Walker Scotch. I lifted the bottle and directly under it was the piece of music for which Doc had asked.

On Friday afternoon after lunch I had gone to see Mrs. Boxall in the library to give her the Kommandant's message.

"Whatever do you think they're up to, Peekay?" she had said.

"At twelve o'clock they are going to fetch the Steinway and take it to the prison. Doc asked me to be there to help him."

"My God! He's going to give a concert! The professor is going to give a concert in the market square. How perfectly thrilling!" I had never seen her so excited.

It was suddenly also clear to me. "I don't think he's very happy about it. He said Mr. Van Zyl was trying to be a smarty pants with the people of the town."

Mrs. Boxall, in her excitement, appeared not to have heard me. "I once checked up on our professor. He turned out to be terribly famous." Her eyes shone. "There's something dark and mysterious about it all, if you ask me. Why would a famous European pianist give it all up and bury himself in a tiny dorp in Africa giving lessons to little girls?"

"I think he just likes collecting things like cactus and aloes and climbing in the mountains," I said.

"Peekay, did he ask you to do anything when he said he needed your help?"

"He asked me to get out Beethoven's Fifth Symphony."

"Jolly good show! Beethoven, eh? What a treat we're in for." Mrs. Boxall clasped her hands and looked up at the ceiling fan. "Oh bliss!"

"He also said I must put what is above the sheet music into his water flask."

"Whatever can he mean?" she said absently. It was obvious her mind was on Doc's concert in the market square. This was no time to attempt to solve one of Doc's conundrums. "Peekay, you'll have to excuse me, I think we're going to have to close early today. I have such a lot of phoning to do. One o'clock, are you sure that's the time Mr. Van Zyl said?" I nodded.

Now I stood holding Doc's music, staring down at the bottle of Johnnie Walker. Why would he keep a bottle in his piano stool? If Klipkop hadn't walked in at the moment he was about to tell me, everything would have been clear. I recalled the last words in the note Doc had sent me . . . *and whisky is getting easier not to have.*

I wasn't at all sure I was doing the right thing but the bottle was directly above the musical score Doc wanted and it was the only item in the piano stool that you could pour into a water flask. When I had last interfered with Doc's whisky, the repercussions had been enormous. I took the water flask and the bottle of Johnnie Walker into the cactus garden, where I dug a hole in the ground and planted the flask with its neck protruding. I must say it was a good plan and I spilled hardly any. After that I planted the bottle upside down in the hole.

I returned the flask to the piano stool, placing Doc's musical score over it. Then I put the key in my pocket.

I was waiting at Doc's cottage by nine on Monday morning. Dee and Dum had cleaned everything and the place was spotless. The Steinway shone like a mirror. The girls had spent an hour cleaning the whisky from the keys. Seated on the two piano stools, they had giggled fit to burst at the cacophony they made.

I passed the time waiting for Doc clearing weeds from the garden. After a couple of hours I heard the low whine of a truck and the less agonized sound of a light van as they made their way up the steep road to the cottage.

The black prison flattop was a Diamond T. The van, coming

along behind it, waited a little way down the road while the truck turned to face downhill again. On the back were six black prisoners and two warders carrying rifles. A third warder sat in front. I recognized one of the warders as the young one who had let me into the prison on the previous Friday and I said hello. He jumped down from the back of the truck and stuck his hand out. "Gert Marais, *hoe gaan dit?*" I shook his hand. Just then the van drew up and I could see that Klipkop was driving and Lieutenant Smit was beside him. They stopped in front of the lorry and Klipkop jumped out. Walking to the rear of the van, he unlocked it. To my surprise Doc stepped out. He was dressed in a clean white shirt, blue tie and his white linen suit. The place where his knee had torn through the trouser leg when the sergeant's kick brought him to the ground had been mended, the suit had been washed and pressed and his boots shone. I had never seen him looking so posh. Lieutenant Smit and Klipkop greeted me like an old friend.

I could see Doc was agitated and when Klipkop and Lieutenant Smit moved toward the house he turned to me urgently. "We must talk, Peekay. Today is a very difficult thing for me to do." We followed the two warders into the cottage and Doc pointed to the Steinway and the stool. He was too preoccupied to notice the cleanup and I felt a little disappointed.

Two of the warders came in, and together with Doc they discussed how the Steinway might be safely moved.

Klipkop went to call the prisoners in and Doc asked if he could go and look at his garden, as he couldn't bear to see the piano being moved. Lieutenant Smit laughed and added that it was necessary to have a warder along. "I know Gert Marais. Can he come, please?" I asked. Lieutenant Smit shrugged and signaled for Gert to come with us.

"I can't have you two escaping into the hills, now can I?" he said jokingly. But I was to learn that Lieutenant Smit was a careful man and liked to play things by the book. Gert couldn't speak English, which meant Doc and I could talk safely.

We walked in the garden, following the Johnnie Walker bottles as they meandered through the tall cactus and aloe, Doc stopping to look at plants and bending down to examine succulents close to the ground. It was as though he was trying to memorize the garden, so the memory would sustain him in prison. At last we stopped and sat on an outcrop of rock. Gert stood some little way off chewing a piece of grass, his rifle slung carelessly over his shoulder.

Finally Doc started to talk. "Peekay, these dummkopfs want I should do a recital in the town today. I have not played a concert since sixteen years. Peekay, I cannot do this, but I must."

I looked up at Doc and I could see that he was terribly distressed. "You don't have to, Doc. They can't force you," I said defiantly but without too much conviction. My short experience with authority of any kind had shown me that they always won, they could always force you.

Doc turned to look at me. "Peekay, if I don't play today they will not let you come to see me." I could feel the despair in his voice as he continued softly, "I do not think I could bear that." I hugged him and we sat there and looked at the hills dotted with the aloes in bloom and at the blue and purple mountains beyond them. At last he spoke again. "It was in Berlin in 1925. The Berlin Opera House. I had been ill for some months and I was coming back to the concert circuit. I had chosen to play the score you found in my piano stool. Beethoven's Symphony Number Five is great music but it is kind to a good musician. The great master was a piano player himself and it is not full of clever tricks or passages which try to be schmarty pantz.

That night I played the great master goot, better than ever until the third movement. Suddenly, who knows from where, comes panic. In my fingers comes panic, in my head and in my heart. Thirty years of discipline were not enough. The panic swallowed me and I could not play this music I have played maybe a thousand times when I practice and forty times in concert. Nothing. It was all gone. Just the coughing in the crowd, then the murmuring, then the booing, then the concertmaster leading me from the stage." Doc sat, his head bowed, his hands loosely on his knees. "I have never played in front of an audience again. Every night for sixteen years I have played the music, the same music and always in the third movement it is the same, the music in my fingers and my head and my heart will not proceed. It is then the wolves howl in my head and only whisky will make them quiet. Today, in one hour, I must play that music again. I must face the audience or, my friend, I lose you."

I cannot pretend to have understood the depth of Doc's personal dilemma. I was too inexperienced to understand his pain and humiliation. But I knew he was hurting inside. "I will be there with you, Doc. I will turn the pages for you."

Doc took out his bandanna and blew his nose. "You are goot friend, Peekay." He gave one of his old chuckles and rubbed a hand through my hair and then examined one of my hands, dirty from weeding between the cactus. "Better wash in the tank if you are going to be my partner. We must look our best." He rose. "Come, Peekay, we go now."

On the journey into town Doc and I sat in the front of the van with Lieutenant Smit while Gert sat in the back. Klipkop drove the truck. The Steinway had been loaded onto the flattop and roped. Even so, five prisoners were arranged around it to hold it firmly in place, while one sat with Doc's piano stool between his legs.

About half a mile from the market square the Diamond T stopped and the two warders herded the six blacks off the truck. One of them climbed back on while the other started to march the prisoners out of town toward the prison. We entered the top of Crown Street about three hundred yards from the market square. The main street was deserted, as quiet as a Sunday afternoon. "God, I hope this doesn't backfire on the Kommandant," Lieutenant Smit said. I noticed all the shops were closed. We turned the corner into the square and my eyes almost popped out of my head.

The market square was packed with hundreds of people, who had started to cheer as they saw us. A warder signaled us to a space that had been kept clear under a large flamboyant tree. Lieutenant Smit told Gert to stay with the van but not to show his rifle. Then he jumped out and, walking in front of the Diamond T, he guided it into a roped-off section in the center of the square.

Several warders scrambled up a stepladder onto the flattop and untied the ropes securing the Steinway. One put Doc's piano stool in place while another rigged up a microphone.

The moment we saw the crowd, Doc began to shake. "Peekay, did you do what I said about the water flask?" he asked in a tight voice.

"It is in the piano stool, Doc."

"Peekay, you must take it and when I ask, you must hand it to me, you understand?" I nodded.

When we drew to a halt under the flamboyant tree the Kommandant was waiting for us. He opened the van door and Doc got out.

Kommandant Van Zyl took him by the elbow and held him firmly. "Now then, Professor, remember you are a German, a member of a glorious fighting race. We of the South African Prison

Service are on your side, you must show these Rooineks what is real culture, man!"

Doc looked round fearfully to see if I was by his side. "Do not forget the flask, Peekay," he said. We walked to the center of the square.

The excitement of the crowd could be felt around us. Nothing like this had happened on a dull Monday since war was declared. We reached the flattop to find that some twenty rows of chairs had been placed behind the ropes on either side of it. They formed a ringside audience of the posh people in town. Mrs. Boxall was in the front row. She was dressed in her best hat and gloves, as were the other town matrons of social rank. At the back end of the lorry sat the prison warders and their wives, the men in uniform and the women wearing their Sunday best. It was obvious they were very pleased with themselves.

Doc had pulled himself together a little by the time we reached the truck and he and I climbed the stepladder onto the flattop.

The Kommandant stood in front of the microphone.

"*Dames en Heere,* ladies and gentlemen," he began. But from then on he spoke in English. "As you all know from reading the newspaper, there has been a very big fuss made about one of our most distinguished citizens, Professor Karl Von Vollensteen, a professor of music from across the seas. The good professor, who has lived in this town for fifteen years and has taught many of your young daughters to play the peeano, was born in Germany. It is for this alone that he is being put under my custody." Several pockets of people in the crowd had started to boo and someone shouted, "Once a Jerry, always a Jerry!" which brought about a little spasmodic laughter and clapping. The Kommandant held up his hand. "I am a Boer, not a Britisher. We Boers know what it is like to be robbed of our rights!"

Considerably more booing started and the same voice in the crowd shouted, "Put a sock in it!"

The Kommandant, as though replying to the heckler, continued. "No, it is true, I must say it, you took our freedom and now you are taking the professor's!"

This time the booing started in earnest and suddenly Mr. O'Grady-Smith, the mayor, stood up and shouted: "Get on with it, man, or we'll have a riot."

The booing continued, for Mr. O'Grady-Smith was no more popular than the Kommandant. He strode from his seat, mounted the stepladder and walked over to the microphone and waited until the booing stopped. "It's high time we moved the jail and the nest of Nazis who run it out of Barberton," he shouted. "This town is loyal to King George and the British Empire. God save the King!"

Most of the crowd clapped and cheered and whistled and Mr. O'Grady-Smith turned and looked at the Kommandant, a smug, self-righteous expression on his face.

From where I stood on the flattop I could see about a dozen men making their way through the crowd toward us. "Some men are coming," I said to Lieutenant Smit, who was now standing beside the stepladder with Klipkop to discourage any further townsfolk from emulating the mayor. They quickly mounted the flattop, pulled up the ladder and placed the microphone next to the Steinway so that the bottom half of the flattop was clear. The mayor and the Kommandant were hastily pushed to the top end to stand beside the seated Doc and me.

There was a good ten feet between the truck and the first row of seats. The attackers crossed this strip and swarmed onto the back of the flattop. Lieutenant Smit and Klipkop held the high ground while the other warders took the clearing between the lorry and the seats. The flattop and the apron around it were filled with fighting men and the screams of the ladies as they tried to back away from the brawl. The Kommandant ventured out from behind the Steinway and received a punch on the nose. Fat Mr. O'Grady-Smith was crouched on all fours halfway under the piano.

Just then Doc tugged me on the sleeve. "The flask, Peekay." His hand was outstretched. I handed the flask of whisky to him and he unscrewed the cap and took a slug and handed it back to me. "When I make my head like so, you must turn the page." He turned to the score in front of him and paged quickly to the beginning of the fortissimo movement, which in Beethoven's Fifth occurs at the end of the second movement. Then he started to play. The microphone had been knocked down and its head now rested over the piano. It picked up the music, which thundered across the square.

Almost immediately the crowd grew quiet, and the fighting stopped. The flattop cleared and the men around the apron slipped back into the crowd. The mayor squeezed out from under the Steinway; he and the Kommandant were helped down the replaced stepladder. Even the sobbing ladies grew quiet.

On and on Doc played, through the second into the third movement and, hardly pausing, into the fourth, his head nodding every time he wanted the page turned. It was a faultless performance as he brought the recital to a thunderous close.

The audience would remember Doc's performance for the rest of their lives. Mrs. Boxall was weeping and clutching her hands to her breast.

Lieutenant Smit shouted at several of the warders, who began to clear a way for the truck. He shouted for Klipkop to get into the truck and drive away; then he jumped into the passenger side of the cabin as the big Diamond T started to move. Doc, who had been bowing to the crowd, fell back onto his seat. With a flourish of the keyboard he began to play Beethoven's *Moonlight* Sonata.

I had never seen him as happy. He played all the way back to the prison, not stopping when we got to the gates and reaching the final bars as we drew up outside the administration building. Then he took a long swig from the flask and rose from the piano and looked out over the prison walls to his beloved hills.

I quickly opened the piano stool and put the flask into it together with the score. I locked it and slipped the key into my pocket.

Doc rubbed his hand through my hair. "No more wolves. Absoloodle," he said quietly.

ELEVEN

Dee or Dum woke me up at a quarter to five every morning with coffee and a rusk. Shortly after five I strapped my leather book bag to my shoulders and was off at a trot to the prison.

I was let in the gates without equivocation. The guards, with an hour and a half to go before the night shift ended, waved from the walkway on the wall. I was the first tangible sign after the gray dawn that the long night was almost over.

I learned that the greatest camouflage of all is consistency. If you do something often enough and at the same time in the same way, you become invisible. One of the shadows. The prisoner enjoys the advantage over his keeper of continuity. Warders change, get promoted, move elsewhere. But old lags, those prisoners with long sentences, have the advantage of time to plan. The warder unwittingly depends on the old lags to run the prison system, for it is they who restrain the younger prisoners who lack the patience to go along with the system or who see violence as the only solution to getting what they want. A prison without this secondary system of authority can be a dangerous and unpredictable place.

I found myself a part of this shadow world, brought into it with great patience over a long period by an old lag known as Geel Piet.

Translated from Afrikaans, his name simply meant "Yellow Peter." Geel Piet was a half-caste, or a Cape Colored, neither black nor white, treated as a black man but aspiring in his soul to be a white one. He was also an incorrigible criminal who freely admitted that it was hopeless for him on the outside. Geel Piet was the old lag who exerted the most influence in the shadow world of the prison.

My prison day began in the gymnasium at five-thirty where the boxing squad assembled. There were twenty of us and this included four other kids between eleven and fifteen. Seniority went by weight, with Klipkop, who had defeated Jackhammer Smit on points over ten rounds and was now the lowveld heavyweight champion, the most senior, down to myself, the utter nobody of the boxing squad.

Lieutenant Smit stood in the boxing ring with a whistle in his mouth and we would perform a routine of exercises interspersed with push-ups and sit-ups. Lieutenant Smit was a big believer in push-ups to strengthen the arms and the shoulders and sit-ups to strengthen the gut muscles. The boxers from Barberton prison were known throughout the lowveld and as far as Pietersburg and Pretoria as tough men to take on.

Lieutenant Smit was true to his word and for the first two years he would not allow me to step into the ring. "When you can throw a medicine ball over Klipkop's head, then you will be ready," he said. The first of my goals was set, and for the fifteen minutes after exercises, when all the other boxers were paired off with sparring partners, I worked until I could no longer lift my arms.

After a five-minute shower I reported to the prison hall for my piano lesson with Doc, and at seven-thirty we would both go in to breakfast at the warders' mess.

Doc had a special status in the prison. While he lived in a cell, he could come and go as he pleased. He ate in the warders' mess, and wasn't required to do any special work. "You just play the peeano, Professor," Kommandant Van Zyl had said, "that's your job, you hear?"

Doc often wandered into the gymnasium to watch the squad going through its paces. He knew that I yearned to box against another person in the ring. While he made it clear that he didn't understand why I should have such a need, he respected my ambition and soothed my impatience. "In music you must first do the exercises. If you do the exercises goot then you have the foundations. I think with this boxing business it is the same."

And so I practiced on the punch bag until the whole armory of punches was as familiar to me as the piano scales. That old punching bag took a terrible hiding on a daily basis over those first two years. I would imagine it cowering as it saw me approach, sometimes even whimpering, "Not too many of those deadly uppercuts today, Peekay!" Or, "I can't take any more right crosses." I'm telling you, that big old punching bag learned to respect me, all right.

But it was the speedball I grew to love. Gert, the young warder who spoke no English, was also on the boxing squad and we'd become firm friends. He'd modified an old punching ball so that it stood low enough for me to reach.

I can remember the first day when, after many weeks of practice on the speedball, I achieved a continuity of rhythm, the ball a blur in front of my boxing gloves.

After several weeks Lieutenant Smit walked over to watch me. My heart pounded as I concentrated on keeping the speedball flurried, a blurred, rhythmic tat-tat-tat of leather on leather. "You're fast, Peekay. That's good," he said, and then walked away. They had been the first words he had specifically directed at me in the six months I had been on his squad.

Doc's Steinway was kept in the prison hall. There was also an upright Mignon piano, for Doc's Steinway was not to be used except to play classical music. This was an express order from Kommandant Van Zyl, who pointed out that a peeano of such superior qualities should not be expected to play *tiekiedraai* or to accompany the banjo or accordion. The Steinway became a symbol of something very superior, which, in the eyes of the prison officers and their families, gave them a special social status. Doc and I, the only two people who played on the Steinway, were included in this status. The fact that the great German professor of music gave me lessons was confirmation that I must be a budding genius. Doc was kind enough never to contradict this opinion.

I visited the cactus garden most days on my return from school and every Sunday after church I went with Dee and Dum to Doc's cottage. Doc and I discussed the progress of the cactus garden in detail from a chart prepared by him of every species that grew there. There were several thousand. Taking a small patch of garden at a time, I reported on its progress. Doc made notes and instructed me when to thin or separate plants. The separated plants I brought to the prison, where Doc had started a second cactus garden.

Marie, the little nurse from the hospital, had become firm friends with my mother. She loved needlework and would sit for hours chatting away to my mother and doing buttonholes. It seemed certain she would soon fall into the clutches of the Lord. She taught Dee and Dum to cook pumpkin scones and corn bread and they soon became my favorites.

Marie brought sweet potatoes for me from her farm, and fresh eggs, sometimes even a leg of pork or home-cured bacon. She always brought a large bunch of cured tobacco leaf for my granpa. He smoked a blend called African Drum and hated the raw, unblended tobacco from Marie's farm, though he was much too polite to tell her. He would hang it from the ceiling of the garden shed. The supply grew alarmingly. Eventually it was to become one of the most important factors in my rise within the prison system.

For the first year Geel Piet, the half-caste, was a part of morning piano practice, for he was always in the hall on his knees, polishing the floor, a shadow in the background who greeted Doc and myself with "*Goeie môre, baas en klein baas.*" He followed this with a toothless smile and then a soft cackle. Doc and I both returned his greeting. It was forbidden to talk to any of the non-European prisoners and our replies must have been a great encouragement.

Geel Piet was small and battered-looking. His nose had been flattened and his face was crisscrossed with scars. He stood around five foot two inches on his buckled legs. Had he been able to straighten them he might well have been four or five inches taller. In the process of surviving, Geel Piet had worn out his luck in the outside world, if indeed he'd ever had any. Born in Cape Town's District Six, he had been in and out of jail for forty of his fifty-five years. He took pride in the fact that he knew every major prison in South Africa, and he was the grand master in the art of camouflage. Should a warder beat him for whatever reason, Geel Piet bore no animosity, no hatred. He regarded a beating as self-inflicted because it resulted from some piece of carelessness. He had long since realized that, for him anyway, freedom was an illusion. He had accumulated years of sentences, and was realist enough to know that he was unlikely to survive the system at his age and with his deteriorating health.

Geel Piet ran the prison black market, in tobacco, sugar, salt and *dagga* (cannabis). He also had an encyclopedic knowledge of boxing.

My relationship with Geel Piet was built upon small conversations eked out over weeks until an understanding formed that eventually led to the conspiracy that made me present him with a leaf of tobacco.

I had put cuttings of *Euphorbia pseudocactus* from Doc's cottage garden in a bucket from the garden shed at home. I had lined the bottom of the bucket with a large tobacco leaf, which was covered by the thorny cactus for Doc's prison garden. Something must have made me do it: perhaps Geel Piet, with his snatches of seemingly unconnected dialogue. Tobacco is, after all, the greatest luxury and the most essential commodity in the prison system. With the war on, the normal shortage behind the walls had become severe; it was more highly prized than ever.

I was never searched as I entered the prison, although on this particular day, as I was carrying a bucket rather than a bag, a mildly curious guard had come over to take a look. I had entirely forgotten about the tobacco leaf. "Funny how he likes all these ugly plants, hey?" the guard said, for Doc's cactus garden was directly outside the warders' mess and was the butt of many a joke.

I had taken the bucket through to the hall after the squad workout and Geel Piet took it with the cuttings to Doc's garden. When he returned, his broken face was wreathed with smiles. "I will help you to be a great boxer," he simply said. And that was how it all started.

I broached the subject of the tobacco to my granpa when I returned home that afternoon after school. I did not really think about the moral issue involved. After a year of going in and out of the prison each weekday I had come to understand the system. War existed between two sides and I could see the odds were heavily biased toward one of them. The prison warders were an extension of the kids at the boarding school: a brutal force confronting a defenseless one.

My granpa, between much tamping, tapping and lighting of his pipe and staring into the distance, and after ascertaining that I was never searched, decided that the prisoners should have the tobacco.

"Poor buggers, most of them are in for crimes that deserve no more than a tongue lashing."

He was wrong. Barberton was a heavy-security prison and most of the prisoners had committed crimes worthy of formal punishment in any society. It was the administration of the prisoners' life that was the real crime. It was not unusual for a prisoner to be beaten to death for a comparatively minor infringement of prison rules.

Doc had requested to remain in Barberton prison rather than be transported to an internment camp in the highveld. The thought of being away from his beloved mountains, his cactus garden and his piano was more than he could bear, and I'm sure our friendship also played a large part in his reluctance to leave Barberton. Kommandant Van Zyl, who had come to regard Doc as the personal property of the prison and a constant thorn in the side of the English-speaking town, was more than happy to cooperate, and Doc spent the remainder of the war under his benign supervision.

Doc was coconspirator in what became a sophisticated smuggling system. Being in the prison constantly, he was there when the work gangs returned at night and left again at dawn. He was a compassionate and fair-minded man and the unthinking brutality of the warders offended him deeply. Man brutalized thinks only of his survival. The power the tobacco gave Geel Piet was enormous, and he used it as ruthlessly as the warders used their white superiority.

Geel Piet successfully contrived to get into the gymnasium while the squad was working out. At first he was a familiar shadow, hardly noticed, polishing the floor or cleaning the windows. Then gradually he became the laundry boy, picking up the sweaty shorts and the boxing boots in the shower room and returning them the next day freshly laundered and polished. By the time I could throw a medicine ball over Klipkop's head, Geel Piet had established himself as an authority on boxing. The lieutenant gave him the job of supervising the progress of the kids in the squad.

The standard of the young boxers improved under Geel Piet's direction, for the old lag was a maker of boxers. When he hadn't been in prison he'd worked in gymnasiums, and somewhere in the dim past had been the colored lightweight champion of the Cape Province. He had a way of teaching that made even the Boer kids respect him, though at first it was only their fear of Lieutenant Smit that prevented them from refusing to be coached by a blerrie yellow kaffir.

From the first day Lieutenant Smit agreed that I could begin to box I was under Geel Piet's direction. From day one he concentrated on defense. "If a man can't hit you, he can't hurt you," he'd say. "The boxer who takes chances gets hit and gets hurt. Box, never fight, fighting is for heavyweights and domkops."

It wasn't what I had been waiting for two years to learn. But Doc persuaded me Geel Piet was right.

It was some weeks before I was allowed to get into the ring with an eleven-year-old from the squad. The boy's nickname was Snotnose Bronkhorst. He was a big kid and a bully but he had only been with the squad for a few weeks and lacked any real know-how. He had pushed me away from the punching ball, and I had tripped over a rubber mat and fallen. Picking myself up, I had squared up to him, when Lieutenant Smit, seeming not to have noticed the incident, said he wanted to see us in the ring. My heart thumped as I realized that the moment had come.

We climbed into the ring and it was Hoppie and Jackhammer Smit all over again, in size if not in skill. But I had absorbed a great deal over the past two years and even more over the six weeks Geel Piet had been coaching me. Snotnose chased me all over the ring, taking wild swipes, any of which, had they landed, would have lifted me over the ropes. I managed to make him miss with every blow while never even looking like landing a decent punch myself. After three minutes Lieutenant Smit blew his whistle for the sparring session to stop.

I noticed for the first time that most of the squad had gathered around the ring and when the whistle blew they all clapped. It was one of the great moments of my life.

Peekay had completed his two-year apprenticeship. From now on it was all the way to the welterweight championship of the world.

I turned to walk to my corner before climbing out of the ring and, sensing something was wrong, I ducked just as a huge fist whistled through the air where my head had been a second before. Without thinking I brought my right up in an uppercut, using all the weight of my body behind the blow. It caught Snotnose Bronkhorst in the center of the solar plexus. He staggered for a moment and then, clutching his stomach, crumpled in agony onto the canvas, the wind completely knocked out of him. The cheers and laughter from the ringside bewildered me. Looking over the heads of the squad, I saw Geel Piet, unseen by any of them, dancing a jig in the background, his toothless mouth stretched wide in delight.

Throwing caution to the winds, he yelled, "We have one, we have a boxer!" The colored man's intrusion into the general hilarity caused a sudden silence around the ring.

Lieutenant Smit advanced slowly toward Geel Piet. With a sudden explosion Smit's fist slammed into his face. The little man dropped to the floor, blood spurting from his flattened nose.

"When I want an opinion on who is a boxer around here, I'll ask for it, you hear?" Then, absently massaging the knuckles of his right hand, Smit turned back to the squad. "But the yellow bastard is right," he said. "Bronkhorst, you are a domkop," he added as Snotnose rose shakily to his feet.

Still standing in the ring, I watched Geel Piet crab-crawl along the floor, making for the doorway. When he reached it he got unsteadily to his feet and looked directly at me. Then he grinned, and gave a furtive thumbs-up sign. To my amazement, the expression on his battered face was one of happiness.

On my way to school that morning Snotnose Bronkhorst sprang from behind a tree and gave me a proper hiding.

It had been my experience that the Snotnoses of this world were a plentiful breed and I thought it might be a good idea to learn street fighting as well as boxing. Geel Piet, I felt sure, would show me how to fight dirty.

But I was wrong. Geel Piet knew the corruption that turns a boxer into a fighter and a fighter into a street brawler.

"Small *baas,* if I teach you these things a street fighter knows, you will lose your speed and caution and when you lose your caution you will lose your skill."

I was disappointed. Being tough was one of the ambitions I had set for myself. How could you be tough if you had to bob in and out like a blowfly? "Please, Geel Piet," I begged, "just teach me one really rotten dirty trick." After some days of nagging he agreed.

"Okay, man, I will teach you the Sailor's Salute. It is the best dirty trick there is. But you got to know timing to get it right. A boxer can know this trick and still be a boxer. The police use it all the time so they can say in the charge book they never laid hands on you. Its other name is the Liverpool Kiss." He held the flat of his hand three inches from his brow and with a lightning-fast jerk of his head his forehead smacked loudly onto the hand. "Only you do this against the other person's head, like so." He drew me toward him and in slow motion demonstrated the head-to-head blow. Even in slow motion he nearly took my head off and my eyes filled with tears. It was the head butt Jackhammer Smit had used to floor Hoppie, and now I knew why Hoppie had gone down so suddenly.

"Do it to me also," Geel Piet said, patting his forehead with the butt of his hand. I did so and received a second severe blow to the head. I was beginning to have misgivings about street fighting.

But over the next few weeks I perfected the Liverpool Kiss. The quick grab of the punchbag and a lightning butt to the imagined head of an opponent. Every now and again Geel Piet allowed me to practice on him and he grinned when I got it right. "Once you got it, you got it for life. But only use it quick and as a surprise."

School had one disadvantage. I was two classes higher than my age group and so friends were hard to make. The kids of my own age thought of me as a sort of freak. In fact, with my early school background and now my prison experience, I was a lot tougher than any of them. Doc and the jaw incident had made me somewhat of a celebrity but I kept mostly to myself, being a shy kid and the smallest in my class. I was left pretty much alone. I wasn't aggressive, and when a challenge came from a boy called John

Hopkins and his partner Geoffrey Scruby, supposedly the two toughest kids in my class, I tried to avoid the fight they demanded. The Judge and even the jury had been so much tougher than these two that it never occurred to me to be frightened of them. The English-speaking kids at school had no idea of my boxing or prison background, as the small contingent of Afrikaans kids in the school seldom mixed with the English. Hopkins and Scruby badgered me for some days and I took the problem to Geel Piet, who immediately understood my dilemma.

"Small *baas*, it is always like this. This is what you must do. You must make them feel you are scared. Tell them, no way, man. Let them get more and more cheeky. Even let them push you around. But always make sure this happens when everyone is watching. Then after a few days they will demand to fight you and they will name a time and a place. Try to look scared when you agree. You understand?" Geel Piet held me by the shoulders and looked me straight in the eyes. "More fights are lost by underestimating your opponent than by any other way. Always remember, small *baas*, surprise is everything."

It happened just as he said, a constant badgering during break, then a few pushes in front of everyone. Protests from me that I didn't want to fight. Finally a demand that I be behind the town cinema after school, where I could choose either of them to fight.

When I got to the small yard behind the cinema where all the official school fights took place, it was packed with at least fifty kids. All of them were English-speaking with the exception of Snotnose Bronkhorst, who had somehow got wind of the fight. To my surprise he stepped up to me and said in Afrikaans, "I'm here to be your second. These are all Rooineks, you can never tell what they'll do."

I looked at him in surprise. "I'm also a Rooinek."

"Yes, I know, man, but you're a Boer Rooinek. That's different."

I elected to fight Hopkins, who seemed delighted as he was the bigger of my two tormentors and had not expected to be chosen.

The kids formed a ring and Snotnose, who didn't know a lot of English, simply said, "Okay! Make quiet! Fight!"

Hopkins threw a haymaker at me and missed by miles and I landed a blow to his ribs. He looked surprised and came rushing in again, swinging at my head. I ducked in under his punch and caught him hard on the nose. He stopped dead in his tracks and brought his hand up to his face. I hit him with a left and then a right to the solar plexus and to my astonishment he started to cry.

"All over!" Snotnose held up my hand as Hopkins, sniffing and thoroughly humbled, walked back into the crowd. I pointed at Geoffrey Scruby. "Your turn now, Scruby," I said, feeling a rush of adrenaline as I saw his fear.

"I'm sorry, Peekay," he said softly. I had won. Just as Geel Piet said.

Then Snotnose stepped up. "Does any of you Rooineks want to fight him?" he asked. There was complete silence and nobody stirred, not even the bigger kids. "You're all yellow, you hear!" he snarled; then he turned and looked at me with a grin on his face. I grinned back. He seemed an unlikely ally but he had stood by me. "Okay then, I will," he said. There was a murmur of apprehension through the crowd. They were clearly shocked at the idea. I must say I was pretty shocked myself.

"It's not fair. You're much bigger than him," Geoffrey Scruby said. "And older," someone else shouted.

Snotnose turned and squared up to me.

It had been four months since we'd first met in the ring and he'd learned a fair bit about boxing in the meantime. I tried to stay out of his way, dancing around him, making him miss. But he hit me a couple of times and it hurt like blazes. I was connecting more often than he was, aiming my blows carefully, but I knew it was only a matter of time. *First with your head, then with your heart, first with your head, then with your heart,* Hoppie's words drummed through my brain as I tried to stay alive. Snotnose had tried to come in close on one or two occasions, but soon learned that this evened things up. At close range I was much the better boxer. So he stood his distance and picked his shots, knowing that a big punch had to get through sooner or later. All I could do was to try to make him miss. The kids were yelling their heads off, trying to reach me with their encouragement. But I think they all knew the Boer was too tough and that the outcome was inevitable.

"Come closer, Boer bastard. Are you scared or something?" I taunted. Snotnose stopped in his tracks and his eyes grew wide. With a roar of indignation he bore down on me. I stepped aside at the last second and he missed knocking me over. As he turned to come back at me his head was lowered so it was on a level with mine. He had his back to the cinema wall and I had mine to the crowd. I stepped in, and using both hands grabbed him by the shirtfront and gave him a perfectly timed Liverpool Kiss. The blow was so perfect I felt nothing. Snotnose simply sat on his bum, completely dazed, quite unable to comprehend what had happened. The crowd hadn't seen it either. They were behind me and my hands flying up to grab his shirtfront must have looked like a two-fisted attack. Forever afterward it was retold that way: "Then Peekay said, "Come closer, you Boer bastard," and with two dazzling punches to the jaw he knocked Snotnose Bronkhorst out."

To my surprise Snotnose started to sniff and then got up unsteadily and made his way through the crowd. He stopped halfway down the alley and shouted in Afrikaans, "I'll get you back for this, you Rooinek bastard!" The English kids jeered as he walked away, but I knew better. One doesn't allow a Boer to lose face and expect to get away with it. Though, to my amazement, even Snotnose came to believe that he had been punched.

After the fight with Hopkins and Snotnose my status at school improved immeasurably. While there were no more than sixty Afrikaans pupils, they tended to be bigger than the English kids and much more aggressive. Most of the English boys had at some time or another suffered at the hands of one of the Boers. I was seen as the one kid who had successfully fought back.

The prison kids explained that it was acceptable to be beaten by me as I was a sort of honorary Boer who spoke the *Taal* and was also one of them. Even Snotnose left me alone unless we were sparring in the gym, when he would go all out to try to hurt me.

And then there was the tobacco crisis. The tobacco crop on Marie's farm failed. This left a period of three months when the curing shed was empty. Marie kept apologizing for this; the more my granpa protested that he didn't mind the more guilty she seemed to become. By this time Geel Piet had become undisputed quartermaster for the prison. To tobacco we had added sugar, salt and a letter-writing business that was getting news in and out of the prison to and from all over South Africa. Postal orders would come in from outside contacts. Prisoners would order sugar, salt and tobacco and Geel Piet would add thirty percent to the groceries and charge threepence a cigarette. Tobacco was by far the greatest luxury. The little I brought in leaf form was carefully rolled into slim cigarettes. Somehow I understood how such a small thing as a cigarette, a tablespoon of sugar or a teaspoon of salt made the difference between hope and despair.

Letters were becoming a big thing at the prison and Doc wrote most of them as Geel Piet dictated to him. The little man could remember the contents of entire letters, together with the addresses of a dozen or more black prisoners at a time. Doc would write them at night. He would then write out a sheet of music theory for my homework and attach the letters to the back of it.

The letters were much of a muchness, men telling their families they were all right and inquiring after the health of the wife and kids. It was not unusual for a family not to know that a husband had been arrested or where he was detained. So the letters provided a vital link in the spiritual welfare of the prisoners.

Mrs. Boxall acted as postmistress. The letters would be dropped in after school. With the stamp used for marking the books, which said: BARBERTON MUNICIPAL LIBRARY, de Villiers St., Barberton, we stamped a blank envelope, attached a postage stamp to it and included it in the original letter with instructions to the receiver to use it as the return envelope. We also wrote the name of the sender on the inside of the return envelope. This was done because we often received letters which started *Dear Husband* and carried no other identification. Finally Mrs. Boxall or I would address the outgoing envelope and send it off.

She explained these elaborate precautions to me. "If we get a lot of letters addressed to the library in primitive handwriting, the postmaster just might smell a rat. I've been sending out overdue notices to country members for years. The notices include return addressed envelopes using the library stamp. He won't suspect a thing." And he didn't. The system worked perfectly and returned letters were taken into the prison and locked in Doc's piano stool, to which only he and I had a key, though I'm sure Geel Piet could have picked the lock anytime he chose to do so.

The money prisoners received from outside was generally in the form of a postal order for two shillings. As all incoming mail was opened by Mrs. Boxall, she cashed the postal orders and put the money back into the envelopes and wrote the name of the recipient on the front.

And so a regular mail system in and out of the prison was established with Mrs. Boxall cheerfully paying for the stamps and stationery. She would often sit and read a letter to one of the prisoners from a wife, written by someone who could write in English, and as she read it to me the tears would roll down her cheeks. The letters were mostly three or four lines.

My Husband Mafuni Tokasi,

How are you? The children are well. We have no money only this. The baas *says we must go from this place. There is no work and no food. The youngest is now two years. He looks same like you. We have no other place to go.*

Your wife Buyani

A postal order in the letter meant that the whole family might not have eaten for two days or more. Mrs. Boxall would wipe her eyes and say even if she was arrested she knew she was jolly well doing the right thing. She badgered friends and people coming into the library for clothes and these she sent off to needy families, even sometimes sending off a postal order of her own. She referred to prisoners' families as "innocents, the meat in the ghastly sandwich between an uncaring society and a vengeful state." Her code for these families simply became the word "sandwich." "We need more clothes for the sandwiches," or, "Here's a poor sandwich for whom we'll have to find some money." She kept a forty-four-gallon drum in the library that had a wide slot like a huge money box. On the side was written: "Cast-off clothes for the Sandwich Fund." People brought lots of stuff and no one ever asked what the Sandwich Fund was.

"People feel they ought to know, so they don't dare ask," she would say. She once told me that the sandwich was named after the Earl of Sandwich, who was always so busy gambling he had no time to take meals. To overcome the problem his butler had made him two hunks of bread with something between them. These were the first sandwiches. "If anyone ever asks we'll say it's the famous Earl of Sandwich Fund for the poor."

Eventually the Earl of Sandwich Fund became the most social of all the war effort funds in Barberton. At the Easter and Christmas fêtes held in Coronation Park, Mrs. Boxall and I ran a sandwich stand where cakes donated by the town's leading families were sold. My mother sent pumpkin scones baked by Dee and Dum, who were also allowed to work at the stand. The rather snobbish Earl of Sandwich Fund sandwich stand earned enough to pay for the entire mailing system and to send money and clothing to a great many destitute families.

When the tobacco crisis came we solved it through the Earl of Sandwich Fund. Mrs. Boxall sent a note to the headmaster of our school requesting that children bring in cigarette butts from home. She even managed to get the butts from the sergeants' mess at the army camp. Everyone assumed the recycled tobacco was going to the prisoners of war as Mrs. Boxall simply referred to them as prisoners. The bags of butts were taken to Doc's cottage, where Dee and Dum spent Sunday afternoon shredding the week's tobacco supply. Geel Piet never had it so good. When the new crop came from Marie's farm, with some dismay he was forced to switch back to straight tobacco leaf.

What I didn't know was that little by little the prisoners had pieced it all together and I had been given the credit for everything. I was enormously surprised one day, as I passed a gang of prisoners digging a large flower bed in the town hall gardens, to hear the chanter who was calling the rhythm so the picks all rose and fell together change his song at my approach.

"See who comes toward us now," he sang. "Tell us, tell us," the rest of the work gang chanted back. "It is he who is called the Tadpole Angel," the leader sang. "We salute him, we salute him," they chorused.

I glanced around to see who they were singing about, but there was no one. The warder in charge, who recognized me, obviously didn't know Zulu. He called out to me, "How are things going, man?" and I replied, "Very good, thanks." He obviously wanted me to stop for a chat.

"He who is a mighty fighter and friend of the yellow man," the leader continued. "The Tadpole Angel, the Tadpole Angel," the chorus replied, their picks lifting on the first "Tadpole Angel" and coming down on the second. I realized with a shock that they were talking about me.

"I hear the lieutenant is going to let you fight in the under-twelve division in the lowveld championships in Nelspruit this weekend."

"Ja, I'll be the smallest, but he thinks I'll be okay."

"We thank him for the tobacco, the sugar and the salt and for the letters and the things he sends to our people far away," sang the leader. "From our hearts, from our hearts," came the chorus.

"Nine is not very old, man. Eleven can be blerrie big with a Boer kid."

I shrugged my shoulders. "I am ten in two weeks. Look, I have to go, I'm late for the library." I wanted only to get away from the chanting of the prison gang.

"You'll be okay, man, I seen you sparring." He looked at me and grinned. "You is a funny bloke, Peekay. Why you blushing like mad, hey?"

"He is the sweet water we drink and the dark clouds that come at last to break the drought," the leader sang. Up came the picks, "Tadpole Angel." Down they went in perfect unison, "Tadpole Angel. We salute him, we salute him." I started to run toward the library, my embarrassment consuming me.

I tackled Geel Piet about the matter the next morning and he admitted that this was my name. "It is a great compliment, small *baas*. For them you are a true angel."

Doc was listening, as Geel Piet and I now spoke in English when we were with him. "Ja, and for you we are all angels, Geel Piet." He chuckled. "You are a rich man, I think, ja?"

Geel Piet made no attempt to deny it. "Big *baas,* it is always like so in a prison. If I am discovered I will be killed, so I must have something for risking my life."

Doc, like Mrs. Boxall, had come to realize how important the letters were and how the small amount of contraband made life bearable for men who were shown no compassion and whose diet of mealie meal and a watery stew of mostly cabbage and carrots was only just sufficient to sustain them. He had also come to accept the role Geel Piet played in the distribution system, knowing that without it chaos would ensue. "Inside all people there is love, also the need to take care of the other man who is his brother," Doc would say. "When man is brutalized in such a place like this, the smallest sign that someone is worried for him is like a fire on the dark mountain.

When a man knows somebody cares he keeps some small place, a corner maybe of his soul, clean and lit."

While the food allocated for each prisoner was insufficient to keep a man doing hard physical labor, whoever hired a gang was expected to supply a meal at noon. It was this meal that kept the prisoners alive, for the regulations required it to be a vegetable and meat stew consisting of eight ounces of meat per prisoner and a pound of cooked mealie pap.

While no more than a quarter of the prisoners were Zulus, they held the highest status in the prison. Work songs were mostly composed in Zulu and it was always a Zulu who called the time and set the working pace. Zulu is a poetic language and the ability to create spontaneous lyrics to capture a recent incident or pass information on was almost always handled by a Zulu prisoner whose gift for poetry was greatly respected.

Knowing there was some reason for "Tadpole" before "Angel," I persisted in questioning Geel Piet about it. "It is like this, small *baas*. The professor is known as *Amasele* (the Frog), because he plays his peeano at night when the prison is quiet. To the Zulus the frog makes always the loudest music at night, much louder than the cricket or the owl. So it is simple, you see. You are the small boy of the frog, which makes you a Tadpole."

TWELVE

While Geel Piet was growing rich, he had also become indispensable to the boxing squad, a demanding and resourceful coach. The squad kids had been turned into clever boxers, natural aggression combined with real skill. The Barberton Blues hadn't lost a fight in two years.

How I got my first real fight was a matter of sheer luck. The championships in Nelspruit were in August, only days before my tenth birthday. I had tried to persuade anyone who would listen that ten was almost eleven and one year wasn't much to forfeit. But Lieutenant Smit wasn't the sort of man who changed his mind. The two under-twelves were Snotnose Bronkhorst and Fonnie Kruger, both two years my senior and much bigger.

Geel Piet claimed he saw intelligence and speed in me that more than made up for my lack of size. He was a fanatic about footwork. "You must learn to box with your feet, small *baas*. A good boxer is like a dancer: he is still pretty to watch even if you look only at his feet." He taught me how to position myself so the full weight of my body was thrown behind a punch. "If they do not respect your punch they simply keep going until they knock you down, man. A boxer must have respect."

I longed to have a real fight against an unknown opponent. In two years I had never missed a day of boxing and I had worked with all my heart and soul for the moment when I could climb into a boxing ring with an opponent whose every blow, unlike those of my sparring partners, could not be anticipated.

On the Monday of the week of the championships Snotnose didn't turn up at the gym. After the session Lieutenant Smit and Geel Piet talked earnestly for quite a time, every so often looking in my direction. Finally Geel Piet came over to me. "Ag, man, I'm a heppy man today, small *baas*. You got your first fight, man! Bronkhorst he is sick, you got his place."

I couldn't believe my ears. Snotnose had jaundice, which had been going around school. I went to hug Geel Piet, but he quickly sidestepped. "No, no, small *baas,* the lieutenant will come over and beat me." He grinned. "Better go over quick, man, and thank him."

I ran over to where Lieutenant Smit was talking to Klipkop. "Th-thank you for the fight, Lieutenant Smit," I stammered. "I will try my hardest."

"That won't be enough," he said in a brusque voice. "You're going to get your head knocked in, but it will do you good. Nobody should win their first fight."

Geel Piet told me to bring my *tackies* in the next morning so they could be properly cleaned for me to wear at the fight. Using a piece of string, he measured my chest and waist. When I got home after school I told Dee and Dum my *tackies* should be put next to my satchel so I wouldn't forget them, as Geel Piet needed to clean them. Dum got up quietly from the floor. She returned a few moments later with my *tackies*. They were spotless. "Who does this yellow man think he is?" she asked. "Does he think we let our *baas* go around in dirty things?" I had to explain that Geel Piet did all the things for the boxers. "He will not wash your clothes or clean your *tackies*," Dee said. "It is a woman's work and we will look after the clothes of him who belongs to our own *kraal*," Dum added.

I wasn't at all sure how my mother would take the news of my inclusion in the squad. Boxing was never mentioned, and as far as she was concerned my early-morning journey to the jail was in order to take piano lessons. She had been very busy lately with a commission to make three ball gowns. I knocked and entered the sewing room. It seemed full of a plum-colored taffeta gown that was almost finished. My mother rose and held it against her body and she looked just how I imagined Cinderella must have looked when she went to the ball. The skirt billowed from the narrow waist and as she moved, the taffeta caught the light and rustled.

"Such an extravagance. I can't imagine where they found the material in the middle of the war." She kicked the skirt to reveal a second layer of net in peacock blue.

"You look beautiful," I said, not thinking to flatter her.

My mother laughed. "That's the trouble with the things of the devil, they are often tempting and very pretty," she said with a sigh.

I had forgotten for a moment that dances were high on the Lord's banned list. My heart sank. If dancing was frowned upon by the Lord, what would he think of a boxing match? I immediately consoled myself with the knowledge that God was a man, and therefore He'd like boxing a lot better than dancing.

"You've come about the boxing, haven't you?" my mother said.

"Yes, Mother." I was unable to conceal the surprise in my voice.

"Lieutenant Smit, a very nice man, came to see me this morning, though I'm not sure I liked what he had to say. I've spoken to your grandfather and I made it the subject of my quiet time with the Lord after lunch. He gave me no clear guidance on the matter, though your grandfather seems to think it can't do you any harm." Her head jerked back in a sudden gesture of annoyance. "Oh, how I wish you'd stick to the piano. It's clearly the Lord's wish that you do so or He wouldn't have made it possible for you to learn under such trying circumstances. Lieutenant Smit seems to think you have a natural talent as a boxer, which is more than the professor has admitted about your music."

"Doc has said my Chopin is coming along extra good," I said.

My mother sighed. "You'll have to sleep on Friday afternoon if you're going to be up that late on Saturday night."

I jumped with joy. "Thank you, thank you," I cried, and gave her a hug and a kiss.

On Friday morning, Lieutenant Smit called us all together around the ring. "I want to tell you first a few things," he said. He turned to the five kids standing to one side with Geel Piet. "The rules for under fifteen say, you get knocked down, you out. No use getting up, man, you finished. So don't get knocked down, hey." He indicated Klipkop, who was standing on his right. "Sergeant Oudendaal is a semipro so is not allowed to fight, so Gert will fight in the heavyweight division and Sergeant Oudendaal and me will be your seconds. You all know the rules, the most clean blows landed wins, that's how Geel Piet here taught you." He was turning to leave the ring when his eye caught something at his feet. He stooped and picked up a small blue singlet, on the front of which in yellow were the letters BB, standing for Barberton Blues. He turned the singlet around to face us; on the back, in neat cut-out letters, we saw PEEKAY. "Welcome, Peekay," he said, and everyone clapped. "Welcome to the Barberton Blues." My throat ached as I choked back the tears. Lieutenant Smit bent down again and picked up a pair of blue shorts with a yellow stripe down the side, and bundling shorts and singlet together, he threw them at me.

I showed Doc my singlet and shorts and he seemed very pleased for me and I told him about the three rounds. "Do you think you can go three rounds with Mr. Chopin, Peekay?" he asked. I nodded, determined to show Doc that his precious music was not taking a backseat. Out of the corner of my eye I saw Geel Piet enter the hall. It was unusual for him to come into the hall at this time. I always put the day's mail in the piano seat and later, when he came in to polish the Steinway, he would retrieve it. We had decided the three of us should never be seen together near the postbox. He stood pretending to clean a window and finally Doc noticed him.

"You must not come when we practice," he admonished.

The battered little man trotted toward us. "Please, *baas*, it is very important." Geel Piet withdrew a parcel wrapped in a piece of cloth. "In the bootmaker's we have made for the small *baas* a present." He opened the cloth to reveal a pair of boxing boots. I gasped. They were beautiful, the black leather brought to a soft sheen and the soles the bluish white of raw new leather. "It is from all the people, a present for the *Onoshobishobi Ingelosi,* so that you will fight a mighty fight tomorrow, small *baas*. It is why I asked you for the *tackies,* small *baas*." He gave me a big, toothless smile. "It was to know the size."

I leapt from the piano stool and quickly pulled my school boots off and put the boxing boots on. The leather was soft and pliant and the boots felt light as a feather and fitted perfectly. "Geel Piet, they are the nicest present anyone ever gave me, honest."

"They are from all the people. It is their way to thank you."

Without warning he dropped to his knees and, using the cloth in which the boxing boots had been wrapped, he started to polish the floor around my feet. Some instinct in him that never rested had sensed danger. A good five seconds elapsed before the warder actually stood at the entrance to the hall.

He was a new sergeant; his name was Borman and he had been transferred to the lowveld from Pretoria.

He stood, one hand holding the door frame. "Professor, the Kommandant wants to see you. Report to administration after breakfast, you hear?" He turned to go, then caught sight of Geel Piet. "Kom hier, kaffir!" he rapped.

The little man ran across the hall. "Ja, *baas,* I come, *baas,*" he cried.

"What you doing in this place?" the warder demanded.

Doc bent down and picked up one of my school boots. "The boy got some kak on his boots. He come to clean them," he said, waving the boot at the warder and then pointing to where Geel Piet had been cleaning the floor. "Also some was on the floor when he walked in."

Sergeant Borman grinned. "Next time make the black bastard lick it clean." He turned and walked away.

Geel Piet came padding over to us, his bare feet making hardly any sound. "Thank you, big *baas,*" he said with a grin. He turned to me. "Box with your feet, small *baas,* punch clean so it is a scoring shot. No clinches, that way a bigger boxer can push you over. Good luck, small *baas,* the people are with you."

"Thank you, Geel Piet, tell the people I thank them."

"Ag, man, it is nothing, the people love you, you are fighting for them." He was gone.

Doc cleared his throat to break the silence. "Maybe now we can play Chopin, yes?"

I gave him a big hug. "That sure was quick thinking, Doc."

He chuckled. "Not so bad for a brokink-down old piano player, ja?" He frowned suddenly. "I wonder what wants the Kommandant?"

We were to leave for Nelspruit, a distance of some forty miles, at eight the following morning. Though I avoided having to rest on Friday afternoon, I had been ordered to bed at six o'clock. I woke as usual just before dawn and lay in bed trying to imagine the day ahead. What if I was beaten first off? With seven Eastern Transvaal teams competing, I had to win twice to get to the final. I had never boxed six rounds in my life, and even if I got through them I would have to box another three in the finals!

I quickly dressed and ran through the garden. In a little more than ten minutes I was on top of the hill sitting on our rock.

It was early spring and the dawn wind was cold. I shivered a little as I watched the light bleed into the valley and merge with the darkened town below me, smudging the darkness until the roofs and streets and trees were rubbed clean. Patches of bright red from spring-flowering flamboyant trees already dotted the town. I tried to think how Granpa Chook would have looked at the situation. He would have taken things in his stride, just like any other day. Granpa Chook remained a sort of checkpoint in my life. A reference on how to behave in a tight spot. I thought of Hoppie too. If only Hoppie could have been there to see me. "First with your head and then with your heart, Peekay." I could almost hear his cheerful and reassuring voice.

I made my way back down the hill as the sun began to rise. When I got back to the house Dee and Dum had prepared breakfast: porridge, fried eggs and bacon. On the kitchen table stood my school lunch tin. I wondered what they'd packed to sustain me, hopefully for nine rounds of boxing. They opened the tin to show me six pumpkin scones neatly wrapped in greaseproof paper. "We baked them last night, your favorite!" Dum said.

I packed all my stuff into my satchel, including my beautiful boxing boots. At half-past seven I had already said my farewells to my granpa and my mother and was sitting on the front wall waiting for the blue prison ute, which was to pick me up. I could have gone to the prison but Gert said, "It's only a few minutes out of our way, save the energy for the ring!" Gert wasn't like the other warders. He liked to help people and he once told me he only hit kaffirs if they really did wrong. "A kaffir hurts also, maybe not like a white man, 'cause they more like monkeys, but they hurt also when you hit them."

I saw the ute coming up the hill with Gert at the wheel. Next to him someone sat reading a newspaper; I couldn't see who it was. Gert stopped outside the gate. "Jump in the back with the other kids, Peekay," he said cheerfully. I climbed into the back, Gert changed gears and we pulled away. A fourteen-year-old called Bokkie de Beer was in charge and he told me no one was allowed to stand up. All the other kids were giggling and splurting into their hands as they looked at me.

"What's so funny?" I shouted above the sound of the wind and the roar of the engine. Bokkie de Beer pointed to the rear window of the driver's cabin. There, framed in the window, wearing his unmistakable panama hat, was the back of Doc's head. All the kids fell about laughing at my astonishment. I just couldn't believe my good fortune.

It was the first time since my arrival by train three years earlier that I had left the small town. It was a perfectly clear spring morning as we traveled across the valley toward a row of distant hills. The thornveld and the flat-topped acacia had already broken into electric green leaf.

By nine-thirty we'd reached Nelspruit and drew to a halt in a parking lot behind the town hall. I rushed to open the door of the ute for Doc. His blue eyes were shining and I think he was almost as excited as I was.

"We are together outside again, Peekay. It is goot, ja? Absoloodle."

"How did you escape?" I asked clumsily.

He chuckled. "With the permission of the Kommandant. That's what he wished to see me about yesterday." He saw me frown; we both knew the way of the prison system, where nothing is given unless something is taken in return. Doc shrugged. "It is not too much he wants, only that I should play a little Chopin when the brigadier comes from Pretoria next month."

I knew how Doc felt about playing in public. While he had overcome his fear when he triumphed at the Beethoven recital in the market square, Doc was a perfectionist and it gave him great pain not to meet the standards he demanded for himself.

"You should have said no!" I said.

"Tch-tch, Peekay, then I would not see you in your début. One day I will say, I was there when the welterweight champion of the world made his boxing début. Absoloodle! I will play Chopin to this brigadier. That is not so hard, ja?"

We entered the town hall and walked down a corridor until we reached a room that said Barberton *Bloue* on a piece of paper stuck on the door. The room smelt of dust and sweat. Lieutenant Smit and Klipkop were both there.

"This morning are the preliminary fights for the kids and this afternoon for the weight divisions," Lieutenant Smit announced. "Tonight, starting at six, the finals. We come here to win and that is what we going to do! Okay, so what's our motto?"

"One for all and all for one," we all shouted. Doc put his hand on my shoulder and I felt very proud. "I wish Geel Piet was with us," I whispered. Then Doc, who was in charge of first aid, left to fetch the towels and the first-aid kit but promised to be right back.

Klipkop grinned. "Today, man, I'm Geel Piet."

"Does that mean we can hit you and you can't hit back?" Bokkie de Beer said cheekily, and we all laughed.

Klipkop smiled. "You can all get changed now and I'll fetch you in fifteen minutes."

I found a corner and put my boots on first. All the kids crowded around. "Where'd you get those, man?" Bokkie de Beer exclaimed.

"My—my granpa made them," I stammered.

"Boy, you lucky having a bootmaker for your granpa," Fonnie Kruger said.

"Well, he's not really a bootmaker, more a gardener."

I rolled my gray socks down so they made a collar just above the boots. Then I put my blue singlet on and the boxing shorts with the yellow stripe down the side. Geel Piet had sized the waist perfectly but the bottoms of the shorts went way past my knees. When I stood up the other four kids broke up. Maatie Snyman and Nels Stekhoven even rolled on the floor. I must have looked pretty funny with my sparrow legs sticking out, but I also felt terribly proud.

Fonnie Kruger and myself were the first of the Barberton Blues to fight as we were in the under-twelves, the most junior division. We followed Klipkop into the town hall. Kids from other towns in the Eastern Transvaal were standing in groups and they too were changed and ready. I looked around, wondering who among them I would have to fight.

Doc entered the hall and moved over to me. I think he was more nervous than I was. He had taken out his bandanna and was wiping his brow. "I think examinations in the conservatorium in Leipzig when I was so big as you was not so bad as this. Absoloodle."

"I'll be okay, Doc. I'll dance and everything, just like Geel Piet says. Lieutenant Smit says I'm blerrie fast. You'll see—they won't hit me, for sure."

"It's nice of you to say this, Peekay. But what happens when comes one big Boer and connects?"

I grinned, trying to make him feel better. I repeated Hoppie's comment. "Ag, man, the bigger they are the harder they fall." I felt pretty corny saying it and I knew now why Hoppie had said it to me. He must have felt pretty corny too.

Doc groaned. "Peekay, I want you should be very careful. In that ring are not nice people."

Klipkop and Lieutenant Smit were standing with a large bald man who wore long white pants and a white singlet. A few feet from them stood two adults and a kid. The kid was quite a bit bigger than me, though not as big as Snotnose. He wore a red singlet and on the front was the word "Sabie." That was the town where Klipkop had his *nooi,* to whom he had recently become engaged.

The big man in the singlet looked at me and then at Lieutenant Smit. "He is not very big. Are you sure you want him to fight?"

The lieutenant nodded. "It will be good for him."

The big man looked at the boy from Sabie and then looked doubtfully back at me. "His opponent is eight inches taller and has probably got five inches more reach, man."

"If I think he's getting hurt I'll pull him out."

"I hope you know what you doing, man," the big man said, shaking his head. The two men from Sabie were grinning and I could hear what they were saying inside their heads. They were glad their kid was going to get an easy fight first up.

Klipkop turned to me. "This is Meneer de Klerk, Peekay. He is the referee and also the judge. He just came down from Pretoria last night."

"Good morning, meneer," I said, sticking out my hand. The referee shook it lightly.

"You got nice manners, son," he said.

Then Meneer de Klerk examined both sets of boxing gloves and declared them suitable. "Ten-ounce gloves. I don't want to see no kid hurt," he said. "Okay, glove up. We on in five minutes." He turned to a man sitting at a table directly beside the ring. The man nodded and consulted a large pocket watch in front of him. He also had a bell and was obviously the timekeeper.

Klipkop and Lieutenant Smit both worked on lacing me up. I felt very important.

"Remember, Peekay, boxing is a percentage game. Just make sure you hit him clean and more times than he hits you. No clinches, in clinches he can throw you off your feet. Stay out of the corners, stay off the ropes."

The man at the table rang the bell and we walked over to the ring. Klipkop helped me through the ropes and then he and the lieutenant climbed in after me. There was a proper stool in the corner and Lieutenant Smit told me to sit on it. I felt a bit silly because the kid from Sabie was standing up and punching into the air and I was sitting like a little kid on a chamberpot.

"Right! Both in the middle," Meneer de Klerk called, and climbed into the ring. "What's your names?"

"Du Toit, meneer."

"Peekay, meneer."

"I want a clean fight, you hear? No clinches. When I say break, you break. No hitting below the waist or behind the head. One knockdown and the fight is over. You understand, Peekay? Du Toit?"

"Ja, meneer," we both said.

"Right, when you hear the bell you come into the center of the ring, touch gloves and start boxing. Good luck."

I walked back to my corner. Because it was the first fight of the day, all the teams were gathered around the ring. It was my first boxing crowd and my heart was beating. Du Toit was looking around too. I don't think either of us wanted to make eye contact. He seemed very big, but I had waited too long for this moment to be afraid.

The bell rang. "Box him, Peekay, you hear," Klipkop said as I jumped from the stool.

We touched gloves in the middle of the ring, and as he pulled away I darted in and snapped a left and a right to Du Toit's jaw. His eyes widened in surprise. I could see that the punches hadn't hurt him, but nevertheless my early aggression had caught him unawares.

He was a good boxer and didn't lose his composure but circled around me. He threw a straight left, which went over my shoulder and flew past my ear. I went in under the arm with a quick uppercut and caught him in the ribs. I knew I'd hit him hard. He caught me with a right on the shoulder and spun me around. I anticipated the left coming at me and ducked under it and got another good body blow on exactly the same spot as before. His arms wrapped around me and I was in a clinch, which I wasn't supposed to be in. I hit him furiously in the ribs with both hands, but my blows were too close to be effective and I knew he could hold me as long as he liked.

"Break!" I heard the ref say, and as Du Toit's arms slackened I got right out of the way. For the rest of the round I let him chase me. I was much the faster boxer and had much better footwork. Toward the end of the round I could see by the way he set his feet which punch was going to come next. Just as the bell went I got inside with a short right and clipped him neatly on the point of the chin.

I had heard nothing during the fight and now realized that the crowd was making quite a noise and that my name was being shouted in encouragement. At the end of the round there was a lot of clapping and one or two whistles.

"You done good, Peekay," Klipkop said. Lieutenant Smit wiped my face with a towel. "He's missing with the right cross, but not by much. Watch it, man. If that kid finds his range he's going to hurt you bad. Keep your chin buried in your shoulder, that way if he gets one through you'll take most of it on the shoulder."

The bell went for the second round and I let Du Toit chase me around the ring. He must have been told to try to get me into a corner because he would work me carefully toward one but at the last moment I'd feint left and duck out right and his right cross would miss by miles. But then I did it once too often and he caught me with a left uppercut in the gut and had it not been for the ropes behind me I might have gone down. He knew he'd hurt me and was trying for the big hit. All I could do was duck until I could use my feet to get out of trouble.

To my surprise, in the second half of the round he seemed to be tiring. He'd thrown a lot of punches, most of them landing on my gloves, though he did hit me a good body blow that hurt like hell. I began to move in quickly and pick him off. Toward the end of the round the crowd was beginning to laugh as I seemed to be able to hit him almost at will. A look of desperation had crept onto his face. I don't think I was hurting him much but I was making him very tired and very frustrated, just the way Geel Piet had said it must be done. The bell went and I was sure I had won the round.

"You don't have to hit him again to win," Lieutenant Smit said.

"Just stay out of his way, you hear? Just counterpunch, no attack. You going to win this clear, man, unless he cops you a lucky one."

The bell went for the final round. Du Toit must have had instructions to nail me because he kept rushing me, throwing wild punches. I'd nail him with a straight left or a right hook as he passed, but I was careful not to get set to throw a big punch. The crowd was laughing as I made him miss and I was beginning to feel pretty good. I had outboxed him and hadn't been hurt; the bell would go any moment and I'd won. The right cross came at me and I couldn't move out of the way. It smashed into my shoulder and into my face and I felt as though I had walked into a telegraph pole. I felt myself going and grabbed at the ropes behind me to stop myself falling. The next blow came but I managed to get my head out of the way; then Du Toit threw another right and it just grazed my face. But my legs felt okay and my head had cleared. I ducked under a straight right and danced out of the way just as the bell went.

"Phew!"

Doc was at the ringside jumping up and down. "Eleven out of ten. Absoloodle!" he yelled at me. It was the happiest moment of my life.

I had started to move back to my corner when Meneer de Klerk called us both into the center of the ring. We shook hands and I thanked Du Toit for the fight but I think he knew he'd lost as his eyes brimmed with tears and he didn't reply. Then Meneer de Klerk took us both by the hand and said: "The winner three rounds to nothing is Gentleman Peekay!" He held my hand up and the crowd clapped and laughed at my new name. The Barberton Blues all yelled and whistled.

"That was good," Lieutenant Smit said. "But it's early times; you were lucky, man. When I tell you to stay out of the way you stay out of the way, you hear? That right cross nearly brained you. Two like that early in the next bout and we throw in the towel, you understand?"

I nodded and tried to look contrite. As Klipkop pulled the big mitts off my hands I suddenly felt light, as though I were going to float away. It was a wonderful feeling. It was the power of one stirring in me. I jumped down from the ring feeling ten feet tall.

Doc gave me a big hug. "Peekay, I am very proud today! Absoloodle! Such a dancer, already. Absoloodle." I had never heard so many absoloodles.

Fonnie Kruger won his fight against a kid from Boxburg and so did Maatie Snyman in the under-thirteens, Nels Stekhoven in the under-fourteens, and Bokkie de Beer in the under-fifteens. I'm telling you, we were a pretty proud lot in the Barberton Blues; every one of us had advanced to the semis. As Fonnie Kruger and I were both in the under-twelve division, if we got through the semis we'd be in the final together. But our hopes were soon dashed. There was a kid from Lydenburg called Kroon who was the biggest eleven-year-old I had ever seen, at least a foot higher than me and twice as wide. He wasn't a boxer, but he polished off a kid from Nelspruit in the first round when he sat him on the canvas after about one minute. We instantly dubbed him Killer Kroon. We all got scared just looking at him and Bokkie said he was glad he wasn't fighting in the under-twelve division.

Fonnie Kruger got Killer Kroon in the semis and managed to go one round before he was sat on his pants, seconds after the second round had begun. I think he was glad that it was all over. Killer Kroon had closed his right eye. "It's like boxing a blerrie gorilla," he said when he climbed down from the ring.

Just before lunch I entered the ring again to fight a kid from Kaapmuiden. He was a square-built sort of bloke and very strong around the shoulders but not a lot taller than me. It was the first time I had stood up to another boxer whose chin level wasn't above my head. It was a good fight and my speed saved me from taking the weight of his blows. He hit hard and straight, but I was able to move away as the punch came so the sting had gone out of it. Nevertheless, he landed quite a lot of punches and was scoring well. Before the final round began, Lieutenant Smit wiped my face.

"You're not doing enough to make certain of this fight. Watch his straight left, he keeps dropping his right glove after he's thrown the left. Get in under the blow and work him with both hands to the body. I want to make certain you got enough points."

We touched gloves for the final round and Lieutenant Smit was quite right. The kid, whose name was Geldenhuis, threw his left and then curiously dropped his right. I went in underneath and got five or six good blows to the body before he pushed me away. The final bell went and Meneer de Klerk announced for the second time that day, "The winner in two out of three rounds, Gentleman Peekay!" The crowd laughed and clapped and the Barberton Blues went wild.

Doc could hardly contain himself. "Not even one scratch, black eyes not even one. Perfect. You should play Chopin as good as this, ja?" He laughed and handed me a towel. "Lieutenant Smit says you must have a shower and change into your clothes again. Tonight, six o'clock, we fight again." He suddenly grew serious. "Peekay, in the finals is a big Boer, you must dance very goot. You must box like a Mozart piano concerto, fast and light with perfect timing, ja?"

After lunch Doc made me lie down. Despite the heat he threw a blanket over me, and to my surprise I fell asleep. It was five o'clock when he came to fetch me and I felt a little stiff and sore. He made me have a warm shower before I changed into my boxing things again. By the time we got back into the hall it was almost six and the preliminaries were over. Bokkie de Beer said five of the Barberton Blues were through to the finals, including Gert. I went over to Gert to congratulate him.

"Ag, it wasn't too hard, Peekay. I think I got lucky. But like you, man, I got a Boer in the finals as big as a mountain, a super-heavyweight. He won both his fights on knockouts in the first."

"You got the speed, speed is everything," I quoted Geel Piet.

"Not if he gets me in a corner," Gert said solemnly.

"Then stay out of corners, man!" I said flippantly, but the advice was meant as much for myself as for him.

"You on soon, Peekay. You can do it, I'm telling you." But I could hear him talking in his head and he was very worried about me.

Fonnie Kruger came over and said that Lieutenant Smit wanted me.

Lieutenant Smit and Klipkop were in earnest conversation with Meneer de Klerk.

"The Boer kid has thirty, maybe forty pounds on yours. I don't like it one bit," the referee was saying.

"You saw him in the other two fights. He hardly got touched; our kid's a good boxer," Klipkop said.

"He's the best I've seen in a long time. But he's a midget compared to Kroon. Kroon dropped both his opponents in the first. That's a bad kid. I work with young boxers every day; I'm telling you, this kid is not a sportsman." Meneer de Klerk threw his hands open. "There's plenty of time. Let the boy grow a bit. Wait till next year. He's champion material, too good to spoil with a mismatch."

I could see a hesitant look cross Lieutenant Smit's face. The voices going on inside his head were confused. My heart was going boom, boom, and there was a huge aching lump in my throat. Then he squinted at the bald referee. "I make you this promise, Meneer de Klerk. If my boy even looks like being hurt we throw in the towel. You don't know Peekay. That kid has worked three years for this fight. I can't pull him out without giving him a chance."

"I'll give him one round, Smit. If he even looks like being hit in the first round I'm giving the fight to Kroon on a TKO, you understand?"

Lieutenant Smit nodded his head. He turned and saw me and I grinned at him. They had to give me a go. I had to fight Kroon. Kroon was no bigger to me than Jackhammer Smit was to Hoppie. I could take him, I knew it. "We got to glove up now, Peekay," Lieutenant Smit said.

I climbed into the ring and sat on the little stool and Killer Kroon also sat on his. He stared directly at me. Shit, he was big! He had a grin on his face and I could hear his conversation to himself, "I'm going to knock this little kid out first round."

With the arrival of the townspeople for the finals, the town hall was at least half full. I remembered Doc's words, "You must box like a Mozart piano concerto." In my head I could hear the way Doc would play a Mozart concerto, no arpeggio, fast and straight, the timing perfect. It made sense to box Killer Kroon in the same way.

"Never mind his head, Peekay. You just keep landing them to the body. Quick punches in and out with both hands. Scoring shots. Stay out of reach and don't let him get you against the ropes. You box him in the middle of the ring. Make him work, make him chase you all the time, you hear?"

I listened to them carefully, but I knew the real answer came from Geel Piet. That I had to box with my feet. I had no idea what sort of a boxer Killer Kroon was. His first opponent had lasted less than a minute and Fonnie went down a few seconds into the second round but had spent all of the first backpedaling.

As I sat there waiting, Kroon stared at me with an evil grin and the feeling of being in front of the Judge came back to me and the ring became the dormitory and the audience the jury.

I closed my eyes and counted from ten to one. I stood on a rock just below the full moon, the roar of the falls in my ears. The river and the gorge and the African veld stretched out below me in the silver light. I was a young Zulu warrior who had killed his first lion and I could feel the lion skin skirt around my hips, the tail of the lion wrapped around my waist. I took a deep breath and jumped the first of the falls into a pool lashed with white spray, rose to the surface and was swept to the rim of the second, plunged downward and rose again to be swept to the edge of the third pool, where I fell again, rising to the surface at the bottom of the falls, where the first of the stepping-stones shone wet in the moonlight. I crossed the ten stones to the other side and opened my eyes and looked directly at Kroon. Killer Kroon saw something in my eyes that made him turn away and not look at me again.

The referee called us up, and taking us by the wrists, he held our hands in the air. "On my left, Dames and Heere . . . Gentleman Peekay of the Barberton Blues." The crowd gave me a big hand, although this was mixed with laughter as they saw my size next to Killer Kroon. "On my right, from Lydenburg, Martinus Kroon." The crowd had already chosen sides and with the exception of the Lydenburg squad the clapping was only polite.

The bell went for the first round and I sprang from my stool while Killer Kroon got up slowly, almost disdainfully. We moved to the center of the ring, and he threw a left at my head, which only came up to below his shoulder. I could see it coming for miles and let it pass my ear. He followed with a right and I ducked under the punch. It was almost the same opening Du Toit had used and I followed it the same way with a left and a right under Kroon's heart. I got some body behind the two punches but he didn't even seem to notice. I danced quickly out of the way and a clumsy uppercut with his left missed my chin by six inches.

I stayed in the center of the ring, moving around Kroon, who threw four more punches and missed. He threw another right that parted my hair but the punch was too hard, throwing him off balance. I moved in fast and hit the same spot under the heart with a left and right combination, which I repeated. Four good short punches. But I'd been too greedy getting the extra two punches home. His huge arms locked around me and, lifting me bodily, he threw me away from him. I was sent spinning across the ring, my legs working like pistons to keep me on my feet. I bounced into the ropes, and grabbed the middle one with both arms to steady myself. I was wide open as the straight right came at me. It should have been an uppercut. I was against the ropes and would not have been able to move out of the way. To put everything he had into the punch, Killer Kroon had pulled his shoulder back just a fraction too far. It allowed me a split second to move my head to the right. The blow caught my ear and it felt like a branding iron had been pushed into the side of my head. But I'd taken worse from the Judge and I feinted left and moved off the ropes under his right arm. He turned quickly but my feet were already in position and he walked into a perfectly timed right cross, coming at him with the full weight of my body behind it. The punch landed flush on the point of his chin and his head snapped back. I knew I had hurt him. It was the best punch I had ever thrown by far. Gert said later, had I been nearer to Killer Kroon's size, he'd have been out for a week.

Kroon shook his head in bewilderment. He was hurt and he was mad and he came looking for me. I stayed out of his way, taking a straight left on the shoulder moving away, and managed two more good punches to the spot under his heart, which had developed a red patch. The bell went for the end of round one, and as I returned to my corner I could see a grin on Meneer de Klerk's face.

Doc was standing outside the ring in my corner as Lieutenant Smit and Klipkop climbed in to attend to me. He had his bandanna in both hands and was twisting it round and round.

"You done good," Klipkop said. Lieutenant Smit smeared Vaseline over the ear where Kroon had glanced his big hit off me. He covered my good ear with his hand.

"Can you hear me, Peekay?" He spoke from the side I'd been hit on.

"Ja, lieutenant, I hear you good," I replied.

"If a thick ear is all we get out of this fight we'll be blerrie lucky." He turned to Klipkop. "Give him another half-glass of water. Rinse only, don't swallow. Now listen good, Peekay. It looks like this gorilla's only got four punches. Straight right, straight left, right cross and left uppercut. He's a fighter and he's never needed any more than those; every one is a good punch and he throws them well, except the left uppercut is a bit clumsy and he tries to hit too hard with the right cross so you can see it coming. You done good to move under it and hit him under the heart. He's very strong but if you can get in enough of those they'll count in the end and you'll slow him down for the third. You must keep moving, you hear? Make him work; he's not as fit as you; and keep hitting him on that spot under the heart, okay?"

I had never heard Lieutenant Smit talk so fast, and listening to what he wasn't saying, I could see he now thought I had a chance. "No more attack, you hear? Only counterpunch." I nodded and the bell went for the second round.

Kroon came storming out of his corner and I could see from the look in his eyes that he wanted to finish the fight. For the first half of the round I ducked and weaved and backpedaled and moved him around. He must have thrown fifty punches without landing even one. The crowd was beginning to laugh as he repeatedly missed. Toward the second half of the round he slowed down a little and his right cross wasn't coming quite so fast. He was breathing heavily. I moved up a little closer and started coming in under the right cross again, to land on the same spot under the heart time and time again. I couldn't believe his lack of imagination. His breathing was getting heavier and heavier and he grunted as I landed a left and a right and I realized that my punches were beginning to hurt him. I was getting pretty tired myself when the bell sounded for the end of the second round.

The crowd stood and clapped. As I returned to my corner I looked toward Doc. He had the bandanna in his mouth and was chewing on it.

"He's going to try and finish you this round, Peekay. You got both rounds, you miles ahead on points. He is going to try to put you down." Lieutenant Smit's usually calm voice was gone. "Stay away, man. I don't care if you don't land a single punch, just keep clear, you hear? Keep clear, you got this fight won. *Magtig!* You boxing good!" His eyes were shining.

The bell for the final round went and we met in the center of the ring and touched gloves. Killer Kroon was still breathing hard and his chest was heaving. As we moved away he said, "I'm going to kill you, you blerrie Rooinek."

Geel Piet said you always had to answer back, so they know you're not afraid. "Come and get me, you Boer bastard!" I shot back at him. He rushed at me and I stepped aside but his swinging arm caught me as he passed and knocked me off my feet. It wasn't a punch, it was the inside of his arm, but it sat me down. I couldn't believe it had happened. One knockdown and you lose the fight! I had opened my mouth to talk, lost my concentration and lost the fight! I couldn't believe it was me sitting on the canvas. There was a roaring in my ears and a terrible despair in my heart.

"No knockdown, continue to box!" I heard Meneer de Klerk shout as though in a dream. I was coming to my feet but the thought of defeat had drowned my senses. Killer Kroon rushed in and that clumsy left uppercut just missed my chin. This time he should have used the right cross as I couldn't move upward to my feet and sideways at the same time. A right cross would have caught me flush on the chin and finished me for keeps. Instead I simply moved my head backward and the uppercut whizzed safely past the point of my chin. I was back on my toes and dancing out of reach, moving around him. He couldn't box for toffee. No way was he going to get a second chance at me.

I began to realize that there was something wrong with him. His breath was coming in rasps and his chest was heaving; his punches had lost their zing. I moved up and hit him as hard as I could with a two-fisted attack to the spot under his heart and his hands fell to his sides. His gloves came around my waist but there was hardly any strength left in him and he leaned heavily on me, his gloves working up and down my waist. The thumb of his glove must have caught the elastic band of my boxing shorts, for they slipped neatly over my hips and fell to my ankles. I didn't know what to do. I couldn't step backward for fear of falling; anyway his weight made it impossible to move. So I just stood there and hit him again and again, my bare arse pointed at the crowd. Then he gave me a last desperate push and I tripped over the shorts and fell down. I tried to pull my pants up with my boxing gloves but without success. The crowd was convulsed with laughter and Killer Kroon was standing over me with his hands on his knees, rasping and wheezing and trying to take in air.

"No knockdown!" Meneer de Klerk shouted. "Get back to your corner, Kroon!" He jerked me to my feet and pulled my pants up. I had been covering my snake with my gloves. In those days nobody wore underpants. But I didn't care. The only thing that mattered was Killer Kroon in the ring with me. "Box on," Meneer de Klerk said. I turned to face Killer Kroon's corner. He was standing with his back to me and his chest was still heaving. Suddenly a towel lofted over his head and landed at my feet. Kroon's corner was throwing in the towel; the fight was over! Meneer de Klerk moved quickly over to me, and with a huge grin on his face held my hand aloft. "Winner on a technical knockout, Gentleman Peekay!" he announced. The crowd shouted and cheered and Lieutenant Smit and Klipkop jumped into the ring. Klipkop lifted me high above his shoulders and turned around in the ring and everyone went wild.

Meneer de Klerk had moved over to Kroon's corner and now he came back to the center of the ring and held his hand up for silence. Klipkop put me down again. "The Lydenburg squad want me to say that Martinus Kroon retired because of an asthma attack." A section of the crowd started to boo and there was general laughter. "More like a Rooinek attack!" someone shouted. The referee held up his hand once more. "I just want you to know that I had the fight scored two rounds to none for Gentleman Peekay and I also had him ahead on points in the third round. The technical knockout stands. Let me tell you something, this boy is going to be a great boxer; just remember where you saw him first." The crowd whistled and stomped and cheered and Lieutenant Smit held my hand up and then we left the ring.

"I think Geel Piet and the people will be very happy tonight," Doc said as he handed me a towel. "I go to get you a soft drink? What color do you want?"

"But we haven't got any money," I said.

"That's what you think, Mister Schmarty Pantz!" Doc fished into his pocket and produced two half-crowns.

"Five shillings!" I said in amazement.

He grinned slyly. "I am making this bet with a nice man from Lydenburg."

"A bet! You bet on me? What if I'd lost? You couldn't have paid him!"

Doc scratched his nose with his forefinger. "You couldn't lose, you was playing Mozart," he said.

I asked for an American cream soda. It was the drink Hoppie had bought me in the café at Gravelotte and it was still my favorite. It was also the closest I could come to sharing my win with Hoppie. If Geel Piet and Hoppie could have been there, everything would have been perfect. Not that it wasn't perfect. But more perfect.

THIRTEEN

By the time we got to the last fight of the evening, the Barberton Blues had won five of the eight finals and only the heavyweight division remained. Gert was matched with a giant called Potgieter from Kaapmuiden.

Potgieter was a better boxer than he first appeared and in the first round he had Gert hanging on twice, but Gert won the round by landing more clean punches. In the heavyweight division a knockdown did not mean the end of the fight and in the second round Potgieter connected with an uppercut and Gert dropped to the canvas. The bell went at the count of five.

In the final round Gert started hitting Potgieter almost at will. The big man knew he was behind on points so he dropped his defense, confident he could take anything Gert dished out. Finally Potgieter managed to trap Gert in a corner. The uppercut caught Gert on the point of the jaw. The warder was out cold even before his legs had started to buckle. The referee counted him out and Klipkop and Lieutenant Smit lifted him unconscious from the floor and carried him to his corner. Gert had, as usual, fought with too much heart and not enough head.

It was after ten when we left Nelspruit. We kids huddled

together in the back of the *bakkie*. The indigo night was pricked with sharp cold stars. We'd spent what energy remained in lavish praise of each other and of the glorious Barberton Blues, and now we were silent and sleepy. Klipkop drove as Gert had gone home with Lieutenant Smit.

I was enormously tired but couldn't doze off. In my mind each of my three fights kept repeating itself. I played them all back in sequence as though they were scenes on a loop of film that I was able to edit in my imagination, remaking the fights, seeing them as they should have been.

I didn't know it then, but this ability totally to recall a fight scenario made me a lot more dangerous when I met an opponent for the second time.

It was nearly midnight when we stopped outside our house. Everything was in darkness. I crept around the back because the kitchen door was never locked. A candle stub burned on the kitchen table and on the floor, each rolled in a blanket, lay Dum and Dee. I tried to tiptoe past but they both shot up into sitting positions.

They were overjoyed at my return and switched on the light to examine me. They burst into tears when they saw my swollen ear and it took some effort to calm them. Despite my protests, for I was almost too tired to stand up, Dum sat me down and washed my face, hands and feet. At last I was allowed to totter off to bed.

Geel Piet had not expected me to win through to the finals in Nelspruit. The most he had hoped for was a berth in the semis. His delight at the Monday-morning training session knew no bounds. "The people are very happy. I'm telling you, since we heard the news they have talked of nothing else, man." He laughed. "The Zulus say you are surely a Zulu chief disguised as a white man, for only a Zulu can fight with this much courage."

At my piano lesson, Doc found an excuse for Geel Piet to come into the hall and I played back the three fights blow by blow to him. He nearly died laughing when I told him about my pants falling down.

That morning Lieutenant Smit had made a short speech. "I'm proud of you all, you hear? Not one boxer let us down; even those of you who lost, you fought good. The under-twelve finals was the best boxing match I have ever seen." Fonnie Kruger punched me in the ribs and I didn't know how to stop my face burning. "No, honest, man, if you all want a lesson in boxing then watch Peekay." He paused and looked directly at Geel Piet standing behind us. "Geel Piet, you just a yellow kaffir, but I got to hand it to you, you a good coach."

We all looked round to see Geel Piet cover his face with both hands and dance from one foot to another as though he were standing on hot coals.

The prison photographer came into the gym and Lieutenant Smit announced we were going to have our picture taken but not our fingerprints. We all laughed and the photographer lined us up. There was an explosion of light as he took the picture, and then he said he wanted to take another. Lieutenant Smit looked about him as Doc entered the hall. "Come, professor, stand here," he invited, and then to everyone's surprise he beckoned to Geel Piet. "You too, kaffir," he said gruffly.

Klipkop stepped out of the photographer's former arrangement. "No way, man! I'm not having my photo taken with a blerrie kaffir!"

Lieutenant Smit brought his hand up to his mouth and blew a couple of breathy notes down the center of his closed fist. "That's okay, Sergeant Oudendaal," he said pleasantly. "Anybody else want to step out?"

Geel Piet stepped out of where he was standing on the edge of the group. "I am too ugly for a heppy snap, *baas*." He grinned.

"Get back, kaffir!" Lieutenant Smit commanded.

Geel Piet returned to the group, whereupon the remainder of the adult boxers stepped out with the exception of Gert; then Bokkie de Beer moved away, followed by the other kids. I could see they were real scared. Only Doc, Gert, Geel Piet and I were left when Lieutenant Smit stepped back into the picture.

The photograph captured the exact moment when I understood with conviction that racism is a primary force of evil.

We were all given a ten-by-eight photograph of the Barberton Blues and the photographer gave Doc, Gert and me a copy of the second photograph. The lieutenant refused his copy, which I begged from the photographer and gave to Geel Piet privately. He kept it in the piano stool and looked at it every day when he collected the prisoners' mail.

Some weeks later Lieutenant Smit was promoted to captain and people even started to talk about him being the next Kommandant. He called me aside one morning and asked if I would return the second photo and get Doc's copy back as well. I had no option but to obey, and Gert did the same. Captain Smit tore them up but forgot about the extra copy. He obtained the plate from the photographer and destroyed this also. A man cannot be careful enough about his career.

Between Doc and Mrs. Boxall, my education was in fairly safe hands. Mrs. Boxall consulted with Doc by note and they decided on my serious reading. She was the expert on English literature and he on the sciences, music and Latin. The Barberton library, apart from containing Doc's botanical collection, had been the recipient of two more good private collections and Mrs. Boxall said it was choked with intellectual goodies for a growing mind. Both Doc and Mrs. Boxall were natural teachers. Doc set exams and Mrs. Boxall conducted them in the library on Tuesday and Friday every week. I grew to love this time spent with Mrs. Boxall.

Two of me were emerging, a small boy approaching eleven who climbed trees, used a catapult, drove a billycart and led an eager gang in *kleilat* and other games, and a somewhat precocious child who often left the teachers at school unable to cope with the fact that I was well in advance of anything they had to teach.

In my tenth year a new teacher, Miss Bornstein, arrived at the school. She taught the senior class, getting them ready for the leap into high school, and while I was still two classes below the seniors she had summoned me to her classroom after school one Friday.

"Hello, Peekay, come in," she said.

"Good afternoon, miss," I said, entering a little fearfully.

"Miss Bornstein, please, Peekay. They tell me you're rather clever." She looked up and smiled and my head began to zing as though I'd been clocked a straight right between the eyes. Miss Bornstein was the most beautiful person I had ever seen. She had long black hair and huge green eyes and a large mouth that shone with lipstick. She was dazzling.

Miss Bornstein tried me on Latin vocabulary and verbs. It was pretty simple stuff but as Latin was only taught in high school she seemed impressed. She then handed me the book she had been reading. "Do as many of these as you can in ten minutes," she instructed.

The book was full of little drawings and sentences with missing words and trick questions where you had to pick the answer from several choices. It was like old homework for me. Doc had a great many books on logic and thinking, as he would call it, out of the square. Miss Bornstein's book was for beginners and I finished the whole thing in under five minutes.

I had to wait while she marked the answers. After the first page she looked up and tapped her pencil against her beautiful white teeth. Then she said, "I wouldn't say you were stupid, Peekay." She turned to the last page and marked it. "No, I wouldn't say that at all. I think you and I are going to see quite a lot of each other." She thanked me for coming and said that on Monday I was to report to her class.

Miss Bornstein, who had been lecturing at the university in Johannesburg, had returned home because her mother was dying of cancer. Miss Bornstein's father and mother had come to South Africa from Germany in 1918, and were the only Jews in Barberton. Mr. Bornstein was in partnership with Mr. Andrews as the town's only solicitors. I heard all this from Mrs. Boxall who, it turned out, had known Miss Bornstein "since she was a gel."

I told Doc about the whole incident on Monday morning and at the end he asked a question. "Tell me, Peekay, how bad in love are you?"

I told him that I didn't know much about love but it was like being hit in the head with a really good punch.

"I think maybe you in love bad, Peekay. Absoloodle."

With Lieutenant Smit's promotion to captain, Sergeant Borman became the new lieutenant. This was not a popular promotion.

Lieutenant Borman was too old to belong to the boxing squad, but he often talked big about the fighter he had once been. Gert said that a man who talks about how tough he is is probably yellow. But, while the warders didn't like Borman, they respected him for being a professional. If there was any trouble in the prison, the

Kommandant had soon learned to put Sergeant Borman in charge. It was his ability to terrorize the prisoners, both physically and mentally, that made him the Kommandant's choice to take over when Lieutenant Smit was promoted.

Lieutenant Borman deeply resented the freedom Geel Piet had achieved in the gymnasium under Captain Smit, and Geel Piet was careful to keep out of his way. When Borman entered the gym, unless he was in the ring actually coaching one of the kids, Geel Piet would quietly slip away. Lieutenant Borman's eyes would follow him as he crept out. "He will get me. One day, for sure, he will get me. I hope I come out the other side alive," the battered little colored man confided in me.

Captain Smit would watch Geel Piet leave the gymnasium when Borman entered, but he remained silent. Borman saw the alliance of Doc, Geel Piet and myself as a basic breakdown of the system. Because he was a professional, he was quick to realize that such a break in the normal discipline of the prison could lead to other things. As a sergeant his influence did not carry to the Kommandant. But as a lieutenant his power increased enormously.

Had it not been for the Kommandant's desire to keep Doc sweet for the biannual visit of the inspector of prisons, our freedom within the prison would have been severely curtailed. Doc at his Steinway was to be the cultural component of the inspector's visit. The Kommandant had no intention of allowing Lieutenant Borman to disrupt his careful plan.

The war in Europe was rapidly drawing to a close. The Allies had crossed the Rhine and were moving toward Berlin. Doc was terribly excited. After four years' incarceration he had a deep need for the soft green hills, the windswept mountains and the wooded *kloofs*. We would talk about walking all the way to Saddleback Mountain on the border of Swaziland. In these last days of the war we spent most of our hour together discussing our plans for Doc's release and talking about the photos we needed for his book.

Doc's second book on the cacti of Southern Africa had been written while he was in prison. This one was in English, each page edited by Mrs. Boxall, who in the end had to confess that there was more to the jolly old cactus than she could possibly have imagined.

Doc, Geel Piet and I had discussed the matter of my love for Miss Bornstein and, I must say, neither of them was a lot of help. Among the three of us we knew very little about women. The two of them finally decided that regular bunches of roses from my granpa's garden was a good idea.

"I think maybe just let the roses do the talking, Peekay," Doc advised.

My granpa seemed much more informed on the subject of love. His own had been of the highest quality, involving the building of an entire rose garden. When I said that I was not prepared to give up being world welterweight champion for Miss Bornstein, amid a lot of tapping and tamping and staring into space, he announced that the quality of my love was certainly worth a dozen long-stemmed roses a week but fell short of a whole garden. I accepted this verdict, although I knew it was impossible to love anybody more than I loved Miss Bornstein.

The Kommandant promised Doc he would be released the day peace was declared in Europe. We were already into the first days of summer, and Doc and I had talked about being out of prison in time for the firebells, the little orange lilies flecked with specks of gold, which bloomed throughout the hills after the bushfires. Doc was disappointed when the firebells came and went and VE, or Victory in Europe, day had not arrived.

We had already arranged for a new depository for the tobacco leaves, sugar and salt and, of course, the precious mail. These were placed in a watering can made out of a four-gallon paraffin tin. The can had been doctored by Geel Piet. A false bottom had been inserted, leaving a space cunningly fitted with a lid to look like the real bottom. Filled with water, the watering can looked perfectly normal, and would even work if it became necessary to appear to be watering plants. It was left standing in Doc's cactus garden and on my way to breakfast I would simply pass through the garden and put the mail and whatever I'd brought into the false bottom of the can. It was natural enough for me to go to the warders' mess via Doc's cactus garden as I often brought new plants. The warders almost never came this way and habitually used the passage in the interior of the building to get to the mess. We had been using this method for some months as the idea was to make it routine before Doc left and the piano stool with him. The Kommandant decided the cactus garden would remain as a memorial to Doc's stay, also allowing that Geel Piet could maintain it. As I would be continuing with the boxing squad, the new system was nicely designed to work without Doc.

The writing of the letters proved to be a more difficult task. Geel Piet wrote with difficulty. Without Doc to take dictation, the prisoners would be unable to get messages to their families. This was solved when Geel Piet and I approached Captain Smit to ask if, for half an hour after boxing, I could give Geel Piet a lesson to improve his reading and writing. Captain Smit was reluctant at first but finally gave his consent.

A strange relationship had grown up between the captain and the little colored man. They only spoke to each other on the subject of boxing and Captain Smit would occasionally belittle a suggestion from Geel Piet to one of the boxers, but you could see that he respected Geel Piet's judgment and it was only to show who was the boss of the squad. In the months that followed my win against Killer Kroon I continued to enter the ring against bigger, stronger and older opponents, yet had never lost a fight. Captain Smit saw in me the consummate skill Geel Piet had as a coach.

I knew this because Bokkie de Beer said Captain Smit had told his pa that I would be the South African champion one day, ". . . because, man, he is getting the right coaching from the very beginning."

Under the guise of learning how to read and write, Geel Piet would stare into a schoolbook and dictate the prisoners' letters to me. His facility for remembering names and addresses was quite remarkable.

We had the new system up and running well before VE day and while it wasn't as foolproof or convenient as the piano stool, it worked well enough. Geel Piet was too old a lag not to maintain absolute caution and he would never let me get careless or less mindful of the risks involved. For instance, on rainy days I would bring nothing to the prison as the idea of my taking the outside path in the rain would seem both silly and, to an alert warder like Borman, suspicious. Nor would the drops be made every day or on the same days. Geel Piet created a random pattern for my drops, even allowing that on some dry days I would take the interior passage to the mess.

It was very fortunate that Doc was smart enough to initiate the new system some time before he left.

One morning, shortly after he had been promoted to lieutenant, Borman wandered into the hall while we were practicing. This was simply not done. The Kommandant's orders were that we should not be disturbed, two geniuses at work. Lieutenant Borman walked over to us, his boots making a hollow sound on the sprung floor. I continued to play until his footsteps ceased as he came to a halt just behind me.

"Good morning, Lieutenant Borman," we both said.

"Morning," Borman said in a superior way. He was carrying a cane not unlike the one Mevrou had carried and with it he tapped the leg of the piano stool. "Stan' up, man," he said to me. I rose, and he bent down and with his index finger and thumb he measured the seat. "A bit deep, hey, maybe something lives inside this seat?" He got down on all fours and put his head under the seat. "Maybe a false bottom, hey?" He tapped the bottom of the piano stool, which gave off a hollow sound. "Very inter-res-ting." Doc rose from his stool, inserted the key into my stool and raised the lid. Lieutenant Borman started to rise. Halfway up he could see that the seat was filled with sheets of music. Remaining in a crouched position, he stared at Doc and me for what seemed like a long time. "You think this is playing a funny joke on a person, hey?"

"No, lieutenant," Doc said, his voice surprisingly even. "I think only you should ask before you look. Inside lives only *Klavier-Meister* Chopin." He opened the lid of his own stool, "And here lives also Herr Beethoven, Brahms, Mozart and Bach and maybe are visiting also some others, perhaps Haydn, Liszt and Tchaikovsky, but not Strauss, definitely not Strauss. Like you, my dear lieutenant, Strauss is not welcome when I am teaching."

Lieutenant Borman rose to his full height. The two men stared at each other. The lieutenant was the first to drop his eyes. He laid the cane on top of the Steinway and hitched his pants up. "You think I don't blerrie know things is going on? I got time, I got plenty of time, you hear?" He picked up the cane, then brought it down hard against the open lid of my piano stool, knocking the lid back into place. The sound of the cane against the leather top echoed through the hall. He pointed the cane at Doc so that it touched him lightly on the breastbone as though it were a rapier. "Next time you try to be cheeky you come off secon' bes'." He turned and stormed out, his heavy boots crashing and echoing through the empty hall.

"Phew!" I sighed as I closed the lid of Doc's piano stool and sat down weakly on my own. Doc also sat down, reached over to the Chopin Nocturne No. 5 in F sharp major on the Steinway music rack and commenced to fan himself with it. He was silent for a while, lost in thought, then said softly, "Soon come the hills and the mountains."

FOURTEEN

We were reasonably safe for the month after the piano stool incident as the inspector of prisons was due to arrive and Lieutenant Borman had the job of seeing that the place was spick-and-span, with fresh whitewash everywhere you looked. Much to Doc's annoyance, even the stones bordering his cactus garden were whitewashed. Painting stones seemed to him an insult against nature. The prison corridors smelt of polish and the cells of disinfectant. Window ledges were painted prison blue and everywhere you went smelt of new paint.

The rapidly approaching VE day was a matter of concern to the Kommandant. If it arrived before the brigadier's visit then the cultural part of the program would disappear with the release of Doc. He had tried to elicit a promise from Doc that, should this occur, he would return to the prison and play for the inspector. But Doc had learned the rules of prison life, where everything is in return for something else. The *Goldfields News* had already printed a piece by the Kommandant saying that the moment Germany surrendered Doc would be released. The Kommandant couldn't go back on his word without losing face. Doc's price for staying over, if necessary, caused an uproar among the warders but as far as the

Kommandant was concerned no price was too high for a smooth visit. Doc asked if he could give a concert for all the prisoners.

On Sundays the prisoners did not go out in work gangs. Instead they were locked in their cells and fifty at a time, tribe by tribe, were allowed in the exercise pen, a high-walled enclosure. First the Zulu, followed by the Swazi, then the Ndebele, Sotho and Shangaane. The Boers understood the antipathy each tribe has for the other, and by keeping the tribes separated they maintained the traditional tensions between them. This was thought to lessen the chances of a mass uprising or a prison strike.

Doc told me how each Sunday he would take a position in the guard tower overlooking the exercise pen to listen to them. Each tribe would use much of the ninety minutes allotted to them singing together, and he soon learned which tribal song each tribe liked best. He had written out the music for it, and then he had composed a piano concerto that represented, in melody terms, each of these songs. Doc said that he had never heard such magnificent harmony. Even though he did not understand the words, he could hear in the songs the people's longing for their homes, their people, the comfort of their fires. He called his composition Concerto of the Great Southland. It was this that he hoped to play to all the prisoners as his tribute to them before he left the prison.

The idea was for Doc to play the concerto through first, each movement in effect being one or more of a particular tribe's songs. Then on the second time through the tribe whose movement it was would sing the song to Doc's accompaniment. In this way each of the tribes in the prison would participate in the concert.

Once the Kommandant had agreed the concert could go ahead, a great deal had to be done. No rehearsal was possible, of course, but through Geel Piet each of the tribes was told which song was needed and the exact time it should take to sing. At night Doc would play the various songs fortissimo with all the hall windows open so the sound carried to the cell blocks. The warders claimed you could hear the cockroaches scratching as the prisoners strained to hear the music.

Doc decided I should conduct. This I would do in the simplest sense, signaling the piano breaks and the pianissimo as well as the fortissimo to the choir. Doc and I went through the concerto during morning practice until I knew what every shake and nod of his head meant. Geel Piet had also taken basic instructions back to the prisoners so they knew what my hand signals would mean. Had Doc proposed that I assume the role of conductor in front of a white audience I could not have done so, but such was the nature of white supremacy in South Africa that I thought little of standing up in front of three hundred and fifty black prisoners and directing them.

Geel Piet informed me of the mounting excitement among the inmates. When the news spread that the Tadpole Angel would be directing the people in the singing *indaba,* it was immediately assumed the concert had a mystical significance. Work time was used as practice and farmers and the people at the sawmills who hired gangs spoke of singing from dawn until dusk. Even the dreaded quarries rang with the songs of the tribal work gangs. The Concerto of the Great Southland was being wrought into being, a musical jigsaw. On the big night, all the pieces would be brought together under the magic spell cast by the Tadpole Angel.

Captain Smit seemed to have decided that the concert was a good idea, perhaps for no other reason than that it was opposed by Lieutenant Borman. The two men had never liked each other and

Captain Smit was said to have been bitterly opposed to the elevation of Borman to lieutenant.

The concert was to take place on the parade ground, and a platform had been built to raise the Steinway above the level of the prisoners. Each tribe would form a semicircle around the platform with ten feet separating each group. Two warders carrying *sjamboks* would be stationed in this corridor to stop any monkey business. A double shift issued with extra ammunition would be on guard duty on the walkways along the wall, and spotlights would be trained on the prisoners.

The concert was scheduled for Monday, May 7, 1945, and all the warders had been placed on full alert. Prisoners were never paraded at night and rumors were rife of tribal vendettas being settled in the dark, as well as an attempted prison break by the Zulus. Lieutenant Borman lost no opportunity of telling anyone who was prepared to listen that trouble was on its way.

It was difficult to get my mother to agree to my staying up late for the concert. Finally, after consulting the Lord and receiving a note from Miss Bornstein that assured her that my school career would not be affected by one late night, she gave her permission.

Doc asked me how I would dress as conductor. The choice was limited: khaki shirts and shorts and a pair of black boots with gray school socks were the entire contents of my wardrobe. Then Geel Piet suggested that I dress in my boxing uniform, wearing the boots the people had made for me. Doc thought this was a splendid idea and I must say I quite liked it myself. It would be awkward for me to wear boxing gloves as it would make it difficult to conduct. Geel Piet suggested that I should wear gloves and then just before the concert began, remove them.

Thus, on the night of the concert, all the myths Geel Piet had so carefully nurtured among the prisoners about the Tadpole Angel would harmonize in my appearance as their leader, uniting all the tribes in the great singing *indaba* .

In any other society Geel Piet would have been a great promoter. The Tadpole Angel would appear to the people dressed as a great fighter who would lead them in their tribal songs, crossing over the barriers of race and tribe. Was he not already a slayer of giants? Was he not the spirit of the great chief who bound Zulu with the Swazi and the Ndebele and Shangaane and Sotho so that they all sat on one mat in a great singing *indaba* ?

As with Mrs. Boxall's Earl of Sandwich Fund, Doc's wonderful Concerto of the Great Southland was appropriated by the prisoners as being my work and my doing. Geel Piet had seen that it would be more appropriate if it was presented in this way.

The night of Doc's concert arrived. The moment I passed through the gates I knew something in the prison was different. The feeling of despair was not in the air. The sad chattering that was in my mind the instant I stepped within the grounds had ceased. The thoughts of the people were calm. I felt a thrill of excitement. Tonight was going to be special.

A full moon had risen just above the dark shadow of the hills behind the prison walls, and the parade ground was flooded with moonlight. Doc's Steinway stood sharply outlined on the platform.

As I stood looking at the Steinway, the floodlights, bright and sudden, came on. When my eyes had adjusted to the harsh, raw light I could see that around the platform in a semicircle on the ground, whitewashed lines denoted the area for each tribe. A dozen warders carrying *sjamboks* came out of the main building and walked toward the piano, their boots scrunching on the gravel.

I made my way to the hall. Doc was sitting at the Mignon

upright, absently tapping at the keys. He looked up as I entered. "Geel Piet is late; he should be already here," he said. Doc regarded Geel Piet as an essential part of the entire operation. Without him working with the prisoners, a concert still fraught with the potential for unrehearsed disaster would have no chance of succeeding.

"He'll be here any minute, you'll see," I said to cheer him up. "I'll go and get my gloves." I hurried from the hall toward the gym. An old lag was coming toward me carrying a huge coffeepot; another followed him with a tray of mugs. They were taking coffee to the warders in the parade ground. "Have you seen Geel Piet?" I asked one. I spoke in Shangaan for I could see from the cicatrization on his cheeks that he was of the Tsonga tribe. "No, *baas,* we have not seen this one," he said humbly. As I departed I heard him say to the lag behind him, "See how the Tadpole Angel speaks the languages of all the tribes. Is he not the chosen leader of the people?"

When I reached the gymnasium I switched on the lights. I put on my boxing singlet, shorts, socks and boots; then I loosely tied together the laces of the gloves I liked to use and slung them around my neck.

I returned to find Doc still alone in the hall, concern showing clearly on his face as he absentmindedly gloved me up. "It is too late to wait longer; we must go now. I will tell Geel Piet I am very cross because this happens."

The door I'd used to enter the building couldn't be opened from the inside, so we walked into the main administration building, which led out to the parade ground. We passed through the small hallway where I had first entered the prison four years earlier. The lights were out in what was then Lieutenant Smit's office but which was now occupied by Lieutenant Borman. I moved over and peered for a moment into the darkened office. In the half-light my eyes wandered around the room and rested on a thin strip of light showing under the door of the interrogation room off the main office. The door must have been slightly ajar, because I heard the unmistakable thud of a blow and a sudden sharp groan such as men make when they receive a hard punch to the solar plexus. It was not an unusual occurrence but it seemed inappropriate on this full moon night of the playing of the Concerto of the Great Southland.

The prisoners were already seated in their marked-off sections when we arrived, the warders walking up and down striking their *sjamboks* against the sides of their legs. The prisoners avoided looking at them, almost as though they were not there. Talking was not allowed, but as we passed I could see the people smiling as Doc and I stepped onto the platform.

The Kommandant arrived shortly after us and stood on the platform to address the prisoners. Lieutenant Borman was to have done the translation into Fanagalo, a made-up language rather like Pidgin English, which was understood by all the tribes, but he seemed not to have arrived. The Kommandant, clearly annoyed by this, started to speak in Afrikaans.

"Listen to me, you hear," he said, and I quickly translated into Zulu. He looked surprised. "Can you translate, Peekay?" I nodded. "Okay, then I will speak and you can translate when I have finished. Stop after every sentence."

The Kommandant spoke too loudly and too harshly. "This concert is a gift to you all from the professor, who is not a dirty criminal like all of you, you hear! I don't know why an important person like him wants to make a concert for kaffirs, not only kaffirs, but criminals as well. I just want you to know it won't happen again and I don't want any trouble, you hear. You just listen to the peeano and you sing, then we march you back to your cells." He turned to me. "That's all. You tell them what I said now."

I said the Kommandant welcomed them and that the professor welcomed them and thanked them for coming to his great singing *indaba* . He hoped that they would sing each tribe better than the other so they would be proud. They should watch my hands, and I took my boxing gloves off to demonstrate the hand movements. When I had finished, the sea of faces in front of me were smiling fit to burst and then spontaneously they started to clap. "You done a good job, Peekay," the Kommandant said, pleased at this response to his speech.

Doc played the Concerto for the Great Southland through entirely and the prisoners listened quietly with nods of approval as they heard the melodies of their own tribal songs. At the end they all clapped furiously.

I then stood up and showed them how I would bring each tribe into their part and stop them by fading their voices out or simply ending a song with a downward stroke of the hands.

Doc played the prelude, which was a musical medley of each of the melodies, and then I brought in the Sotho singers. Their voices melded into the night as though they had caused the air to vibrate with a deep harmony before they broke into song. They seemed instinctively to understand what was required of them and followed every gesture as though anticipating it. They were followed by the Ndebele, who carried a more strident melody and whose voices rose deep and true. The Swazis followed as beautiful as any, then the Shangaane. Each tribe sounded different, separated by a common refrain that was hauntingly African and seemed somehow to be a mixture of all. The Zulus took the last part, which rose in power and majesty as they sang the victory song of the great Shaka, using the flats of their hands to bang on the ground as the mighty Zulu Impi had done with their feet, until the parade ground appeared to shake. The concerto lasted for half an hour, the last part being the by now familiar refrain, which all the tribes hummed in a glorious finale. Never had a composer's work had a stranger début and never a greater one. Eventually the composition would be played by philharmonic and symphony orchestras around the world, accompanied by famous choirs, but it would never sound better than it did under the African moon in the prison yard when three hundred and fifty black inmates lost themselves in their pride and love for their tribal lands.

Doc rose from the Steinway and turned to the mass of black faces. He was crying unashamedly and many of the Africans were weeping with him. Then without warning came a roar of approval from the people. Doc would later tell me that it was the greatest moment of his life, but what they were saying was "*Onoshobishobi Ingelosi!* Tadpole Angel!" chanted over and over again.

The Kommandant looked worried and some of the warders had started to slap the *sjamboks* against the ground. "*Onoshobishobi Ingelosi! Onoshobishobi Ingelosi!*" Doc had risen from his seat to take a bow and I jumped up onto it and started to wave my hands to indicate that the chanting must stop. Almost instantly there was silence. Doc looked up surprised, not sure what had happened. I said, "The great music wizard and I thank the people for singing. You are all men who tonight have brought honor to your tribes and you have brought great honor also to the music wizard and to me." I would have lacked the maturity to make such a speech in English but the African tongue is gracious and fits such words easily. "You must go quietly now in the names of your wives and your children, for the

Boers grow restless." My voice was a thin piping sound in the night.

Suddenly a shower of stars sprayed across the sky above the town and then another and another, single red and green stars that burst high, cascades that danced in the heavens. The prisoners looked up in awe, some even covering their heads against the magic. A warder came hurrying up to the Kommandant, whispered in his ear, and the Kommandant turned toward Doc and then extended his hand. "You are free to go, professor. The war in Europe is over. The Germans have surrendered." He pointed in the direction of the town. "See the fireworks, the Rooineks are already celebrating." A final cascade of stars burst against the dark sky and the black men cried out; they had never seen such a happening before.

Was this not the final sign? The myth of the Tadpole Angel was complete. Now it could only grow as legends are wont to do. I had become a myth.

Each tribe rose when they were commanded to do so and marched silently away until the parade ground was empty but for the guards who manned the walls, and the Kommandant.

"*Magtig!* I have never seen such a thing in all my life, man," the Kommandant said, shaking his head. He turned to Doc. "Your music was beautiful, man, the most beautiful thing I have ever heard and such singing we will never hear again. Peekay, someday you will make a great Kommandant. I have never seen such command of black men. It is as though you are some kind of witch doctor, hey?"

Quite suddenly there was a single voice in the night as though from the direction of the gymnasium, "*Onoshobishobi Ingelosi!*" I heard it just the once and the sad voices in my head began chattering; the trouble in this place had returned.

Doc was overwhelmed by the news of the German surrender and the excitement of the concert, and he sat on the piano stool for a long time. The Kommandant bade us goodnight. The floodlights had been switched off so that the moon, which had risen high in the sky, ruled the night again. Then I remembered Geel Piet. I turned to Doc, who looked up at me at the same time. We were thinking the same thing.

"Geel Piet never came. I cannot understand it. He would not have stayed away," Doc said. I could see he felt guilty for not having thought about his absence sooner.

There was a scrunch of footsteps on gravel and Gert appeared out of the darkness. "Captain Smit says it's late and school tomorrow, so I must drive you home now, Peekay."

I was surprised, for I had expected to walk home as always. "I'll go and get changed and take the gloves back," I said.

"It was a wonderful concert, professor," I heard Gert say in his halting English as I ran into the dark. I entered the side door to the gym and switched on the light, moving past the wooden horse and the medicine balls and giving the punching bag a straight left and a right hook. The big box in which we kept the gloves was just to the side of the ring. I had tied the laces of my gloves together and strung them around my neck as before. Now I threw them toward the box from halfway across the gym. It was almost a good shot with one glove landing inside the box while the other hung over the rim. I moved over to drop the glove in and suddenly, with a certainty I knew always to trust, became aware that something was terribly wrong. I ran over to the wall opposite and turned the ring light on. For a split second the sudden blaze of light blinded me; then I saw the body in the center of the ring.

Geel Piet lay facedown, as though he had fallen, his arms

stretched out to either side. His head lay in a pool of blood. Without thinking I jumped into the ring screaming, although I could hear no sound coming from me. I fell to my knees beside him and started to shake him; then I rose and took him by one of his arms and tried to pull him to his feet. I began bawling at him, "Get up, please get up! If you'll get up you'll be alive again!" But the little yellow man's body just flopped at the end of his arm and his head bounced in the pool of blood. I kept trying to make him come alive. "Please, Geel Piet! Please get up! If you can get up you'll be alive again! It's true! I promise it's true!"

There was a trail of blood as I pulled him across the ring. And then I saw that in his other hand he held the picture of Captain Smit, Doc, Gert, himself and me. I dropped his hand and fell over his body and sobbed and sobbed. Then I felt myself being lifted by Captain Smit, who rocked me as I sobbed uncontrollably into his chest. "Shhhh, don't cry, champ, don't cry," he whispered. "Shhhh. I will avenge you, this I promise. Don't cry, little brother."

The festivities in honor of the inspector of prisons were held on the following Saturday night. Doc tried to get out of playing; the death of Geel Piet had upset him dreadfully and the idea of returning to the prison, even for the concert, filled him with apprehension. The Kommandant didn't quite see it the same way. Geel Piet was simply another kaffir. "No, man! Fair is fair! I gave you your kaffir concert, now I want my brigadier concert! I let you leave the prison the morning after Germany surrendered. A man's word is his word."

Doc's return to his cottage had been an emotional business. Dee and Dum had scrubbed and polished and his home had never been as clean and neat. Gert dropped Doc at the bottom of the hill, as the roadway to the cottage had eroded over the four years he'd been away. The very next day Klipkop sent a prison gang to repair the road so that it would be ready on the day after the concert for the Steinway to be returned.

Mrs. Boxall had ordered groceries and had made sure that the municipal ratcatcher had been to check the outside lavatory hole to see that no snakes or anything else had made their home down there in the past four years. She also gave me a bottle of Johnnie Walker for Doc. After my jaw incident and all the mentions I'd heard of the demon drink down at the Apostolic Faith Mission I wasn't at all sure that Mrs. Boxall was doing the right thing.

For several weeks before Doc's release Mrs. Boxall had been sending the boy from the library to the cottage with his bike basket filled with Doc's books. She referred to these books as simply having been "borrowed for the duration." When anyone mentioned the word "duration" you knew they meant the duration of the war. When Doc returned to his cottage he found it exactly as it had been four years before, with only the Steinway missing. He told me later that he sat down on the *stoep* and wept because his friends had all been so lovely to him.

After school on the first day of Doc's freedom I found him in his cactus garden cutting a dead trunk from a patch of halfmens; their proper name is *Pachypodium namaquanum;* they look like large, prickly elephant trunks.

I made coffee and we sat on the *stoep* for a while. Neither of us had mentioned Geel Piet, both unwilling to share our grief. After a while Doc brought up the loss by saying, "No more letters for the people. No more anything." Then we talked about the garden and Doc pointed to an overgrown hedge of krans aloe. "We are being invaded by *Aloe arborescens.* I will attack soon, ja in one week." I could see he loved the idea of making plans again, of being free to decide the divisions of the days and the weeks ahead.

He rose from his stool to refill his coffee mug and groaned. I looked up to see him trying to conceal his pain with a smile. "I am a dumkopf, Peekay. This morning I climb the hill to our rock but such a small climb has made me very stiff. It will take maybe a month before we can go into the hills again." He walked stiffly toward the kitchen, and for the first time I saw that Doc had become an old man.

He planned to visit Mrs. Boxall at the library on Saturday morning—the day after school broke up for the June holidays and the day of the Kommandant's concert. Mrs. Boxall was in quite a tizz when I told her. I also told my granpa of Doc's visit to the library and early on Saturday morning he cut two dozen pink and red roses for Doc to give to Mrs. Boxall. "He can't go giving her a bunch of cactus flowers now, can he?" he declared a little smugly. My granpa saw no virtue whatsoever in a cactus garden.

We arrived at the library just as the clock on the magistrates' court tower struck nine. The library boy was sitting on the step outside. "The missus, she be come soon," he said. Doc started to stride up and down the footpath. Then I saw Charlie, Mrs. Boxall's little Austin Seven, coming down the road toward us. "Here she comes!" I yelled, and thrust the bunch of roses at Doc. He grabbed the flowers with both hands. Charlie lurched to a halt outside the library and the engine died with a clunking sound. Mrs. Boxall stuck her head out of the window.

"Come along, Peekay, give a gel a hand, there's a good chap," she said cheerily. I hurried to open the door of the Austin. "Now that the war is over we can all go back to having nice manners," she said, stepping out of Charlie. She looked up at Doc and gave him her best smile. Doc thrust the roses at her in an awkward movement, as though he didn't quite know how it should be done. "And here's the man with the nicest manners of all," she said, burying her nose into the pink and red blossoms and breathing deeply. "Thank you, professor." She took another shy whiff of the roses; then she stretched her hand out toward Doc. "Roses say so much without having to say anything at all." Doc immediately clicked his heels together; then he bowed stiffly and, taking her hand, lifted it high above her head and kissed it lightly.

"Madame Boxall," he said.

"Oh dear, I have missed you, professor. It is so very nice to have you back." She buried her head in the roses again and then looked up brightly. "A cup of tea for Peekay and me and for you, professor, I have some fresh-ground Kenya coffee." She reached into her handbag for the keys to the library.

Once we were inside it was like old times. The four and a bit years slipped away and it was the same old Doc and Mrs. Boxall. Doc spoke with some consternation of returning to the prison that evening to fulfill his obligation to play for the brigadier, and Mrs. Boxall volunteered to drive us over. Doc then suggested that she might like to attend the concert and she seemed thrilled at the idea. We phoned Captain Smit, who said that Mrs. Boxall was most welcome.

We then talked for the first time about Geel Piet. Mrs. Boxall had never met him but he was almost as real to her as he had been to Doc and me. Doc lamented the fact that the Sandwich Fund was effectively finished and to our surprise Mrs. Boxall would hear of no such thing. "Just a temporary hiccup. We can't have Geel Piet thinking we're a bunch of milksops. I have a plan." She gazed at us steadily. "I'm not prepared to reveal it yet, not even to you. But I can tell you this much. I had proposed taking the train to Pretoria but now, by golly, Pretoria seems to have come to us." She wore one of her tough expressions and so we didn't question her any further. "It's my plan, and if it doesn't work, then only I shall look a proper idiot," she declared.

On the night of Geel Piet's death, Captain Smit had led me sobbing and hiccuping to the blue Plymouth, where Gert was waiting to drive me home. The captain told me that I needed a break from training and was not to return to the prison until the boxing exhibition that had been planned for the brigadier on Saturday night. As prospective welterweight champion of the world, it worried me that I wasn't in training. It hadn't yet occurred to me that I would return to a boxing squad that was now without Geel Piet, and that from now on I would simply be the most junior boxer under Captain Smit's concerned but preoccupied care.

On Saturday night we arrived at the prison just before seven and made our way to the hall. Doc's piano recital was the first item of the evening: it was thought best to get the cultural part of the evening over with while everyone was still well behaved. After that, the audience would go through into the gym for the boxing exhibition and then back to the hall for the *tiekiedraai* and *braaivleis*. The air smelt smoky from the *braaivleis* fires that had been lit on the parade ground. Someone was already playing a piano accordion in the dark.

Mrs. Boxall, Doc and I found three seats in the front row. I hadn't seen Gert since he had driven me home four days before and he now made a special point of coming over to me, and we moved off into a corner for a chat. Gert told me again how sorry he was about Geel Piet and how it wasn't the same without him on the boxing squad.

"Man, I don't understand. He was only a kaffir but I miss him a lot," he confided. He also told me that the brigadier's inspection was an all-time success and that Lieutenant Borman was up to his eyeballs in the Kommandant's good books right up until late that afternoon.

"What happened this afternoon?" I asked, delighted at the suggestion that Lieutenant Borman might have fallen from grace.

"The brigadier stood up and said to us all that he had never seen a prison in better shape. But that also Pretoria had heard of the kaffir concert." He paused and his eyes grew wide. "I'm telling you, man, we knew who had told them about it and we thought we were in a lot of trouble. But it wasn't like that at all. The brigadier said that it was a piece of proper prison reform, an example to the rest of the country, that Barberton led the way and the Kommandant was to be congratulated. You should have seen Borman's face, man, he was furious."

Snotnose came over and said Doc wanted me. Gert told me he'd see me later in the gym. Doc had decided to play Chopin's Nocturne No. 5. I knew the music well enough to turn the pages for him and that's why he had sent for me. Doc had agreed to play two pieces for the concert. He said the second piece was to be a surprise and that after the Chopin I was to return to my seat beside Mrs. Boxall.

The hall was almost full, and the warders and their wives and guests from the town had all taken their seats when the Kommandant walked to the front and stood beside the Steinway.

"Dames and Heere," he began, "it gives me much pleasure to welcome you all to this concert in honor of our good friend Brigadier Joubert, Transvaal Inspector of Prisons. The brigadier this very afternoon said nice things about Barberton prison and I just want to say to all my men that I am proud of you. We thank him for his visit and now it is our turn to say nice things about the brigadier. It is men like Brigadier Joubert who make the South African Prison Service a place where good men can hold their heads up high." He paused and seemed to be examining the gold signet ring on his hand before looking up again. "The concert we held for the black prisoners last week, the brigadier was kind enough to say, was a good example of prison reform. It was just a little idea I had and it worked. But the brigadier is a man of *big* ideas that work, a man who gives us inspiration and strength to continue." I could feel Mrs. Boxall's arm trembling against my own and I turned to see her trying hard not to laugh. "He is a God-fearing man dedicated to the prison service." The audience broke out in applause. "He is also a cultured man, which brings me to the first item on the program for tonight." He cleared his throat. "All of you know that we have had in this prison as our honored guest for the past four years, a man who is a musical genius. Last week he helped us with the prisoners' concert and tonight he is giving a personal one in Brigadier Joubert's honour. I ask you now to welcome Professor Von Vollensteen." Doc rose and did a small bow to the audience and gave me a nod and with the applause continuing we moved over to the Steinway.

The Kommandant was still on his way to his seat when the first notes of the Chopin nocturne filled the hall. At first the music was wonderfully relaxed, deceptively simple and straightforward, and then the melody line became more and more ornamental. In the middle section the music became more complex, fast and urgent, leading to a long crescendo and frenzied climax where Doc could shake his head a lot and bang furiously at the keys, which he knew the audience would like. The nocturne ended with an elegant descent toward a rustling, almost muted final chord.

The audience stood up, clapped and seemed very pleased. Doc rose and took a bow and nodded for me to return to my seat. Then he removed several sheets of music from inside his piano stool and fixed them carefully on the music rack. He turned to the audience and cleared his throat.

"Ladies and gentlemen. Tonight I would like to dedicate this next piece of music, which I have played once only before, to a very good friend. I have named this music by his name and it is for him. I give you 'Requiem for Geel Piet'!"

Without further ado Doc commenced the Concerto of the Great Southland, which he had now renamed. The melodies of the tribal songs seemed to take over the hall, as the Ndebele song followed the Sotho. The Swazi melody followed and then the Shangaan, each separated by the haunting refrain that linked them together. Finally came the victory song of the great Shaka and the Steinway seemed to build the drama of the magnificent Zulu Impi, the chords crashing as they marched into battle. The requiem closed with the muted and very beautiful compilation of the songs of the tribes. The music seemed to swell as all around us from the cells beyond the hall the voices came as the tribes completed the requiem. Geel Piet, who had had no tribe, whose blood was the mixture of all the people of southern Africa—the white tribe, the Bushman, the Hottentot, the Cape Malay and the black tribal blood of Africa itself—was celebrated in death by all the tribes.

There was a special kind of silence as the performance ended. To our own was joined the silence of the listeners beyond the hall. We had all been a part of the lament for Africa. "Requiem for Geel Piet" was a lament for all of us, the tears shed for South Africa itself.

During the applause Brigadier Joubert rose from his seat and moved to the front of the hall. He raised his hands and the hall grew quiet again. Taking a khaki handkerchief from his trouser pocket, he slowly wiped his eyes and began to speak.

"Tonight, Dames and Heere, we have heard a work of true genius. Whoever this Geel Piet was, we know from his name that he was an Afrikaner who is honored by this music. He was also the spirit of Africa and as Afrikaners we should all honor him." He folded the handkerchief neatly and put it back into his tunic pocket. "All I can say is that he must have been a great man for the professor to write a piece of music just for him. I now ask you all to stand and to bring your hands together once again for the professor." I saw that Captain Smit had a big smile on his face and was clapping madly. Even the Kommandant was clapping for all he was worth.

Doc stood with his head bowed and I knew he was crying for Geel Piet. But I also knew Geel Piet would have found this moment very funny.

"Ag, man," he would have said, "why must a man wait until he is dead for such a clever joke to heppen?"

Then the warders, wives and guests moved into the gym to watch the boxing exhibition.

Captain Smit had worked out a routine that was pretty clever. All the boxers were seated in a row facing the ring and he was in the ring with a whistle round his neck, acting as referee. When the audience had filled the gym he blew his whistle and I climbed into the ring with Snotnose. We shook hands and Captain Smit blew his whistle again and Snotnose and I started to box. The idea was that after every round, one of the boxers would step down and another would replace him. As the youngest I stepped out first and Fonnie Kruger came in. Then Maatie Snyman replaced Snotnose and then Fonnie stepped down and Nels Stekhoven came in and so on right up to the heavyweights, where Klipkop fought Gert and then as a joke I stepped in and fought the final round with Klipkop. It all went like clockwork. The crowd really enjoyed it and there was a lot of cheering.

Afterward I went over to Doc and Mrs. Boxall to tell them that I had to change and would see them at the *braaivleis*. Mrs. Boxall said that she wanted to have a word with the inspector chappie and that she'd be obliged if Doc would go with her for moral support. As I turned to go she called me back.

"Peekay, I must say I've never been too keen on your boxing. But you do seem to be rather good at it and I do believe you will be a welterweight champion of the world someday. Jolly well done is all I can say!"

We were all in the showers changing when Klipkop came in. "Captain Smit wants you all to come back into the gym when you finished. You must be there in the next ten minutes. When you get into the gym only the lights above the ring will be on. Sit in the dark and be very quiet. Not near the door but on the far side of the ring, you hear?" We all nodded and he hurried from the room.

We hadn't been seated long in the darkened gym when one of the double doors opened, spilling a shaft of light from the passage. Caught in the light were Captain Smit, Klipkop and, standing between them, Lieutenant Borman. The door swung back and we could only dimly see the three men walking toward the ring while they would not have been able to see us. Then they appeared suddenly in the circle of light illuminating the ring.

"Climb in, Borman, up into the ring," Captain Smit said.

"What you doing, man, what's happening?" we heard Lieutenant Borman say.

"Just climb in. Everything will be made clear in a minute." Borman climbed up into the ring and Captain Smit and Klipkop followed. A pair of boxing gloves hung from the posts of each of the two boxers' corners and in one of the neutral corners was a piece of rolled-up canvas.

Like Captain Smit, Lieutenant Borman was wearing civilian clothes, an open-neck shirt and long pants. Captain Smit removed his shoes, leaving his socks on.

"Take off your shoes, please, lieutenant," Klipkop said politely.

"Hey, man, what's going on here?" Borman said, with a hint of apprehension in his voice. "I don't want to fight nobody. I got no quarrel with you, Smit. I never done anything personally to you. Why do you want to fight me?"

"Take off your shoes or am I going to have to take them off for you, lieutenant?" Klipkop asked calmly.

"Keep your hands off me, you hear," Borman snarled. "I am your superior, Oudendaal! You should show me respect or you on report, you hear?" Klipkop shook his head slowly and started to move toward Lieutenant Borman. Borman pulled one shoe off and dropped it on the canvas, then removed the other and placed them both in the neutral corner right next to the rolled-up piece of canvas.

From the moment Captain Smit had stepped into the ring he had remained silent, and I could sense this was beginning to unnerve Borman. Klipkop lifted the gloves from the post nearest to the lieutenant and walked over to him.

"Give me your hand, please sir," he said.

Lieutenant Borman folded his arms. "No, man! No way! Let Smit tell me first what I done." Captain Smit had retrieved the gloves in his corner. "Jus' tell me, you hear!" Borman shouted. Captain Smit looked straight at Borman. Keeping his eyes fixed on the lieutenant, he walked over to the neutral corner and picked up the roll of canvas.

He held the roll up to his chin so that it unrolled. My heart gave an enormous leap. The canvas sheet was covered with dry blood. Borman pulled back in horror but then as quickly recovered himself.

"What's this, man? I never saw that before in my life."

Captain Smit began to roll the canvas up again. I had been terrified, when I climbed into the ring earlier, that I might see signs of Geel Piet's blood, but the old canvas had been removed and the ring re-covered. The sight of Captain Smit holding part of the old bloodstained canvas brought back the shock I had felt, and without realizing it I began to sob. Suddenly a large hand covered my mouth and Gert's arm came around my shoulder and drew me in to him.

Captain Smit put the canvas back in the corner. Klipkop pulled Borman's arms open and slipped his gloves on. This time the lieutenant made no move to stop Klipkop, who laced up the gloves.

"I don't know what you talking about, you hear! I swear I was at home the night the kaffir died. I can prove it! My wife had an asthma attack. Everybody saw I wasn't at the kaffir concert. You're mad, I'm telling you, I never done it. I never killed that kaffir!"

Klipkop finished tying Captain Smit's gloves and he walked to the center of the ring. "No butting, no kicking, fight like a man," Klipkop said, and climbed out of the ring, leaving Smit and Borman to fight.

Captain Smit started across the ring, but Borman held up his glove open-handed. "Look, I admit I phoned Pretoria about the kaffir concert. Orright, you got me on that. I thought I was right, I done my duty, that's all."

Captain Smit brushed the open glove aside with a left and drove a hard right into the soft roll of gut that spilt over Borman's belt. The lieutenant doubled up, clasping his stomach with both hands, trying to catch his breath. Smit stood over him, waiting. Without warning, Borman suddenly smashed his gloved fist into Captain Smit below the belt. The captain staggered back, then sank to his knees. Borman was on him in a flash, and catching him on the side of the jaw, he sent Captain Smit crashing to the canvas. Borman shouted, "You kaffirboetie, you nigger lover!" He kicked Captain Smit in the ribs just as Klipkop, who had climbed back into the ring, reached him and brought his arms around him. But Borman was a big man, and he jerked free as Captain Smit was attempting to rise. He caught Smit another solid blow to the side of the head, putting him back on the canvas. Klipkop tried to hold Lieutenant Borman again.

"I killed that yellow nigger, you hear!" Borman shouted. "He wouldn't tell me who gave him the letters, who brought the letters in. I caught him red-handed, two letters, man! Two letters in his pocket. He wouldn't tell me. I broke every bone in his face. I pounded him to pieces with my *sjambok*. He wouldn't tell me!" There were flecks of foam at the corners of Borman's mouth and he began to sob.

Captain Smit had dragged himself to his feet and stood facing Borman, who was no longer trying to get out of the bear hug Klipkop held him in. Bringing his gloves up, Smit signaled to Borman to come and fight. Klipkop released his grip and Borman rushed at Smit, walking into a straight left that stopped him in his tracks. Borman charged in again and Captain Smit stopped him again, repeating the straight left into the face. It was obvious that Borman had never been a boxer. Blood ran from his nose and he brought his arm up to wipe it. A smear of blood covered his arm and he stared down in horror at it. "Shit, I'm bleeding!" he cried.

Then Captain Smit stepped up and smashed his glove into

Borman's face. He dropped to the canvas. Covering his face with his gloves, he wailed, "Don't hit me, please don't hit me!"

Captain Smit signaled to Klipkop to get Borman back onto his feet, but the man refused to get up. His eyes were wide with terror. Then, crawling on all fours toward Captain Smit, Borman held Smit around the legs. "Please don't hit me, captain. I don't understand why you doing this to me. It was only a kaffir, a dirty yellow man. Why you hitting a white man over a kaffir?"

Captain Smit kicked his legs free of Borman's embrace. "You can't even stand up and fight like a man!" It was the first time Smit had spoken since they'd entered the ring. He turned and extended his hands to Klipkop, who unlaced and removed the gloves. Then Smit went over to the neutral corner, picked up the canvas roll and unrolled it beside the sobbing officer. Together Klipkop and Captain Smit lifted him and placed him on the bloodstained canvas and rolled it around him. "This kaffir's blood will haunt you till you die," Captain Smit said. Then he and Klipkop climbed from the ring. Klipkop moved over to the switch and plunged the gymnasium into darkness.

In the darkness from the direction of the swing doors there came a sudden shout, "*Abantu bingelela Onoshobishobi Ingelosi!*" The people salute the Tadpole Angel! The door opened slightly and in the shaft of light we saw a black figure slip quickly out of the gymnasium. The people knew. The curse was fixed. Borman was dead meat.

When I got outside, the *tiekiedraai* was going full swing, with someone on the Mignon hammering out the *Boeremusiek*, accompanied by the man with the piano accordion and a banjo player. Outside, on the parade ground, warders and their wives stood around the barbecue fires now burned down to glowing embers.

Doc and Mrs. Boxall were nowhere to be seen. I was watching the guy beating the Mignon, thankful he wasn't using Doc's Steinway, when I felt a tap on my shoulder. It was Gert. "How you getting home?" he inquired. I explained that Mrs. Boxall had brought us in her old crock, which made a fearful racket, and I was doubtful that it had long to live. "You know where the professor and that lady is, don't you? I seen them going into the administration building with the brigadier and the Kommandant."

Gert always seemed to know what was going on. "Maybe the professor will get a medal or something for the kaffir concert." Then he giggled. "I hope the brigadier never finds out that Geel Piet was only a broken-down old lag." He punched me lightly on the shoulder. "Sorry, man, about shutting your mouth back there." I hung my head, the memory of the bloodstained canvas still sharp in my mind.

"You did right," I said softly.

"So long, Peekay, I'd better kick the dust," Gert said.

At last Doc and Mrs. Boxall came out. I could see Mrs. Boxall was excited.

"By Jove, Peekay, miracles will never cease. I do believe we've done it!" she exclaimed.

"Done what?" I asked.

"Have done what?" she corrected automatically. "We have been given permission to start a letter-writing service. Isn't that grand news? The brigadier says that every prisoner may send and receive one letter a month. It's the first time it has happened in South Africa." She grabbed me by one hand and Doc by the other and we danced around to the sound of the *tiekiedraai* music coming from the hall. "You're going to be needed because you speak three African languages as well as English and Afrikaans. Every Sunday morning after church we'll come out for two hours and take dictation from the prisoners. I say, it's a real victory for the forces of good. The brigadier was most impressed when I told him that it would be done under the auspices of the Earl of Sandwich Fund," she giggled. "The Kommandant assured the brigadier that the Earl of Sandwich Fund was a very respected organization with worldwide contacts." We all started to laugh. Doc finally said, "Madame Boxall, you are absoloodle the best. For this I give you eleven out of ten."

She did a small curtsey and gave Doc one of her extra-special smiles. We hung around for a while longer and finally made our way to the car. As we approached we saw a pair of boots sticking out from under Charlie. Gert got up sheepishly and wiped his grease-blackened hands on the sides of his khaki shorts. He bowed awkwardly to Mrs. Boxall.

"Does mevrou speak Afrikaans?" he asked me.

I shook my head. "I'll translate, if you like?"

Gert nodded. "Tell her she's got more power now. You only had three cylinders firing, but you still got a bad knock in the diff." He turned to Mrs. Boxall. "If you can get it here tomorrow, I'll borrow the Plymouth and drive you home and I'll fix the car up for you." I introduced Gert to Mrs. Boxall and translated what he'd said. Mrs Boxall was very grateful and called Gert "a dear, sweet boy," which I didn't translate.

"Oh dear, I have no idea what a knock in the diff is. Is it something very bad?"

"It's the differential. I think it's pretty bad," I replied.

Pulling up his socks, Gert stammered, "Goodnight, missis," in English and then walked quickly away into the dark.

We zoomed away. The difference in Charlie was amazing. We

dropped Doc off at the bottom of his hill. I think the new four-cylinder Charlie could've made it easily but Mrs. Boxall had never been invited by Doc to his cottage and she said as she drove me home, "This wasn't the right time"—whatever that was supposed to mean.

FIFTEEN

Mrs. Boxall promised to talk to my mother about the new letter-writing arrangements in the prison. I had real doubts about being allowed to partake in them. Sundays were difficult for me: it was a day filled with taboos, beginning with Sunday school and church in the morning and ending with evening service. I wasn't allowed to do anything except the Lord's work on a Sunday, like reading the Shangaan Bible to Dee and Dum. Reading the Bible was regarded as the most superior type of work for the Lord. I was required to read three pages of the New Testament every day and ten pages on Sunday.

So getting to the prison for two hours every Sunday to take dictation wasn't simply a question of Mrs. Boxall asking my mother. A great deal of toing and froing to the Lord would have to take place and my fear was that the Lord was going to be hard put to see that taking dictation from a bunch of criminals was the best possible use of my Sabbath.

My fears proved to be correct and the scheme had to be delayed a month. A major investigation such as this one would begin by looking for a precedent in the Bible. In this regard I scored a direct hit when I pointed out that St. Paul, in his Epistles, had written from prison in Rome. This was just the sort of material my mother liked to take with her when she had a chat with the Lord. My granpa said later that my St. Paul research was a stroke of genius. But, it turned out, the Lord wasn't all that satisfied because Paul was a born-again Christian, converted on the road to Damascus, and he was in prison under an unjust Roman regime. The prisoners in Barberton prison were criminals being punished by a just regime. The point here was that Paul was doing the Lord's work while I was potentially aiding the devil writing letters from hardened criminals.

To my wife, Umbela,

I send you greetings in my shame. Who is putting food in the mouths of our children? It is hard in this place, but one day I will come to you again. The work is hard but I am strong, I will live to see you again.

Your husband,
Mfulu

I wasn't able to tell my mother how innocent the letters really were because she didn't know about the previous letters or the tobacco, sugar and salt. So for the next week I read the New Testament like mad. There had to be something in there to help me.

I took the problem to my granpa, who, after my telling opening move with St. Paul, seemed anxious to see that the debate was conducted fairly. We sat on the steps of one of the rose terraces, my granpa tapping and tamping and staring squinty-eyed through the blue tobacco smoke into the distance. After a long while he said, "The only time I ever heard of the Bible being useful was when a stretcher bearer I was with at the battle of Dundee, when we were fighting the Boers, told me that he'd once gotten hit by a bullet in the heart, only he was carrying a Bible in his tunic pocket and the Bible saved his life. He told me that ever since he'd always carried a Bible into battle with him and he felt perfectly safe because God was in his breast pocket. We were out looking for a sergeant and three troopers who were wounded while out on a reconnaissance and were said to be holed up in a dry *donga.* Alas, a Boer bullet hit him straight between the eyes." He puffed at his pipe. "Which goes to prove that the Bible is good for the heart and not for the head and that God is in nobody's pocket." He seemed very pleased with this neat summary, which nevertheless wasn't a scrap of help to me.

However, on Sunday night three weeks after Mrs. Boxall had first approached my mother, my granpa elected to play a part in the supper debate. Marie was always there for supper on Sundays and she joined in as well. My mother opened by saying the Lord was "sorely troubled" over the whole issue.

My granpa cleared his throat. "Were there not a couple of chaps who were crucified on either side of Christ, thorough scallywags, as I recall?"

"The Word refers to them as thieves who were crucified beside the Lord, though I don't see that they have anything whatsoever to do with the matter," my mother replied, her irritation thinly disguised. "I do not recall it saying in the Bible that they wrote home from jail." I knew that my granpa's opinions on biblical matters were not very highly regarded.

"I seem to remember that Christ forgave one of them, promising him a berth in heaven right there on the spot. Or am I mistaken?"

"Goodness! The Lord does not promise people 'berths' in

heaven," my mother said sharply. " 'Verily I say unto you, today shalt thou be with me in paradise' is what the Lord said."

"It seems to me, from that remark, that Christ has no objections to convicted felons entering the kingdom of God," he declared.

"Of course he doesn't! That's the whole point. Jesus was sent to save the most miserable sinners among us. His compassion is for all of us. Seek His forgiveness and you're saved. You're no longer a murderer or a thief, you're one of the Lord's precious redeemed. The thief on the cross beside Him was saved when he confessed his sins."

"Hallelujah, praise His precious name," Marie offered absently. Marie, under my mother's instruction and with the help of Pastor Mulvery, had become a born-again Christian and she and my mother would give out tracts in the hospital and witness for the Lord to the captive sick whether they liked it or not.

"And the prisoners here in Barberton. Like him, could they also be saved?"

"You know as well as I do they could," my mother said primly.

"How?"

"By accepting Christ into their lives, by renouncing the devil and . . ." My mother stopped and looked straight at my granpa. "You know very well how."

"Oh, I see. You are going to make it possible?"

"Well, no. We've prayed a great deal about this, prayed that the Lord would make it possible for the Apostolic Faith missionaries to spread His precious word and bring the gospel to those poor unfortunate sinners."

"Has it not occurred to you that the Lord may have answered your prayers?" my granpa asked.

"What on earth are you talking about?"

"Well, if the lad has direct access to the prisoners, could he not distribute tracts?"

It was a master stroke. In return for being allowed to take dictation on Sunday at the prison, I was required to take gospel tracts in Sotho and Zulu from the Apostolic Faith missionaries and give one to each prisoner after he had dictated his letter to me. My mother and Marie had scored another major triumph, first in the hospital and now the prison; they were earning recognition as a couple of hard-core fighters in the Lord's army. What's more, my time on a Sunday was counted as first-class work for the Lord.

I don't exactly know how it happened but I did it just the once; then it suddenly got done all the time. One of the prisoners had said that tobacco was sorely missed, and the next week I cut a piece of tobacco leaf exactly the same size as a tract and slipped it inside one. The next thing I knew Dee and Dum were slipping these neatly cut squares of tobacco leaf into every tract, and I would take a whole bunch with me and sort them into their African languages and put them in the drawer of the desk at which I sat, leaving an "innocent" pile of Sotho tracts in front of me. After one of the people had dictated his letter to me I would hand him a tract from the drawer. This was Doc's idea and on two occasions the warder who attended the letter-writing sessions absently picked up a tract, looked at it in a cursory manner and then returned it to the pile on the desk.

Letter writing suddenly became very popular and those of the people who didn't have anyone to write to would ask me to write to King Georgie. When I asked them what they wanted to say to George VI, the King of England, it was almost always the same thing.

Dear King Georgie,

The people are happy because you are our great king. I send greetings to the great warrior across the water.

Daniel Mafutu

After a while a letter to King George was simply a euphemism for a tract. One tract and contents made two cigarettes. Not only had the Tadpole Angel contrived to continue the supply of tobacco into the prison, but the people no longer had to pay for it and it came together with paper to roll it in. For a generation afterward, cigarettes in South African prisons were known as King Georgies. More importantly for the Kommandant, the letter-writing experiment proved a huge success and before the summer was over he had been made a full colonel and received a commendation from Pretoria for his work in prison reform. The Apostolic Faith missionaries kept up the supply of tracts and when I told Doc that King Georgies now came in Swazi and Shangaan he smiled and said, "I think, Peekay, because the people cannot read they now send smoke signals up to God."

It was not long after Geel Piet's death that Lieutenant Borman seemed to be losing weight and Captain Smit advised him to see a doctor.

"It's God's justice," Gert confided to me.

No one said anything but you could see it in their eyes. Those of us who had been in the gym that night all knew Borman was under a curse.

Geel Piet had once told me how prisoners could think so hard that, collectively, they could make things happen.

"Ja, it is true, small *baas,* I have seen it heppen lots of times,"

Geel Piet had said gravely. "Sometimes, when there is enough hate, this thinking can kill. The people will think some person to death. Such a death is always long and hard, because the thinking takes place over a long time. It is the hate; when it boils up there is no stopping it. The person will die because there is no *muti* you can take to stop this hating thing."

Anyone born in rural Africa is superstitious and the warders, who were mostly backwoodsmen, were particularly so. We all watched Borman as he started to shrink. The flesh started to fall off him. He seemed to age in front of our eyes. Then he experienced a severe hemorrhage and was rushed to Barberton hospital, where the surgeon's examination revealed the presence of cancer. In less than a month he was dead.

Within weeks of leaving prison Doc was fit enough to head for the hills and we would climb away from the town at first light every Saturday. We'd breakfast on hard-boiled eggs and bread with a thermos of sweet, milky coffee high up on a ridge somewhere or beside a stream. Sometimes we'd make for Lamati Falls, ten miles into the hills, and we'd wait for the morning sun to whiten the water where it crashed into a deep pool that stayed icy cold throughout the year. Doc was like a small boy. The years seemed to fall away from him as we scampered up the sides of mountains or slid down into deep tropical *kloofs,* where giant treeferns and the canopy of yellowwood turned the brilliant sunlight into twilight.

Doc was busy taking the photographs for his new book and sometimes we'd hunt all day for a single perfect specimen. It was good to be working with Doc again. Some days we'd communicate all day in Latin and in this way Doc gentled me into Ovid, Cicero,

Virgil and Caesar's conquest of Gaul. Mrs. Boxall countered this with the English poets. Wordsworth, Masefield and Keats were her favorites. I asked Doc about German poets, and he replied that Goethe was the only one in his opinion who could be considered worthy, but that personally he found him a terrible bore and that the Germans put all their poetry into music. He declared I should study the English for their poetry and the Germans for their music.

It was a lopsided sort of education, added to by Miss Bornstein, who had been busy preparing me for a scholarship to a posh private school in Johannesburg. An education well beyond my mother's income as a dressmaker. I was not yet twelve, the minimum required age for entry into a secondary school, and I had languished in Standard Six for three years, during which Miss Bornstein had privately educated me in "all those things there's never time to learn at school."

A month before my twelfth birthday I sat for the scholarship exam to the Prince of Wales School, and at the end of the term to my absolute mortification Mr. Davis, the headmaster of Barberton school, announced that I had received the highest scholarship marks this school had ever given. That I would be starting as a boarder in the first term of 1946. Doc, Mrs. Boxall and Miss Bornstein had trained me well. Above all things I had been taught to read for pleasure and for meaning, as both Doc and Mrs. Boxall demanded that I exercise my critical faculties in everything I did. In teaching me independence of thought they had given me the greatest gift an adult can give to a child, besides love, and they had given me that also.

And so the last summer of my childhood came to an end. I also sat for the Royal College of Music Advanced Exams and passed, although my marks weren't spectacular. I think this was as much as

Doc expected from me. He knew I had no special gift for music and what I achieved had been simply out of love for him. For his part he had fulfilled his contract with my mother, for whom my passing the exam was confirmation of my genius. It was one of the major disappointments in her life that at boarding school I would elect to play in the jazz band. Jazz was the devil's music.

Before Geel Piet died he had been teaching me how to put an eight-punch combination together. I worked solidly all summer on this and at the championships held in Boksburg I retained the under-twelve title.

Everyone seemed pleased that I had won a scholarship to the Prince of Wales School in Johannesburg. I kept my apprehension about returning to boarding school to myself; it seemed I would once again be the youngest kid in the school, though this aspect anyway now left me unconcerned. If they had a Judge at the Prince of Wales School, all I could say was he'd better be able to box. In fact, the only question I asked about the school was about boxing. The reply came back that boxing was a school sport and the boxers were under the instruction of an ex-cruiserweight champion of the British Army.

The final crisis of that summer came when the clothing list arrived from the Prince of Wales School. As she read it the tears started to roll down my mother's cheeks. Marie was there on her afternoon off from the hospital so it must have been a Wednesday. My mother read the list aloud. "Six white shirts with detachable starched collars, long sleeves. Three pairs of long gray flannel trousers (see swatch attached). Six pairs gray school socks, long. One school blazer (see melton sample attached), school blazers or blazer pocket badge and school ties obtainable from John Orrs, 129 Eloff Street, Johannesburg. One gray V-neck jersey, long sleeves.

Shoes, with school uniform, brown. Shoes, Sunday, black. Blue serge Sunday suit, long trousers.

"We don't have the money, we simply don't have the money," she kept repeating.

"Ag man, *jong,* where's your faith?" Marie said indignantly, not impressed by my mother's tears. "The Lord will supply everything, just you see. We going to pray right now, so down on our knees and give the precious Lord Jesus Peekay's order. C'mon, let's do it now!"

My granpa rose from the table and excused himself but I was obliged to kneel with Marie and my mother. Marie took the clothing list from my mother and handed it to me. "We going to pray out loud to the Lord. It's always best when you need something bad to pray out loud. When I tell you, you read out the list, okay?"

I nodded.

"Precious Lord Jesus, we got a real problem this time," Marie began.

"Praise the Lord, praise His precious name," my mother said.

"You know how clever Peekay is and how he has won a thing to go to a posh school in Johannesburg for nothing."

"Precious Savior, hear Thy humble servants," my mother said, attempting to bring a bit of tone into the whole affair.

"Well, we got lots of trouble, man, I mean, Lord," Marie continued, "the clothing list arrived today. The cupboard is bare, there are no clothes for school hanging up in it. What we need, Lord Jesus, Peekay is going to say right now, so please listen good and you talk up, Peekay, so the Lord can hear," Marie prayed, cueing me in.

I must say I was quite nervous. "Ah, er . . . six white shirts with detachable starched collars, long sleeves," I read. "Three pairs of long gray flannel trousers (see swatch attached)."

"Show Him the swatch, man," Marie whispered urgently. I didn't know quite what to do so I held the swatch of gray flannel up to the ceiling. When I reasoned the Lord had had a good enough look, I continued, "Six pairs gray school socks, long."

"Only three pairs, man! What about the three pairs you already got for school here?" Marie said in a stage whisper.

"Oh," I said. "Only three pairs, please." My mother had stopped punctuating Marie's remarks and I looked at her. At first I thought she was crying; her face was all squished up and she was holding her hand across her mouth. Then I realized she was desperately trying not to laugh. I started to giggle.

Without opening her eyes Marie admonished me. "Peekay, stop it! It's hard enough asking the Lord for you, you not even being born again an' all that! But if you laugh we got no chance." Her voice became conciliatory. "Sorry, Lord, he didn't mean it. Go on, start reading again. The Lord hasn't got all day, you know!"

I went on reading the list and also showed the Lord the swatch of green melton blazer cloth. When I got to the bit about school badges being obtainable from John Orrs, 129 Eloff Street, Johannesburg, Marie whispered again.

"You don't need to give Him the address, He knows where it is." I finally got to the blue serge suit. "That's his Sunday suit for going to church, Lord," she said. My mother threw in a few more "Praise the Lord, praise His precious name"s and the request for the contents of my clothing list was over.

Marie's eyes blazed with faith. There was absolutely no doubt in her mind that the Lord would provide. My mother also seemed considerably cheered up and called for Dum to make tea. I must confess I didn't share their confidence. All I had was three pairs of gray socks, two pairs of gym pants and the *tackies*. These latter items had appeared in a separate list titled "Sport and Recreation," which included two rugby jerseys, house and school colors, rugby socks, rugby boots, white cricket shirt and shorts Form One and Two, cricket longs Form Three onward. The optional section on this list included cricket boots and white cricket sweater with school colors. It seemed an amazing collection of clothes for one person.

I mentioned the clothing crisis to Doc. Not that he could have helped. Doc, at best, lived hand to mouth with just enough over for an occasional book and film for his Leica camera. But he mentioned it to Mrs. Boxall and Mrs. Boxall mentioned it to Miss Bornstein and the two women went into action.

Miss Bornstein called me over at the end of class and asked me to copy out the clothing list. I did so and handed it over to her. "What about these swatches? Can you get the gray and the green swatch, Peekay? It's absolutely necessary for me to have them." I promised to get hold of the swatches, pleased that the matter of my school clothes wasn't singularly in the Lord's hands any longer.

"We don't have very much money," I said, for the first time in my life realizing that money was important. I knew we were poor but it hadn't seemed to matter much. I'd had the occasional penny to spend on sweets; I'd never really felt poor or needed money. I always somehow managed to save up four shillings for Christmas and old Mr. McClymont at the drapery shop would give me four ladies' hankies and a man's one as well as a red bandanna for Doc. The ladies' hankies would go to my mother, Mrs. Boxall and Dee and Dum, while the man's was for my granpa. They always looked surprised when they got them, but I don't suppose they were. Dee and Dum spread their hankies carefully over the top of their heads in the African fashion. They could never understand why white people would blow the stuff from their noses into such a pretty piece of cloth.

"There are lots of ways to skin a cat," Miss Bornstein said. "This town isn't going to let its *enfant terrible* go to boarding school looking like a ragamuffin."

Between Miss Bornstein and Mrs. Boxall the cloth for my trousers and blazer and blue serge suit just appeared, although I expect Mr. McClymont had a hand in it somewhere. Then Miss Bornstein sprung her surprise. Her grandfather, Mr. Isaac Bornstein, had been a tailor in Germany. He would cut the cloth and do the hand work if my mother would do the machine work. The suit was easy but we needed a blazer to make sure that mine was cut and tailored in the same way as those purchased from Johannesburg. Mrs. Andrews had sent two of her sons to the Prince of Wales School and she still had a blazer, which she gave to Mrs. Boxall. Old Mr. Bornstein took it apart to see how it was made and did a lot of tut-tutting about the poor workmanship. He then cut the blazer to my size and as the badge, which was three ostrich feathers sticking out of a crown, was almost new he cut it carefully around the edges and sewed it onto my new blazer. Mrs. Boxall sent to Johannesburg for two red, white and green striped school ties, which were her special present. All my shirts were cut from a pair of cotton poplin sheets Miss Bornstein said her mother had never used. Old Mr. Bornstein knew just how to make the necklines so that the starch collars donated by Mr. McClymont fitted perfectly. Marie and her mother knitted me three pairs of socks for Christmas.

My mother and Marie testified to the congregation of Apostolic Faith about the Lord's miraculous answer to the prayers. Only the requested V-neck long sleeve gray jersey was missing from my kit, but it was summer in Johannesburg and my mother knew that the Lord would provide in time for winter. Which He did. Four knitted jerseys were pushed into her hands by separate dear, sweet, Christian ladies less than a fortnight later.

Only the brown and black shoes remained, and at the prison Christmas party for all the warders Captain Smit handed me a large parcel from the boxing squad. Inside were a pair of new brown shoes and a pair of black ones and a brand-new pair of boxing boots. "*Magtig,* Peekay, we are all proud of you going to that posh Rooinek school in Johannesburg. Just don't get all high and mighty on us when you get back, heh." Everyone laughed and cheered and I felt the sorrow of leaving people I loved. The Kommandant stood up and recounted the first day he'd met me and said that I had proved that English and Afrikaner were one people, South Africans. That perhaps with my generation the bitterness would pass. He said I was a leader of men and that even the prisoners respected me for my letter writing. There was some more clapping and, shaking at the knees, I thanked them all. I can't remember what I said but I promised I would never forget them. And I never have.

That was the last long, hot summer of my childhood. It wasn't until I went to boarding school the second time that I learned that the business of survival is a matter of making the system work for you rather than attempting merely to survive it. Doc had encouraged me to think, but now I would have to think entirely for myself, invent my own ideas and express my own opinions. I would have to trust myself and my own answers, and be true to my own convictions. If I was to survive I would have to follow the truth as I knew it in my heart. This was for me the power of one and, once it had been attained, I knew nothing could destroy me.

GLOSSARY

(A list of some of the words and phrases in Afrikaans and African languages that occur in the narrative)

❂ ❂ ❂

Abantu bingelela . . . The people salute . . .
Afrikaans language of South Africa, very similar to Dutch
Afrikaner person who speaks Afrikaans and who is of European descent
amasele frog
assegai throwing spear
baas boss
bakkie pickup truck or ute
blerrie bloody
Boer South African person of Dutch descent, also a farmer
boetie brother
braaivleis barbecue
Dames en Heere ladies and gentlemen
dankie thank you
doek handkerchief, cloth, woman's head scarf
domkop stupid
donga deep ditch
dorp small town
een, twee, drie one, two, three

Goeie môre, baas en klein baas Good morning, boss and small boss

Hoe gaan dit? How goes it?

Impi Zulu battalion/s

indaba a meeting of men to talk business

infaan small African boy

Inkosikaan little lord

ja yes

Jy is 'n slimmertjie You are a clever one

kaffir derogatory term for a black tribesperson

kaffirboetie someone who loves black people; literally "kaffir brother"

kêrel chap

Klavier-Meister piano maestro

kloof canyon or valley

koppie small hill

kraal traditional village

kranse cliff

lekker nice

links, regs left, right

magtig my goodness, by golly

mealie corn

meneer mister, sir

mevrou missus, but also Matron

muti medicine

nooi sweetheart, girlfriend

Onoshobishobi Ingelosi the Tadpole Angel

oubas old chap

ounooi my old sweetheart

oupa grandfather

Praat jy . . . ? Do you speak . . . ?

riempie thin leather strap, often used to plait the seat of a small folding stool

Rooinek South African slang for a person of English origin

sjambok plaited leather whip

skattebol fluffy ball (term of endearment)

stoep verandah

stom silent

Taal Afrikaans language

tackies sandshoes

tiekiedraai Afrikaans folk dancing

totsiens goodbye

tsamma native melons

verdomde damned

wonderlik wonderful

wragdig really

A Note from the Author

I do hope you have enjoyed the young adult edition of *The Power of One*. In this version I have told only half of the story of Peekay and his quest to be the welterweight champion of the world. Sometime you may like to read the complete book, which is available in the United States in an edition published by Ballantine Books.

In the meantime, *never* stop reading. A book is just about the best friend a person can have. Absoloodle!

Bryce Courtenay

About the Author

BRYCE COURTENAY is the bestselling author of *The Power of One, Tandia, April Fool's Day, The Potato Factory, Tommo & Hawk, Jessica, Solomon's Song, The Australian Trilogy, A Recipe for Dreaming, The Family Frying Pan, The Night Country, Smoky Joe's Cafe, Four Fires* and *Matthew Flinders' Cat*. He was born in South Africa, is an Australian and has lived in Sydney for the major part of his life.

Further information about the author may be found at www.brycecourtenay.com.